IRON MAN ®

THE ARMOR TRAP

IRON MAN ®

THE ARMOR TRAP

Greg Cox

Illustrations by Gabriel Gecko

BYRON PREISS MULTIMEDIA COMPANY, INC.
NEW YORK

BOULEVARD BOOKS, NEW YORK

This book is dedicated to the
memory of Don Heck.

Special thanks to Lou Aronica, Nel Yomtov, John Betancourt, Mariano Nicieza, and Julia Molino.

IRON MAN: THE ARMOR TRAP

A Boulevard Book
A Byron Preiss Multimedia Company, Inc. Book

PRINTING HISTORY
Boulevard edition / July 1995

ISBN: 1-57297-008-1

BOULEVARD
Boulevard Books are published by The Berkley
Publishing Group,
200 Madison Avenue, New York, New York 10016.
BOULEVARD and its logo
are trademarks belonging to Berkley Publishing
Corporation.

PRINTED IN THE UNITED STATES OF AMERICA

10 9 8 7 6 5 4 3 2 1

Acknowledgments

This novel was written under arduous conditions, and it would not have been possible without the help and inspiration of many individuals. My sincere thanks go to:

Keith R.A. DeCandido and John Betancourt, my editors at Byron Preiss Multimedia Company, for their constant encouragement and faith. (Thanks for all the free comics, Keith!)

Patrick Nielsen Hayden and Sumi Lee for helping me get a new computer up and running. (Like, what's this ''Windows'' thing anyway?)

Martha Soukup for giving me the real scoop on San Francisco. (But I thought all of California was warm and sunny?)

Marina Frants for assistance in the underwater segments. (You mean flounder don't school?)

Stan Lee, Larry Lieber, and Don Heck for creating Iron Man, and to all the subsequent writers, artists, and editors from whose work I have shamelessly cribbed, especially Eliot R. Brown, whose reference work, *The Iron Manual*, was an invaluable source of techno-jargon. (Oh, so *that's* how the repulsors work.)

ACKNOWLEDGMENTS

And, last but not least, Karen Palinko, who did the dishes for two months so that I could type instead, provided me with valuable reference materials I didn't even know I needed, scraped me up off the floor on occasion, fed me, made sure my fingers were constantly tapping at the keyboard, and who patiently listened to me babble about comic books the whole time. (Hey, did you know that Madame Masque hasn't appeared in the comics since 1989 . . . ?)

The humblest citizen of all the land, when clad in the armor of a righteous cause, is stronger than all the hosts of Error.

—William Jennings Bryan (1896)

As for the Iron Man, that metallic hulk who once was Anthony Stark . . . who knows what destiny awaits him?

—Anthony Stark (1963)

CHAPTER 1

FRIDAY. 8:47 AM. PACIFIC COAST TIME.

"Hail Hydra!" the madman cried. At least, Jennifer Coning assumed he was mad.

Far below her, the causeway of the Golden Gate Bridge spanned the bay. On any other Friday morning, the bridge would have been packed with rush hour traffic, but the police had closed this stretch of Highway 101 about an hour ago. Instead, the multilane roadway swarmed with police officers, uniformed and otherwise, while dozens of reporters pushed at the newly erected blue barricades. Local news teams aimed video cameras, telephoto lenses, and long-distance microphones at the tense hostage drama unfolding at the very peak of the bridge. The media eagerly recorded every movement and expression of Jennifer, a twenty-six-year-old blonde woman wearing a navy-blue sweatsuit, sneakers, wire-rimmed eyeglasses—and a look of absolute fright on her face.

Balanced precariously on a narrow maintenance walkway several hundred feet above the sparkling green water of the bay, Jennifer suppressed a scream. She couldn't believe how high she was; it was like gazing down from a skyscraper, but without the comforting restraint of a wall. The milling crowd on the bridge looked like ants, the parked emergency vehicles like miniature toys. Far beneath the bridge itself, the surface of the bay rippled and shimmered, stirred by waves and underwater currents. Her knuckles tightened as she held on desperately to a thick steel cable. Like the rest of the bridge, the cable had been painted industrial orange. The winds blowing over the Golden Gate Bridge sometimes reached as much as one hundred miles per hour, but Jennifer had lucked out; only a mild breeze chilled her bones, one she could easily withstand. A summer fog spread a faint, translucent veil over the scene; the mist was merely cool and moist, yet she shivered as though freezing. Jennifer didn't like heights, but her current altitude was not the source of her terror.

He was standing only inches away: a wild-eyed man wearing a heavy wool trench coat over a brown paramilitary uniform that clung tightly to a body like a professional wrestler's. Jennifer wondered if it was an overdose of steroids that drove him crazy. His coat flapped open in the cool breeze, revealing a sinister insignia, like a stylized octopus, emblazoned on his tunic. His polished black boots rested securely on the narrow walkway. Seemingly unafraid of the vertiginous drop beneath them, he waved a gloved fist at the crowd on the causeway, shouting inexplicable slogans, while his other hand kept an automatic pistol aimed at Jennifer's head.

This can't be happening to me, she thought. One minute she had been jogging across the bridge, with nothing more on her mind than what video to rent that evening after work. *The Joy Luck Club*, maybe, or the new, restored version of *My Fair Lady*. The next she was being forced at gunpoint to climb up a service ladder. She sneaked a peek at the Mickey

Mouse wristwatch she'd bought last summer in Anaheim. My God, it wasn't even nine yet; it felt like she'd been up here for days. *What does he want with me?* she wondered. *I'm just a tour guide at Alcatraz!*

So far, her captor had not made any demands Jennifer could comprehend. Did he want all of California to "hail Hydra" with him? "Please," she said nervously, staring at the muzzle of his gun, "just tell me what you want."

"Silence!" he commanded her. His short, buzz-cut hair was black, edged with silver. He'd shaved a portrait of a squid onto the back of his head, the same ominous octopus displayed on his overdeveloped chest. Stubble darkened his jowls. His eyes were red and bloodshot. His breath, so close to her face, was rancid and foul; Jennifer fought an urge to gag. Raising his voice, he yelled down at the growing media frenzy: "Hail Hydra! We shall never be destroyed!"

Hydra was some sort of terrorist spy group, Jennifer knew that much. She racked her brain, trying to remember more. Weren't they involved in that computer espionage mess in New York last year? She seemed to recall an article in *Newsweek*, and a blurry newsphoto of a couple of super heroes. But, what did that have to do with kidnapping people on bridges? *Perhaps this guy isn't even a Hydra agent at all*, she thought. *Maybe he's just a nut.*

A newscopter buzzed her perch on the bridge. The wind from the rotors blew her hair about wildly, and drove her captor into a killing frenzy. Gunfire exploded in her ears, as the uniformed lunatic fired a round of ammunition at the copter, forcing its passengers and cameras to retreat to a safer vantage point, about a half a mile above.

Yep, Jennifer decided. *Definitely a nut.* All hope seeped out of her, and she knew she was going to die. *It isn't fair*, she thought. There was so much she hadn't done. Visit Europe. Read the complete works of Victor Hugo. Figure out what she wanted to do with her life . . .

Then a hole opened up in the fog, and she glimpsed something descending from the sky towards her. Sunlight glinted off a golden, metallic surface. A tremendous *whooshing* sound grew louder and louder as the flying object zoomed at her. The flare of rockets blasted behind the object, propelling it on a direct path towards the top of the bridge. *Oh my God*, Jennifer thought, panicking. *They've shot a missile at us.*

But the "missile" slowed as it approached her, altering its trajectory and veering away just when it seemed it was about to collide with both Jennifer and her captor. Instead, it hovered in the air opposite them, less than a dozen yards away. Despite the persistent fog, Jennifer could see the gleaming object clearly now, and hope sparked back to life in her heart. Maybe she had a chance, after all; this was no missile, it was Iron Man!

He looked like a robot, but she knew there was a man inside the red-and-golden armor. Everyone in the world had heard of Iron Man, the super-powered bodyguard of millionaire Tony Stark. In person, however, he was even more impressive than the photos and footage Jennifer had seen. Overlapping plates of crystalized iron exaggerated the muscular contours of his body. A golden faceplate, marked only by narrow indentations over his eyes and mouth, formed a grim, intimidating visage. His hands, gloved in crimson metal, clenched into fists. Jets burst from the soles of his boots, holding him aloft.

Jennifer tore her eyes away from this awesome sight to risk a glance at her captor. Her kidnapper glared at Iron Man with hate in his reddened eyes. Foam bubbled at the corners of his mouth. He looked more angry than surprised by Iron Man's unexpected appearance. "Shell-headed stooge!" he hissed vehemently through yellow, scum-coated teeth. "Corporate enforcer!"

A sudden blast of white light left Jennifer blinking. She found herself in the brilliant glare of a spotlight emitted from a beam projector mounted over Iron Man's chest. The intense light cut through the fog, exposing both Jennifer and the madman to view.

"Attention, you on the bridge," Iron Man said. His voice was deep and electronically amplified. "You can't get away. I have at least twelve different weapons systems locked on you at this moment. Surrender now, before I have to use force."

The self-proclaimed Hydra agent spat in reply. He wrapped one arm around Jennifer's waist while firing at Iron Man with the other. "Hydra never surrenders!'' he shrieked. Jennifer struggled to free herself from the man's rough embrace, but his arm was too strong.

Jennifer heard the harsh clatter of gunfire, followed by several metallic *pings*, as the bullets ricocheted harmlessly off Iron Man's armor. In response, Iron Man calmly raised his right hand and unclenched his fist. Jennifer saw a violet glow, like something in a laser show, form in the palm of his glove. ''You have three seconds to release that woman,'' he announced. ''Three . . . two . . .''

Defiantly, the gunman swung his weapon back towards Jennifer, who found herself looking straight down its muzzle. *This is it*, she thought. Despair gripped her once more. *What a stupid, pointless way to die.*

''Avenge this, Avenger!'' cried the man in the Hydra uniform.

A violet ray shot forth from Iron Man's palm, traveling at the speed of light. The violet radiance illuminated the madman's weapon hand. Jennifer waited for the final, deafening gunshot, but instead she saw her attacker's arm suddenly jerk up and away from her, as though yanked by a powerful force. The man howled in rage and frustration. Veins throbbed on his forehead and neck while he struggled to hang on to his gun. After several seconds, he lost the struggle, and she watched in amazement as the deadly weapon seemed to fly out of the man's grip of its own free will.

Jennifer felt the steel cable in her hand vibrate against her flesh. Her wristwatch tugged at her wrist. *Of course*, she realized. The violet ray was some sort of magnetic beam.

The levitating gun followed the beam back to Iron Man's hand. The violet glow vanished instantly, and Iron Man closed his fist around the automatic weapon. Twisted metal screeched in protest, as he crumpled it into a harmless wad of scrap. Jennifer heard her captor gulp as his weapon was destroyed. *Not so confident now, are you?* she thought vindictively. *Hail Hydra, indeed.*

But her smugness was short-lived. Without warning, her captor grabbed on to her with both hands and began to pull her over the edge of the railing. Jennifer tried to fight back, but her ordeal had left her drained and exhausted; she had no more adrenaline left. The walkway beneath her was smooth and even; even if she'd still had the strength, there was no way to dig in her feet. Her glasses came loose, slipping off her nose in the struggle. They fell, but Jennifer never saw them hit the water. Out of the corner of her eye, she spotted Iron Man zooming headfirst towards the bridge, rockets blazing.

"We shall never be destroyed!" the other man yelled. He was over the rail himself now, and pulling on Jennifer with all his strength. Her fingers were torn away from the safety of the cable she'd been clutching for so long; the coiled metal strands scraped the soft flesh of her hands. "Cut off one

limb," he vowed, "and another shall take its plaa-
aaaaaaaaaaaaace!"

His last word dissolved into a scream as he threw
himself off the bridge, his weight dragging Jennifer
with him. In freefall, she felt more than heard the
wind pounding past her ears, saw the surface of the
harbor racing towards her like some immense green
hammer. The clammy touch of the fog shredded into
nothingness against the force of her descent. Her body
slipped free from the clutch of the falling madman
and the small part of her brain that wasn't utterly
reduced to panic thanked heaven that at least she
wouldn't die in her killer's arms.

Then a sparkle of gold and crimson zipped past
her and the surging water beneath her was replaced
by an intense yellow light. Her mouth wide open,
ready to scream, she fell into the light. To her astonishment, the light resisted her fall; it felt almost solid.
Her headlong descent towards death slowed gradually, came to a halt several feet above the bay, then
reversed itself. She felt herself lifted up by a shimmering plane of pure energy, which seemed to grow
more solid and secure every second. It was like a
miracle.

Jennifer's heart pounded in her chest. Gasping for
breath, she looked down through the light and saw
Iron Man directly below her. The life-saving beam,
she observed, came from the same five-sided plate on
his chest that had previously produced the harsh white
spotlight. There seemed to be no end to the wonders

contained in Iron Man's armor. At this point, Jennifer would not have been surprised if harp music and a chorus of angels had emerged from the beam.

The Golden Avenger (as the media sometimes called him) rose up through the light. Powerful, steel-encased arms gently cradled her against Iron Man's chest, at the very moment that the strange, solid radiance disappeared abruptly, like a lightbulb suddenly switched off. "Are you all right, miss?" Iron Man asked. Up close, his voice sounded less like a microphone, warmer and more comforting.

Jennifer nodded. To be honest, she didn't know how she felt after all she'd endured in the last hour or so. She was alive, and intact, and that was enough for now. She gazed up at Iron Man, and saw her own face reflected in his golden helmet. His eyes were hidden behind opaque red lenses. She wondered what he looked like beneath the mask.

"I hope I didn't jar you too much," he said. "I tried to use my repulsor ray to break your fall gradually. Still, there wasn't time to be too subtle about it." His metal arms and chest were cold to the touch, and Jennifer began to tremble once more. "Chilly?" he asked.

Jennifer nodded, amazed that he had even noticed. How sensitive was that armor anyway?

"Let me adjust my thermal units," he volunteered. Almost immediately, the armor grew warmer. After the fog, and the fear, she suddenly felt warmer herself, and more comfortable than she had been since seemingly forever. She snuggled against the armored warrior as if he was an electric blanket or a toasty radiator. His armor was her protection now.

Holding firmly on to Jennifer, Iron Man soared leisurely back to the bridge. Nearsighted without her glasses, she could barely make out the crowd on the bridge; they looked like one big, multicolored blur. She heard cheers and applause from the waiting police officers and reporters as they touched down in the middle of the road. He landed squarely on both feet, tiny gusts of exhaust escaping from his boot-jets. "Ready to face the crowd?" Iron Man asked her quietly.

"I . . . I think so," she answered. Iron Man lowered her carefully onto her feet. Her legs felt a little rubbery, but she managed to keep standing. An emergency worker rushed in from somewhere on the sidelines and wrapped a heavy grey blanket over her shoulders. He guided her towards a nearby ambulance. The flashing red light atop the ambulance was like a beacon in the fog. Jennifer started to go with him, then remembered something. She paused and turned around. "Iron Man," she called.

Iron Man looked deep in discussion with another man: a tough-looking character with a black eyepatch and a cigar. The man wore a black leather jumpsuit with a brown shoulder holster and looked like he hadn't shaved in days. His brown hair had grown white around his temples; Jennifer thought she'd seen him on the TV news. Whoever he was, the man was obviously important, but Iron Man looked up when she said his name. He strode towards her, moving surprisingly smoothly, without any of the clanking or stiffness she would have expected of a man in a metal suit. *He walks like a man*, she observed, *not a robocop.* "Yes?" he replied.

She tried to meet his eyes beneath the lenses. "What happened to . . . *him*?" She looked up at her former perch, twenty-seven feet above.

Iron Man shook his head. Was it just her imagination, or did his narrow slit of a mouth turn downwards at the corners, transforming a neutral expression into something resembling a scowl. "I couldn't save you both," he said, and this time Jennifer was sure she heard regret in his voice.

"I see," she said. Privately, she was glad to hear it. So the creep had fallen to his death instead of her? *Good,* she thought. She felt safer knowing that Mr. Hydra would never come after her again. "I can't thank you enough, Iron Man."

The slit on Iron Man's mask seemed to straighten out, giving his face a less mournful expression, though on reflection, Jennifer probably imagined it. "You don't have to," he said. "I'm glad I could help."

Jennifer watched as Iron Man walked away. He exchanged a few more words with the one-eyed man, whom Jennifer overheard him call "Fury," then took to the skies like a man-shaped missile. Eager paramedics wanted to hustle her into the back of the ambulance, but Jennifer refused to leave the bridge until the receding red-and-gold figure completely disappeared from sight. *Just my luck*, she thought. *I finally meet a real-live super hero and I'm wearing an old, beat-up sweatsuit.*

On ramparts of historic Fort Point, below the southern end of the bridge, a crowd had gathered to watch Iron Man's successful rescue of an unidentified young woman. Among the crowd, one man observed the Golden Avenger's departure with more than usual interest. Dressed like a tourist, with a baseball cap, a souvenir T-shirt, Bermuda shorts, and sunglasses, he looked unremarkable enough, but his high-powered, infrared binoculars tracked Iron Man through the fog and across the bay. Long after the other spectators had lost sight of Iron Man, this single individual monitored his armored target. Very soon, however, Iron Man flew beyond the range of even his binoculars.

The man was unconcerned. He had seen what he needed to see, assuming he now acted with appropriate speed. Lowering his binoculars, he raised a handheld radio to his lips. A flick of a switch put him instantly in touch with his headquarters, on a frequency unrecorded by the Federal Communications Commission. He did not wait for a response or acknowledgment. He knew his superiors were waiting for his report:

"Confirmed: Iron Man is in San Francisco. Activate strike force."

His mission completed, the man put away his radio and exited from the fort. The day was just beginning, but the fog had grown much heavier.

FRIDAY. 11:15 PM. CENTRAL STANDARD TIME.

Tony Stark felt a twinge of pain as he lifted the user interface headset off his skull. *Blast it,* he thought, *this thing always gives me a headache.* Still, the experiment was an unqualified success. Without ever leaving the small office on his private yacht *Athena*, currently anchored in the Gulf of Mexico, he had managed to save a woman's life—and test out a new remote-controlled Iron Man unit. The NTU-151 had performed as well or better than his previous model Neuromimetic Telepresence Unit, even under adverse atmospheric conditions. The Virtual Reality sensors had transmitted the sights and sounds of the hostage crisis with astonishing fidelity; although his real body had been hundreds of miles away, he could actually feel the chill of that San Francisco fog.

Leaning back against his chair, he placed the headset on the polished surface of a mahogany desk. The headset was a lightweight device made of flexible steel and integrated circuitry. The Neurologic Interface Link located on the set's inner surface allowed for direct access to a neural port surgically implanted at the base of Tony's skull, just behind his right ear. An attached microphone and set of earphones had allowed him to speak directly to the kidnapper and his victim.

If only I could have talked him down somehow, Tony chided himself. He regretted any death, even that of a homicidal maniac who had proven all too determined to take his own life. Throughout his long career as Iron Man, and during many hard-fought battles against murderous foes who hardly shared his scruples, Tony had consistently drawn the line at deliberate murder. Given the amount of power his armor bestowed upon him, he had no other choice unless he wanted to pile up a truly horrifying body count. Once he started killing, who knew where it would stop? It would always be easier and quicker to blow an opponent away than to devise a more complicated, less terminal solution, but the worst thing he could imagine was an Iron Man grown callous where the taking of a human life was concerned.

Other heroes felt differently, he knew. In recent years, a new breed of costumed crimefighter had emerged, one more willing to fight fire with fire, to exact a life for a life. Wolverine, the Punisher, Venom, Morbius, Deathcry, even his old friend Jim Rhodes (a.k.a. War Machine) . . . they and many others often crossed the fatal line that Tony had long ago drawn for himself. At times he felt like an anachronism, a knight in shining armor trapped in a more debased and violent age. He suspected many of his old allies and contemporaries, like Captain America and the Silver Surfer, felt the same way. Still, no matter how furious the fray, he wasn't about to abandon his principles now. *If this be chivalry,* he thought, paraphrasing Patrick Henry, *then make the most of it.*

Today, regrettably, he had failed to save one life, but at least he had prevented that psycho from taking an innocent young woman with him in his suicidal plunge, and he'd have to be satisfied with that. He hoped that poor young woman was getting all the care she needed; she'd certainly been through a lot.

But, Tony wondered, *was the dead man really connected to Hydra?* Frankly, he doubted it. He had dealt with Hydra many times in the past, both as Iron Man and as the head of Stark Enterprises, and he knew that this sort of random violence—and very public spectacle—wasn't Hydra's style at all; they preferred elaborate, covert schemes aimed at nothing less than the overthrow of civilization. Baron Wolfgang Von Strucker, an infamous war criminal, had founded Hydra several years ago and Strucker was no fool. A sociopath and an anarchist, perhaps, but there was always a method to his madness, no matter how bloodthirsty his schemes. Why would Strucker want to execute an innocent jogger on top of a major American landmark?

Well, Tony thought, *Nick Fury will doubtlessly look into the matter.* As the Director of the Strategic Hazard Intervention, Espionage, and Logistics Directorate (S.H.I.E.L.D.), the spy agency most responsible for monitoring Hydra and other terrorist organizations, the one-eyed Army veteran had uncovered stranger plots before. Tony Stark had helped found S.H.I.E.L.D. decades ago, after Iron Man foiled a Hydra raid on a Stark laboratory, and he had tapped Fury for the top job. Perhaps the endangered jogger was merely the tip of a far more ominous iceberg. Maybe she was the long-lost daughter of a brilliant molecular chemist on the verge of developing a new super-virus, maybe she was a "sleeper" agent for the alien Skrull Empire . . . or maybe she was only an ordinary American who had had the bad luck to cross the path of just another angry kook with a gun. God knows there were enough of them out there these days. This man who died in the name of Hydra would probably turn out to be no more than yet another disgruntled postal worker or unemployed cokehead. It would be nice to blame all the senseless violence in the world on the likes of Baron Strucker and his ilk, but Tony knew the world was not that simple.

Tony blinked his eyes against the throbbing in his head. *Was the range of the telepresence transmission proportional to the headache it engendered?* he speculated. *Maybe I should plot the severity of the pain against my distance from the NTU, but what sort of scale do you use to quantify headache pain?* Making a mental note to question his neurologist on the subject, he stood up and stretched his arms and legs. Minutes ago he had seemed to be "wearing" a fully automated suit of armor. Iron Man's transistorized limbs had responded directly to his own mental commands. Now he found himself back in a simple pair of blue designer swimming trunks and white tennis sneakers. The floor rocked gently beneath his feet as he trod to the adjacent bathroom to get an aspirin. As he washed two tablets down with a glass of water, he inspected himself in the large, gold-framed mirror over the sink.

His tanned body was in good shape, despite—or because of—the rigors of his secret career as a super hero. The save-the-world exercise plan, he thought of it sometimes. His pencil-thin mustache often evoked comparisons to a young Errol Flynn or Clark Gable, especially in the tabloids and gossip magazines. *How old do I have to get,* he often wondered, *before they stop calling me a "millionaire playboy"? About the same time I drop off the "World's Most Eligible Bachelor" lists, probably.*

Enough speculation about Hydra or whomever, he decided. *I'm supposed to be on vacation.* He ran a hand through his expensively trimmed black hair, making sure it covered the neural port under his ear. *No need to alarm my guest,* he thought. *Not everybody knows that I have an artificial nervous system.*

He locked the headset securely in a desk drawer; a customized memory chip hidden behind the mahogany paneling guaranteed that the drawer would open only to his handprint. In theory, the NTU-151 would respond exclusively to his own brainwaves, but there was no point in tempting fate. Anyway, his usual armor, the Iron Man suit he actually put on over his fragile human body, was conveniently nearby, folded up in an unremarkable-looking brown leather attaché case leaning against the base of his desk. In the unlikely possibility of an emergency, it would be far easier (and more satisfying) to don the armor himself than to summon the remote unit all the way from Frisco. Content that everything was in its place, he walked up a short flight of steps, out of his office and into the bright sunshine of outdoors.

His seventy-foot yacht drifted peacefully in the Gulf of Mexico. Unlike foggy San Francisco, the sky above was blue and cloudless, while the blazing sun baked everything for miles around. Emerging from the air-conditioned office, Tony was briefly startled by the sudden heat. *Forget armor*, he thought, *I need to cover myself with a thick layer of sunblock.* He took a deep breath and tasted salt on the wind. The fresh air did wonders for his headache; he felt better by the moment. Raising a hand to shade his eyes, he saw no other boats in the vicinity. Aside from a family of dolphins frolicking in the waves just off the port side of the yacht, he saw only sea and sky all the way to the horizon.

Almost.

"There you are!" a woman's voice called impatiently from the bow of the yacht. Anastasia Swift, the world-famous supermodel, reclined on an adjustable beach chair near the tip of *Athena*'s spacious upper deck. A stylish wicker hat and designer sunglasses protected her celebrated features from the afternoon glare, but Tony caught a glimpse of her short, blonde bangs peeking out from beneath the brim of her hat. Ana lay on her back upon the deck chair, her well-toned physique barely covered by a skimpy silver bikini. Made of a new metallic fabric developed by Stark's labs, the swimsuit shimmered like a mirage that clung to every curve and contour of the model's famously photogenic torso. Ana had worn the same suit when she posed for a special gift calendar intended only for the stockholders of Stark Enterprises. Tony suspected that bootleg copies were already circulating through every department of his company.

"Hello, Ana," he said, joining her at the bow. "Working on your tan?" Her svelte limbs already seemed darker than he recalled, turning a rich, inviting brown; how long had he been downstairs anyway? Long enough, he reminded himself, to fly the NTU from his lab to the Golden Gate Bridge and back again, plus the time it took to rescue the woman and talk to Fury. He lowered himself into the empty chair beside her. Rungs of sun-warmed plastic supported his back, and he took her right hand in his. Her touch was surprisingly cool and refreshing. As memorable as the photos were, he decided, they were nothing compared to the real thing. Unlike the anorexic waifs that had overrun the fashion industry in recent years, Ana's generous curves made her a wonderful example of a healthy, fit, and well-developed woman in her prime. He looked forward to getting to know her better. *Much* better.

"Finally!" she declared, pouting. Her voice had an exotic, Eastern European accent; Ana had emigrated to the U.S.A. from the Ukraine after the collapse of Communism. She had the sleek, sophisticated air of a woman who had travelled the world and experienced all that life had to offer. "All alone you have left me, with not even seagulls to keep me company."

"Sorry," he apologized. "I had a little work to finish up." He did not elaborate. Like most people, Ana believed that Tony Stark and his armored bodyguard were two separate individuals. Ana seemed like a lovely woman, bright and compassionate as well as beautiful, but Tony wasn't ready to trust her with the secret of his dual identity just yet. *Never on the first date,* he thought dryly. *I'm not that easy.*

Ana didn't seem to notice his evasion. She lifted her sunglasses off her nose, dropping them casually onto the deck beside her chair. She examined him with cool, blue eyes. "You work too hard, Tony," she said, apparently mollified. "Is not healthy."

Tell me about it, he thought. Although not much past his thirtieth birthday, he had already survived and overcome several heart attacks, alcoholism, paraplegia, a complete nervous system collapse, and a temporary case of death, not to mention countless life-or-death battles against the likes of Hydra and the Mandarin. Without meaning to, his fingers played with the hair over his neural port; he felt a hard metal ring, half the diameter of a dime, underneath the dark locks. Only the increasingly sophisticated suits of Iron Man armor had kept him alive and functioning so far; at times, his entire life seemed to boil down to an endless race between technology and mortality.

Languidly, Anastasia leaned over to massage his shoulders. "My God, Tony," she exclaimed. Lush, spectacular eyebrows arched in amazement. "You should feel how tight your muscles are. What were doing down in that office, fighting a war?"

"More like a skirmish, really," he said. Closing his eyes, he let his chin droop onto his chest while strong, confident fingers worked the stiffness out of his neck. He felt the last vestiges of his headache fading away thanks to Ana's gentle ministrations.

"I do not joke about this," she insisted, digging her thumbs in under his shoulder blades. "Your body is telling you to relax. You should listen to it."

Tony sighed. "I'm sure there's truth in what you're saying, Ana." *Then again*, he thought privately, *if I had listened to my body, I would have been six feet under years ago. My* mind *has kept me alive all this time, no matter what damage is inflicted upon my body—by me or anybody else!* For a moment, he felt like railing against all the hardships he'd been forced to endure. Then he opened his eyes, and saw the sunlight dancing over Anastasia's silvery form. Beyond her bare, graceful feet the turquoise sea sparkled on the other side of the white rope guardrail that ran along the perimeter of the deck. A smile formed beneath his mustache. This was far too beautiful a day, and far too enchanting a woman, to inspire such gloomy ruminations. He squeezed her hand and kicked off his sneakers.

"In fact," he said, raising an eyebrow while

bringing his face closer to hers, "I'm listening to my body right now."

"And?" she prompted him. Her throaty voice dropped another octave. A knowing look came into her sea-blue eyes, and a sly smile played over his lips.

"I think it wants to talk to yours," he said.

Abandoning his own deck chair, he shared Anastasia's while they carried on an intense, wordless conversation for many long, luxurious moments. Finally, though, she drew her lips back from his. "When you first suggested a weekend excursion, I had no idea it was to be so wonderfully isolated."

Her hat had long since been discarded, and so Tony stroked her clipped, golden locks, saying, "Mmm. We have the entire sea to ourselves."

An explosion off the bow proved him wrong. Salt water spouted into the air, cascading over the deck and soaking Tony and Anastasia. "What the hell?" he exclaimed, while Ana swore in her native Ukrainian. *Athena* rocked back and forth in the sudden swell, just before she was invaded.

They came over the railings, blasting up from beneath the waves as though shot from undersea cannons. Their flippers slapped loudly on the deck as they deftly boarded the yacht with the smooth, efficient movements of a well-trained fighting squad. *These people are no amateurs,* Tony realized instantly, *whoever they are.*

There were five of them, three men and two women, clad in glistening black wetsuits that covered their bodies from head to toe, making them look like inhuman creatures from some watery abyss. Emerald-tinted visors hid their eyes, compact breathing filters covered their mouths, while some sort of propulsion device was clamped to their backs. A water-propelled jetpack, Tony guessed, the engineer in him intrigued despite the danger. He noted that the suits looked as though they were constructed out of two different materials of different textures: a dull-hued, rubbery substance at the elbows, knees, and other joints and a slicker, harder material elsewhere; perhaps the bulk of the suits were not as flexible as they appeared. Not metal, surely, but maybe a reinforced polymer . . .

Never mind that, he told himself. *They're armed.* All five invaders carried a bronze, cylinder-shaped weapon about the size of a standard speargun, with a coil of red insulated tubing where the spear should have been. Tony didn't recognize the design, but the attached sighting mechanism betrayed its hostile intentions. *My armor*, he thought instantly. He needed his Iron Man armor, but the attaché case containing its components was downstairs in his office. Could he still get to the case in time? Out of the water, perhaps those suits and flippers would slow the invaders down.

"Tony!" Ana cried out, confused and alarmed. She held on tightly to his arm. "Who are these people? What do they want?"

He had no idea, and there was no time to explain even if he did. *Forgive me, Ana,* he thought as he pulled himself abruptly from her grasp and sprang to his feet. He half-ran, half-staggered across the lurching, slippery deck towards the open doorway to the yacht's interior. The explosion of water had left sea water all over the deck. His bare feet splashed through puddles of brine as he ran. *If only I can get to the briefcase,* he thought urgently. *These refugees from* Sea Hunt *would be in for the surprise of their lives then!* Donning the armor was easy; over the years, he'd perfected the technique until he could now transform into Iron Man in less than a minute. When placed adjacent to each other, the modular components of the armor automatically linked themselves together using magnetic connections. Once he opened the attaché case, the armor practically assembled itself, but first he had to reach the briefcase.

Damn, he cursed silently. *I should never have left it all the way downstairs. But who expects a commando raid during a vacation cruise?* He bit his lip in frustration. *I should have, that's who.*

The nearest invader, a large man several inches taller than Tony, rushed to intercept him. He moved faster than Tony expected; either his wetsuit was more accommodating than it looked or the man had logged plenty of hours working in it. He loomed between Tony and the open doorway, brandishing his weapon. "Surrender now, Mr. Stark. You have no choice," he said. His respirator mask muffled the sound of his voice, but Tony thought he detected a German accent.

There was no way to go around the man. *Very well,* Tony thought. He'd won fights without armor before. Running straight at the tall invader, he drew back his fist and delivered a roundhouse punch that caught the man squarely in the jaw. It was like hitting concrete. Tony felt the impact all the way up his arm. The other man didn't budge.

No, not metal, Tony's aching knuckles confirmed. Only plastic, but damn hard nonetheless. *This is bad,* he thought. *Those wetsuits are armored . . . and I'm not.* His mind racing, he scrutinized the black plastic suit, finally recognizing the design as belonging to a contractor that Stark Enterprises occasionally employed—specifically, a design he had rejected. His eyes fell on the dull, rubbery finish of the suit's joints. If he remembered the specs he'd seen right, the joints weren't as hard and stiff as the rest of the suit; this allowed the man to move smoothly about, but also left some of the suit's inner workings vulnerable to someone who knew where to put a well-placed kick. *That's my best shot,* he decided, trying to recall a martial arts move that Captain America had once tried to teach him.

The other man pointed his weapon at Tony. "Don't try to be a hero, Stark," said the man, with an edge of irritation in his voice. The black mask and green visor revealed no trace of humanity of the man's face. "You don't stand a chance."

We'll see about that, Tony thought. *Hope I got this right, Cap.*

Ducking beneath the weapon's obvious line of fire, he swiveled and swung all his weight into a *savate* kick at the miniscule exposure in the man's left leg joint. *If I've figured this wrong,* he thought as the kick struck home, *my foot bones are going to be powder.* A sudden crackle of electricity sounded from the man's armor; all the hairs on Tony's back rose instantly as he felt a discharge of energy pass over him. To his relief, however, the pliable black rubber yielded before his kick. The towering figure before him let out a yelp of pain. He staggered, almost losing his grip on his weapon, and Tony barrelled into him, striking the man in the chest with his shoulder. The armored giant toppled over, and he stumbled onto one knee: the knee with the displaced knee-joint and the exposed wiring, which came into contact with a puddle on the water-strewn deck.

There was a sudden flash, the kind a megawatt lightbulb makes right before it burns out, blinding Tony momentarily. The other man went into convulsions, his body jerking up and down upon the deck like a live trout flopping about on a frying pan. Staring through watery eyes, flashing blue dots obscuring his vision, Tony saw a vicious crack running across the length of the man's visor.

Another wave rocked *Athena*, and the entire yacht tilted to starboard. The thrashing man went sliding across the slippery deck, then underneath the white rope railing. Tony heard the man splash into the sea. With a shock, he realized that this was the second time today he'd witnessed a man go to his death beneath the waves.

"Victor!" a woman exclaimed as her comrade vanished from sight. There were still four pirates onboard the yacht, but none left between Tony and the stairs. Seeing his chance, he dived for the open doorway, only to feel a cold rubber glove grab hold of his ankle. Looking behind him, he saw one of the remaining men right behind him. *Blast,* Tony cursed silently. *He must have charged for me even while his friend was being electrocuted. A pretty cold-blooded character, especially since he could have tried to save the other man instead of grabbing me.*

"You will pay for what you did to Victor," the man said. "Maybe not right now, but before you die I will see to it that you regret the day of your decadent American birth." He was a few inches shorter than the other one, with a leaner physique. *Not to mention a talent for clichéd rhetoric,* Tony noted.

His grip was strong, though. Holding on with his hands to each side of the doorframe, Tony tried to twist his foot free, but the gloved hand held on to him like a vise. He kicked at the pirate with his free leg, but his blow smacked uselessly against hardened plastic. Then another hand grabbed his heel . . . and twisted his foot viciously. Despite himself, Tony cried out in agony. His fingers slipped away from the doorframe, and he fell onto one knee. The other man kicked Tony in the side; the flippers on his boot did little to lessen the blow. *If I had my armor on,* he thought angrily, *I'd make you eat that boot—and wash it down with repulsor rays!*

"Stand up," the thin man commanded, releasing Tony's anguished foot. "Step away from the door." He kicked Tony again for emphasis. *A plain old "or else" would have sufficed,* Tony thought resentfully.

Cautiously, he placed his weight on his injured leg, which protested vehemently but cooperated nonetheless. He stood facing his tormentor, his back to the stairway. As he moved away slowly from the door, the other man circled around him until their positions were reversed. Now the thin man blocked Tony's way just as his late companion had. The pirate raised his weapon and Tony felt a depressing surge of *déjà vu*. He doubted his kickboxing trick would work a second time, especially now that his leg had taken its lumps.

Time to talk my way out this, he thought reluctantly. *If I can.* "Who are you?" Tony demanded, putting on a deliberate display of righteous indignation. "I'll have you know I'm an American citizen, and a close friend of several Senators and the Joint Chiefs of Staff. Have you heard of Iron Man? He's my personal bodyguard, and he's probably on his way this very minute. You and your little zap guns won't stand a chance, so I suggest you surrender immediately. This is sheer piracy, and I want an explanation right now!''

Before anyone could respond to his bluff, Tony heard Anastasia scream. Spinning around so fast that he almost fell once more, he saw her sprinting away from their menacing attackers. Fear filled her sapphire eyes as she ran towards Tony, but she didn't get far. Two members of the cadre—a stocky woman and the third man—ran after her. They captured her quickly, each seizing one of her arms. Her flimsy, two-piece bathing suit made her seem especially vulnerable when compared with the heavy layers of plastic and rubber covering her assailants. Ana struggled to free herself, kicking and shouting, but the armored pirates held her fast between them. Her sunglasses, resting helplessly on the deck of the yacht, crunched beneath a heavy flipper. A third pirate, standing opposite them, raised her weapon and pointed the electrical coils directly at Ana.

''No!'' Tony yelled, even as the thin man took hold of Tony's arms and brutally yanked them behind his back. Tony winced in pain. ''Leave her out of this,'' he begged them. ''Whatever you want, she has nothing to do with me. I barely know her.''

Forgive me, Ana, he thought. *I'm just trying to protect you.*

But no one was listening. Electricity crackled and a coruscating bolt of yellow energy leaped from the pirate's weapon to strike Ana on the forehead. Tony watched in horror as her beautiful, silver-clad body suddenly stiffened, then went limp in her assailant's arms. Her beautiful blue eyes fell shut. He smelled ozone in the air. The invaders dropped her inert form onto the soaked deck as though they were discarding a bag of garbage. Her body lay where it fell, in a still and graceless tangle of limbs. Tony thought he saw her breathing.

"You bastards," he cried. "What do you want?"

"Time to go," said a muffled voice over his shoulder. Like his fallen comrade, the thin pirate had a vaguely Germanic accent. Without warning, the entire cadre charged at him, except for the one who continued to hold Tony's arms pinned behind his back. As Tony twisted and fought to extricate himself, they lifted him bodily over their heads, carted him roughly towards the railing, then flung him headlong into the sea.

What the hell . . . ?

Tony bellyflopped into the waves, swallowing an entire mouthful of water before he could catch his breath. The water was salty and warm and his unexpected immersion came as a shock to his system. A startled fish splashed only a few feet from his head. More splashes exploded all around him, as the cadre dived off the deck, surrounding him. *Where was Ana? What was happening to her?* Fearing for her safety, he scarcely had time to bob once or twice beneath the waves before rubbery hands grabbed onto his legs, arms, and shoulders. At first he thought they were going to drag him under. *Revenge for Victor's acci-*

dental drowning? Then he felt something being injected into his neck. The last light of sunshine, shining through the turquoise water above him, grew ever fainter, receding from view.

Then the sun disappeared, and everything went dark.

Cold. Wet. Dark.

Heart pounding, Tony Stark woke from a dream of drowning to find himself both alive and dry. He sat up hastily, kicking off a set of thin sheets and dropped his bare feet onto a cool tile floor. Harsh white light hurt his eyes. The last thing he remembered was being pulled underwater by a squad of armored scuba divers. *What happened next?* he wondered as the last vestiges of sleep cleared from his mind. *Where is Anastasia?* He looked around at his new surroundings. *For that matter,* he thought, *where am I?*

He was in a stark white cubicle, roughly ten by ten feet in area. The accommodations were spartan: a simple metal cot, on which he now sat; a toilet; a sink (no mirror); and what appeared to be a small computer work station, complete with stool. The entire chamber—walls, floor, and ceiling—was the same dull shade of white. Most alarmingly, the walls appeared perfectly seamless, with nary a crack marring their smooth, antiseptic surface. Tony saw no sign of any doors or windows.

Not exactly the penthouse suite at the Ritz, he thought, *and no exit to boot.* The room and its (minimal) furnishings seemed deliberately barren, utilitarian, institutional. Like a hospital room . . . or a prison cell. Given the circumstances of his arrival, he strongly suspected the latter. He'd seen more welcoming mausoleums.

Tony inspected himself next. His swimsuit had

disappeared, replaced by a short-sleeved shirt and a simple pair of cotton trousers. Both shirt and trousers were white, of course. Basic prison garb. He stood and stretched his limbs experimentally. He felt none the worse for his capture and near-drowning. Even his right hand looked fine, despite its recent collision with the late Victor's armored chin. His ankle twinged a bit when he flexed it, but that was all. No water filled his lungs. *Funny*, he mused. *You'd expect my knuckles to be badly bruised, if not broken.* Punching Victor had been like slamming his fist into a steel girder; even George Foreman would have needed to put his hand on ice after slugging that hard plastic faceplate. Yet Tony's fingers felt as strong and limber as a concert pianist's. It was puzzling.

The computer station also intrigued him. A PC and work area were hardly standard issue features of a dungeon or cell, even in the era of the Internet. The compact PC sat atop a small, one-person worktable mounted flush with the wall. A quick glance in the direction of the station suggested that no support materials had been provided; he didn't see any disks, manuals, or printer. No modem either, naturally. His kidnappers weren't going to make it that easy to call for help. *So what am I expected to do with that computer?* he wondered. *Customize license plates via desktop publishing?* He couldn't afford to indulge his curiosity about the setup just now, however. He didn't know what his jailers were up to, but it couldn't bode well for Stark Enterprises.

More importantly, what had become of Anastasia? The beautiful model haunted his memory; in his mind, he could still see her as she was the instant before *Athena* was boarded: lovely, warm, and happy to enjoy a pleasant, romantic encounter on a sunny and peaceful afternoon. For a few precious moments, they had both been perfectly content with the world. Tony's blood boiled, but he forced himself to think through the situation logically. It was possible that Ana was still in danger, maybe even a prisoner as well. Last he remembered, his surviving attackers had left her unconscious body behind on the yacht, diving off the yacht to drag Tony underneath the waves, but who knows what had happened after they zonked him out underwater? They could have easily retrieved her from *Athena*. Tony felt a prick of guilt for getting the unsuspecting model sucked into this mess in the first place, and cold fury at the unknown enemy who had placed them both in jeopardy.

The mysterious computer waited a few feet away. The technophile in him remained fascinated by the possibilities it presented. He stared at the device, then shook his head. *No,* he decided, turning away from the computer station. Escape had to be his top priority.

He paced along the perimeter of his cell, running his palm over the unadorned white walls. They felt discouragingly sturdy. Plaster over solid concrete, he guessed, and completely unbroken. The entire cell could have been carved out of a single chunk of cement. Still, there had to be a way out somewhere. Every prison has a gate after all.

Besides, he thought, *they had to have gotten me in here somehow. Unless they decided to wall me in, like Fortunato in "The Cask of Amontillado."* Despite himself, he shuddered at the thought of being entombed forever like the Edgar Allan Poe character in this modern dungeon. "For the love of God, Montressor," he whispered to the silent room.

He searched methodically for a hidden door. First, he tapped the walls with his knuckles, listening carefully for the echo that would betray the existence of a secret passageway. He heard nothing, except for the dull thunk of flesh and bone knocking on dense matter several inches thick. He examined the floor, even moving the cot out of the way so he could inspect the air under the bed. Fortunately, the cot was not bolted to the floor as he had feared. He got down on his hands and knees, but found nothing. Placing his ear against the floor, he strained to hear something: pipes, a furnace, voices, anything at all.

Nothing. The floor seemed as firm and impenetrable as the walls. Balancing precariously on top of the stool, he managed to touch the ceiling but found nothing promising there either. He hopped off the wobbly stool, disgusted. He'd found nothing on or near the ceiling, not even a metal grille or ventilation shaft.

For a second, he almost panicked. Where was the air coming from? What if he ran out of air? Tony

flashed back to that terrifying moment beneath the
sea, when he thought he might drown. Had he survived that only to die, gasping for air, in this blasted
white room? A chill ran down his spine, but a moment's thought calmed his fears. Although there was
no clock in sight, and his wristwatch was missing, he
had to have been exploring the cell for over an hour
by now. Plus, who knows had long he had been sleeping in that cot? *If I was going to suffocate,* he concluded, *I would have done so already.* Instead, the air
supply felt fine. He wasn't even breathing hard.

And yet, so far the room had proved completely
airtight. So how was the air getting in and out? For
that matter, where was the light coming from? Tony's
eyes searched the room. No lamps or overhead light-
ing was visible, yet he could see perfectly clearly in
all directions. He scanned the walls and floor for his
shadow, trying to figure out the source of the illumination. But, like Peter Pan in Wendy's bedroom,
Tony had somehow misplaced his shadow. The light
filling the room came from everywhere and nowhere.

Curiouser and curiouser, he thought. *Blast it all.*
Even as a child, he had never liked Lewis Carroll. A
born scientist, he preferred his world to make sense.
Jules Verne and Robert Heinlein were more his speed.
He was missing something; he was convinced of it.
There had to be a logical explanation, if only he could
think his way through it.

First, though: escape.

Perhaps, he theorized, the walls themselves

moved? His fingers probed the corners of the room, feeling for cracks where wall met wall, but again his search yielded negative results. Not even a micron of empty space separated the walls and floor from each other. He almost didn't bother to check the corners of the ceiling, but in the end, after several minutes of dragging the stool all over the cell, and nearly falling every time he stood atop the stool, he had to conclude that his efforts had been wasted.

There was no way in or out. He was thoroughly, undeniably, nigh hermetically sealed in. Trapped.

Good thing I'm not claustrophobic, he thought ruefully. *Nothing like spending half your life in an iron suit to get you used to close quarters.* His Iron Man armor brought him freedom and mobility, however. This cell did anything but.

Discouraged but unwilling to give up, his eyes fell again upon the computer terminal a few feet away. Maybe this PC held some answers, he hoped. No time like the present to find out. Returning the stool to its original position in front of the station, he sat down at the keyboard. Upon closer inspection, the computer turned out to be a modified SE-435, the latest in home computers manufactured by Stark Enterprises. Lots of memory, he recalled, plus plenty of bonus features. A grim smile twisted Tony's lips. *Either my unseen jailer has a cute sense of humor, or he believes in buying the best. Wonder if it's equipped with Tetris? From the looks of things, I may have an excess of free time on my hands.* Monitor and hard drive were combined in a single compact unit. The two disk drives, one for a five-and-one-quarter-inch floppies, one for three-and-one-half-inch, had both been sealed. A single white electrical cord ran seamlessly (what else?) into the adjacent wall.

With the flick of a switch, he turned the machine on. The screen came to life with admirable speed, although Tony couldn't help noticing that the usual Stark Enterprises copyright notices didn't appear the way they were supposed to. *I'll have to call in my lawyers,* he thought ruefully, *if I ever get out of here.* Instead, a single line of white type appeared against an ominous blood-red background:

WELCOME, MR. STARK. PRESS ENTER FOR FURTHER INSTRUCTIONS.

WHO ARE YOU?   Tony typed instead.

The screen did not respond. The same command, PRESS ENTER, flashed emphatically. "Well, why not?" Tony muttered. "We'll play by your rules . . . for now." His finger tapped the appropriate key. Almost instantly, a new message scrolled over the screen:

STARK: YOU HAVE BEEN BROUGHT HERE FOR ONE PURPOSE AND ONE PURPOSE ONLY: TO SHARE THE SECRETS OF YOUR ''IRON MAN'' TECHNOLOGY. USING THIS EQUIPMENT, YOU WILL DESIGN A STATE-OF-THE-ART SUIT OF COMBAT ARMOR, COMPLETE WITH EVERY FORM OF ADVANCED WEAPONRY IN YOUR AR-

SENAL. YOU WILL RECORD ALL SPECIFICA-
TIONS AND INSTRUCTIONS FOR THE CON-
STRUCTION OF THE ARMOR IN THE MEMORY
OF THIS UNIT. YOUR NEEDS WILL BE ATTENDED
TO UNTIL YOUR TASK IS COMPLETED. IF YOU
COOPERATE, YOU WILL NOT BE HARMED. BEGIN
IMMEDIATELY.

Never! Tony vowed silently. Over the years, he
had taken enormous pains and sacrifices to keep his
most potent technology, embodied in the form of Iron
Man's armor, out of the hands of his enemies. He'd
seen firsthand the devastation his inventions could
create when put to the wrong uses. The so-called
''Armor Wars,'' in which he had been forced to battle
a huge assortment of villains equipped with scientific
secrets stolen from Stark Enterprises, had been an ongoing nightmare that nearly killed him . . . and re-
sulted in the death of a Russian adversary of his
known as the Titanium Man. He had gone through
the torments of purgatory, fought friend and foe to
reclaim his technology, and he'd be damned if he'd
now turn over his hard-won secrets to a faceless command on a twelve-inch computer screen.

Hell, he thought, *I've never even patented most
of Iron Man's equipment because that would compromise the armor's security.*

He started to type out an angry reply, then remembered that the SE-435 could be equipped with
voice recognition capability for the price of a small
upgrade. He stared at the machine and shrugged. It

was worth a shot. "Can you hear me?" he asked out loud. *I'm really going to feel stupid if this doesn't work,* he thought.

YES. BEGIN IMMEDIATELY, the PC answered.

"You don't understand. I'm just a figurehead," he lied, stalling for time. "Why, I haven't designed anything more complicated than a press release for years. That's why I employ an entire staff of technicians and programmers."

NONSENSE. YOUR SCIENTIFIC VIRTUOSITY IS WELL-DOCUMENTED. FURTHERMORE, THE DEVELOPMENT OF IRON MAN IS NOT A CORPORATE FUNCTION. HIS CREATION BEGINS AND ENDS WITH YOU.

"Even if I knew how," Tony protested, "I couldn't devise a new suit under these conditions. One silly little home computer to create Iron Man? These days we use genuine artificial intelligences to supervise both the development and construction of Iron Man's armor. The computers design computers to design the armor."

He wasn't entirely bluffing. In the never-ending crusade to improve and perfect Iron Man, the process had grown more and more automated over time, resulting eventually in HOMER, short for Heuristically-Operative Matrix Emulation Rostrum, a self-aware electronic entity capable of manufacturing armor beyond even Tony's own power to devise. The last several generations of Iron Man armor owed as much to HO-

MER as to Tony. *Could I even do it on my own again?* he wondered. *I'm not sure.*

The mystery villain wasn't buying any of it:

THE VISION IS YOURS. ALL ELSE IS MERE LABOR. COOPERATE, OR SUFFER THE CONSEQUENCES.

Resorting to threats already, are you? Tony scowled. His adversary sounded like he was losing patience. *Fine,* Tony thought. *So am I.*

"Forget it, buster," he declared, refusing to bow to extortion. "If you kill me, you'll never get the secrets. And you might as well do your worst now, because I'm never going to come close to cooperating. Got that?"

Tony expected more threats. He didn't care. He wasn't bluffing when he said he rather die than turn over Iron Man to an unknown, malevolent power. Grisly images of armored super-villains wreaking havoc on the world flashed through his mind, steeling his resolve. *Never again,* he vowed silently, awaiting the screen's next dire ultimatum. To his surprise, though, the scarlet background vanished instantly. In its place he saw a high-resolution, full-color image of . . . Anastasia!

She was in another cell, almost identical to his own, except that Ana had not been provided with a computer. Instead of the sparkling silver bikini, she now wore a white prison uniform similar to his own. He watched her pace frantically about the chamber, shouting at the blank white walls. There was no sound, so he could not make out what she was saying, but she was clearly frightened and confused. She walked with a limp, he noticed, and her right arm was wrapped up in a sling. Her forehead was bruised where the lightning bolt had struck her; a dark purple blotch marred the pale smoothness of her brow. A bright red blotch over her shoulder stained the white blouse she wore. *How long has she been bleeding?* he wondered. Tony inspected her legs, looking for the source of the limp. He saw no bloodstains on the cotton trousers, yet Ana winced in pain as she restlessly stalked her prison. She'd been hurt, obviously, but how badly?

"Blast you," Tony snarled at the screen. "What have you done to her?"

A line of white type ran along the bottom of the screen, like subtitles in a foreign film:

BEGIN THE ARMOR OR SHE WILL SUFFER.

Suddenly, the screen went black. The ultimate warning perhaps, implying the threat of total extinction for the unfortunate woman. Tony slammed his fist angrily into his other palm. Now what was he supposed to do? He could not—would not—let anyone as ruthless as the brains behind this vicious operation steal the power of Iron Man away from him, but what about Ana? An innocent hostage, she didn't deserve any of this. Could he really sacrifice her, let her face torture or worse, for the sake of his secrets? He thought of Ana, trapped in that empty cell, cut off from the world without any explanation. *She must be going insane*, he thought.

And yet, he agonized, what of the thousands, maybe millions of people who might be harmed by an army of evil Iron Men? Could the world survive another Armor War?

It was a no-win situation, and one that wasn't going away. The black screen flickered in front of him, waiting for his answer. *I'll beat you somehow, you devil,* Tony vowed, *whoever you are.* In the meantime, though, Ana was still a captive, maybe only a few feet away, on the other side of the wall. Or perhaps she was being held on the other side of the world, thousands of miles away. Wherever her own prison hid, Ana's safety depended on him and what he did next. He scarcely knew her, really, despite their steamy lovemaking aboard his yacht, but that didn't matter now. She was a person in deadly trouble. Tony knew he couldn't let her down.

"You win," he said to the computer. "Open a new file: Iron Man, Stage One."

FRIDAY. 12:36 PM. PACIFIC COAST TIME.

". . . and then I woke up on the deck, and Tony was gone. There was water everywhere, and scorch marks on the deck. I searched the entire yacht, but there was no sign of him. Finally, I managed to activate the emergency beacon in the control room, and a Stark helicopter came and picked me up almost immediately. And that's all I know.''

Anastasia Swift sipped from the cup of hot coffee she cradled in her hands. Steam rose from the black ceramic mug bearing the Stark corporate logo. A yellow Stark Security jacket was draped over her shoulders. She still wore the wet silver swimsuit they had found her in; there had been no time to allow her to change clothes. The minute she'd arrived at the southern California headquarters of Stark Enterprises, she'd been rushed to this heavily guarded debriefing room. Now she sat in a comfortable leather chair surrounded by many of Tony Stark's closest friends and business associates. A large blank monitor screen dominated one entire wall of the chamber, opposite Ana. An impressive bank of controls and communications equipment, full of blinking red and green lights, ran along the bottom of the screen. She scratched her forehead; an ugly red burn above her eyes marred her flawless tan.

Bethany Cabe, Director of Corporate Security, considered the trembling young woman seated before her. Anastasia was bearing up better than Bethany had anticipated; she had expected the model to be something of a hothouse flower, a spoiled, fragile prima donna completely unable to cope with her recent brush with violence. But the celebrated cover girl, although clearly shaken, seemed eager and able to help; her account of the assault on *Athena*, which Ana had already repeated several times, had been both consistent and coherent. Apparently, there was more to Ms. Swift than her miniscule bathing suit revealed.

I should have known better, Bethany thought. *Tony has good taste in women, as I should know better than most.* Bethany leaned back against the front of a desk, supporting her weight with her arms. Where Anastasia, even in distress, possessed a cool, Continental poise and elegance, Bethany bristled with pent-up energy and strength. A statuesque redhead in a skintight black bodysuit, she proudly wore the Stark Enterprises logo, a stylized "SE," on her uniform. Years ago, however, before coming to work for Stark, back when she'd run her own private security firm, Bethany and Tony Stark had been lovers—until his alcoholism and her husband drove them apart. In time, Tony's drinking problem came to an end, as did her marriage, but their relationship had never been the same. Today they were "merely" friends and co-workers. Yet they were still closer, she knew, than many husbands and wives. *I've stood by him, and fought beside him,* she thought, *through hell and back. I've even worn that damn armor of his. And I'll find you now, Tony, wherever they've taken you.*

Besides, that was her job. She brushed back her shoulder-length red hair, and fixed piercing green eyes on the young model, the only known witness to Tony Stark's abduction. *Who is it this time?* she wondered. *The Mandarin? The Controller?*

"Ms. Cabe," Anastasia asked, interrupting Bethany's thoughts. "What's happened to Tony? Do you have any idea?"

"Not yet," she conceded, "but we're working on it." It was true; she had already notified the Coast Guard, the FBI, Interpol, the CIA, Nick Fury, the Avengers, and the Fantastic Four. Force Works, Tony's own privately operated super hero strike force, was on an extended mission in the Kree Galaxy; Bethany couldn't contact them if her life depended on it. And, so far, no one else had any new information on Tony's disappearance, which came as no surprise to Bethany. Notifying the other agencies and super hero teams had simply been standard procedure; she intended to handle this investigation personally. Stark was more than just a cherished friend and ex-lover; he was her boss.

But who could have snatched Tony? The possibilities seemed endless. Unlike Anastasia, Bethany knew that Tony Stark was Iron Man, which probably tripled the number of his enemies. Granted, most of Iron Man's foes were also unaware of his true identity, and a millionaire industrialist/world-class inventor was a tempting target for just about everybody, even if that millionaire didn't also fight super-villains in his spare time. *Hell,* she thought glumly, *this could be a brand-new bad guy for all I know. They seem to spring up like weeds these days, and half of them are mutants.*

"If there's anything I can do. . . ." Anastasia offered, then swallowed another gulp of coffee. Bethany noticed again that the model was cold and wet. *She's had a hard day too,* she recalled. *We're lucky the commandoes didn't take the time to eliminate her.* At the moment, Anastasia was the only lead they had.

"Thank you, Ms. Swift," she said. She walked over and squeezed the other woman's hand. Ana's skin was cold and clammy to the touch. *Probably a touch of shock,* Bethany assumed, although the medic on the rescue team had given her a clean bill of health. "You've been very helpful. You can go now; I'm sure you'd like some rest. We'll contact you if we think of anything else." Bethany helped Anastasia to her feet. "Robert," she said to one of her lieutenants, a tall Asian man fresh out of the Green Berets, "would you see that Ms. Swift gets home safely? Take one of the limos."

Robert began to escort Anastasia out, but the model hesitated in the doorway. "Ms. Cabe," she asked, turning around. She had to take a deep breath before she could speak again. "Do you think Tony's dead?"

Bethany thought a moment before replying.

"No," she said finally. "There was no trace of blood on the yacht, and Stark ships and subs are searching the surrounding waters with ultrasonic scans. Again, no blood and no body." *We haven't even found any trace of the man you saw electrocuted,* she thought. Bethany looked the other woman in the eye and tried to sound as confident as she could. "If whoever's behind this just wanted to kill Mr. Stark, they could have done so easily enough on the yacht, and left the body behind."

Anastasia shuddered, perhaps at the thought of waking on the yacht beside Tony's corpse. Bethany couldn't blame her; it wasn't a pretty picture.

"This smells like an abduction," Bethany reassured her. "I'm sure we'll receive the kidnappers' demands in time." Privately, Bethany was not sure. The Gulf of Mexico was a big place. *We could search for years and not find a body,* she thought. Still, her words seemed to comfort Anastasia.

"I see," Anastasia said, stepping into the hall. "Thank you, Ms. Cabe." Robert closed the door behind her.

I wonder if she knows about Tony and me, Bethany wondered, then dismissed the thought as irrelevant. She faced her colleagues in the room: Felix Ricardo Alvarez, Vice President and Chief Operating Officer of Stark Enterprises; Dr. Abraham Zimmer, Director of Engineering; Dr. Erica Sondheim, Director of Medical Research; Mrs. Arbogast, Tony's Executive Assistant; and Harold "Happy" Hogan, his long-time friend and right-hand man. In Tony's absence, they were the heart and mind of the multinational corporate juggernaut that was Stark Enterprises.

"Well," she addressed them. "That's where we stand. Ms. Swift's eyewitness version of the attack is pretty much our only hard data, and it doesn't tell us anything about Tony's abductors except that they're well-supplied and efficient. So . . . what's next?" *They're all looking to me to solve this,* she realized. After all, she was head of security. But ordinary corporate security didn't stand much of a chance in the super-powered big leagues that Iron Man routinely played in. Too bad the Scarlet Witch and the rest of Force Works were light-years away. *I might need some metahuman assistance before this mess is finished.*

"We have to release some sort of statement," Felix said. A well-groomed Hispanic man in an immaculate three-piece suit, he had distinguished himself as one of America's top lawyers before taking over as COO for Stark Enterprises, winning at least three cases before the Supreme Court. "The press has already got wind of the story. We have a small army of reporters and camera crews parked out front. I haven't seen anything like it since the O.J. Simpson trial."

"No doubt," Mrs. Arbogast sniffed, "that young lady's career as an overexposed pin-up girl only adds to the tabloid appeal of this sorry affair." The middle-aged woman's glasses had slid down her nose. Scowling, she pushed them up again with one firm finger. Mrs. Arbogast had never approved of any of her employer's female companions. *Including me,* Bethany recalled. Beneath her matronly airs, however, lurked the shrewd mind of a savvy and resourceful businesswoman. "Mrs. A.," as she was known and (occasionally) feared around the office, could keep Stark Enterprises running smoothly until Tony was rescued. *If* Tony could be rescued.

Bethany dismissed such pessimistic thoughts from her mind. "Tell the press," she advised Felix, "that Mr. Stark has been reported missing, but that an investigation is underway and we are confident he will be found. Promise them more news as it develops." Another thought occurred to her. "Oh, and somebody offer Ms. Swift a team of security people. She may need protection from the media, if from nothing else."

"What about leaks?" Happy Hogan asked. A burly ex-boxer, he had been at Tony's side since nearly the beginning of Iron Man's career. Only Jim Rhodes had known Tony longer, and Jim no longer worked for Stark Enterprises. Hogan's nickname was pure sarcasm; Happy had a disposition like Winnie the Pooh's melancholy friend Eeyore. Today, it seemed more than appropriate.

"What's to leak?" she asked, letting her frustration show. "We don't know anything!"

"Well, you know some wiseguy is going to say that the boss has fallen off the wagon again, that he's off on a bender.'' Hogan's gaze never left the floor. It obviously bothered him to have to bring up Tony's past battles with the bottle, but Bethany guessed he figured somebody had to say it. She didn't blame him; it was a valid point.

"There's not much we can do about low-minded gossip," Felix said firmly. "Those who want to assume the worst, will. I say we take the high road and ignore the entire issue. Any explicit denials from us will just fan the flames."

Hear, hear, Bethany thought. She was always inclined to trust Felix's instincts where public relations were concerned. Glancing over at Mrs. Arbogast, she saw the small, round woman nodding in approval.

"I'll draft a press release, Felix," Mrs. Arbogast volunteered. The Vice President thanked her, and promised to review the document the minute it came out of her word processor.

"If we hurry," he said, "we can easily make the afternoon news."

Erica Sondheim spoke up. She was in her middle thirties, about Bethany's age, wearing a white lab coat and glasses. "I'm worried about Tony's health. He's in better shape now than he has been in years, but anything could go wrong." Dr. Sondheim knew what she was talking about, Bethany thought. Much of her research, pushing the boundaries of neurosurgery, had been tested on the desperate body of Tony Stark. Working closely with Dr. Zimmer, they had developed the artificial nerve connections that allowed

Tony to walk again after an assassin's bullet severed his spinal cord. And later, after Tony's entire nervous system had been infected by a lethal techno-virus, they had literally brought Tony back to life again. Who else could heal Tony if he was badly hurt? The technology keeping Tony Stark alive was more sophisticated than anything found in the finest hospitals on Earth.

"I wouldn't worry, Erica," Abe Zimmer said. Several years older than Dr. Sondheim, he fit the stereotypical image of a venerable, senior scientist: bald, bespectacled, and vaguely Einstein-ish. (Despite the age difference, however, he and Erica were lovers.) His specialty was cybernetics. Where Erica dealt with the delicate biological connections between mind and body, Abe handled the hardware. Together, they served as Tony Stark's medical support staff, as well as pursuing new breakthroughs in medicine and computer science. "We built Tony's nervous system to last. Why, I offered to give him a money-back guarantee. Besides, don't underestimate Tony's own resources, no matter what situation he may be in. Tony's a 'self-made man,' remember? He programmed most of his nervous system himself!"

Happy Hogan paced angrily. He smacked one meaty fist into the wall. His squashed, homely face bore lifelong souvenirs from countless prizefights. "Programming," he said gloomily, "ain't gonna help him none against goons with guns."

Bethany had to agree. This was not, at the bottom

of it all, a medical crisis or a public relations problem. Stark security had been breached by unknown adversaries who were dangerous and heavily armed. Which made it her responsibility.

"I should have been there," she said bitterly. "I should have had him under heavier guard."

"Er, I think the boss wanted to be alone," Happy said, blushing slightly. He had a point, she conceded. Who wants his ex-girlfriend along as a chaperone, even if that ex was in charge of protecting him? Then again, she reminded herself, more than one of Tony's lady friends had tried to kill him on occasion. The late, unlamented Kathy Dare came damn close to succeeding, shooting Tony in the spine when he least expected it. (Dare subsequently killed herself.) *I'll have to talk to Tony about date security,* she thought, *assuming I ever see him again.*

"Besides," Hogan continued, "Tony can take care of himself. Most of the time, that is."

I hope you're right, Bethany thought. Like her, Happy was well aware that Tony was also Iron Man. Unfortunately, there was one disturbing detail that she could not share with Anastasia or the press: Tony did not have his armor. The locked briefcase containing his Iron Man suit had been found in his quarters on the yacht. Retrieved by her security team, it now rested atop the desk behind her. *Wherever Tony is,* she realized, *he's far away from his best defense.*

"Excuse me," a familiar voice intruded, coming from the overhead intercom system. It was HOMER, the artificial intelligence that, among other things, managed the daily operation of the entire Stark Enterprises complex. His electronically generated voice sounded surprisingly human; Bethany always thought HOMER's deep, booming voice sounded like a cross between Jim Henson and James Earl Jones. HOMER was a joint creation of Tony Stark and Abe Zimmer. *That's probably why I think of him as male,* she reflected. *That, and the voice.*

"I'm sorry to interrupt," HOMER said, "but I'm receiving an urgent communication for all of you."

"From who?" Bethany asked. Had Force Works returned to Earth at last? Maybe Wanda could use her mutant hex powers to locate Tony's whereabouts. That weird blue alien, Century, was a teleporter; he could take them straight there.

"From the kidnappers, I believe," HOMER stated. "I am attempting to trace the transmission to its origin, but the message has been sent through an extraordinarily complicated series of relays. There are indications that the final form of the message may have began as a concealed, mutating virus in an earlier, apparently innocuous transmission."

"Keep working on it, HOMER," Bethany ordered. "In the meantime, patch the message through to this office."

"Understood. Message coming through. . . ."

Bethany and the others quickly turned to face the large monitor at the end of the room. The five-foot square display screen lit up as the monitor hummed to life. A burst of cathode-ray snow and static appeared briefly on the screen, followed by a face Bethany had not seen in years.

Long, lustrous black hair framed a face of solid gold. A metal mask covered the face of the woman on the screen, but, unlike Iron Man's smooth, minimalist faceplate, this mask had all the fine detail and careful craftsmanship of a statue by Michelangelo. Arched eyebrows, a graceful nose, fine cheekbones, and seductive lips had been sculpted with painstaking precision to create a gleaming, polished simulcrum of feminine beauty. A line of delicate rivets along the rim of the mask betrayed its metallic origins, while her burnished forehead was partially divided down the middle by a widow's peak of thick brunette hair. Only a pair of cold blue eyes, gazing steadily out from behind her golden visage, revealed the flesh and blood woman behind the mask.

"Madame Masque," Bethany gasped in surprise. On the huge screen, the masked woman's startling visage seemed larger than life.

As Tony Stark's head of security, and as his one-time lover, Bethany was all too intimate with the infamous history of that name. Instantly, the entire tragic story came back to her:

The original Madame Masque, the first woman to wear the golden mask now on the screen, had been Whitney Frost, yet another of Tony Stark's greatest loves. Once a beautiful socialite, Whitney had inherited from her father, the late Count Luchino Nefaria, control of the Maggia, an international crime syndicate. After an early battle with Iron Man led to an accident in which her face was permanently disfigured, Whitney chose to hide her scarred features forever behind a metal disguise. As Madame Masque, she clashed frequently with Iron Man, while also carrying on a stormy, on-again, off-again love affair with Tony Stark, even after she learned Iron Man's true identity. Despite herself, Bethany felt a pang of jealousy when she remembered the intensity, and obvious passion, with which Tony still spoke of Whitney Frost.

But that was the *first* Madame Masque, she reminded herself. Only a few years ago, an unknown woman had killed Whitney Frost and taken her place as leader of the Maggia. When Whitney's body was found floating in New York's East River, Tony himself had identified the body and arranged for her funeral. But neither Tony nor anyone else had ever discovered the identity of Whitney's murderer, the new Madame Masque.

Who are you? Bethany wondered, staring at the screen. *What do you want with Tony now?*

"I have Tony Stark," Madame Masque said without preamble. Her golden lips did not move when she spoke, and her face remained immobile. The voice that emerged from the monitor was cool and unemotional; Bethany did not recognize it.

"I am willing to ransom him," she continued, "for a price. The organization known as Advanced

Idea Mechanics has developed a new energy chip of almost unlimited power. This device, the size of an ordinary computer chip, can generate enough power to light an entire city—or destroy one. The Maggia wants that chip, but A.I.M. has proven unwilling to part with it. Furthermore, the A.I.M. laboratory where the chip is being kept is heavily guarded by sophisticated technological defenses. My own operatives have had difficulty overcoming these defenses. Iron Man must succeed where they have failed."

"What?!" Bethany exclaimed, joining a chorus of shocked gasps and expletives from her colleagues. She had expected a demand for money, not Iron Man's personal services. Mere money, even millions of dollars, would have been a small price to pay for Tony's freedom. But Iron Man? That was impossible, for more than one reason.

"Well, I never . . . !" protested Mrs. Arbogast. More direct epithets came from around the table. Only HOMER seemed speechless.

"Exactly," Madame Masque declared. Bethany could hear the smirk in her voice even if she couldn't see it on Madame Masque's frozen metal face. "I want Iron Man to steal the energy chip from A.I.M. The location of their hidden lab is now being transmitted to you via a coded frequency. It is now ten minutes after one; you have twenty-four hours to obtain the chip—or you will never see Mr. Anthony Stark again."

"Wait!" Bethany stepped closer to the screen.

"This is ridiculous. Iron Man's not a thief. If you want something from A.I.M., blackmail them instead of us. Mr. Stark has nothing to do with this."

Madame Masque did not acknowledge her arguments. "Send Iron Man now," she repeated. "You have twenty-four hours. I will contact you again regarding the drop-off site. If you don't deliver the chip by precisely one PM on Saturday, Tony Stark will die." Abruptly, the screen went black.

"HOMER?" Bethany cried out. Her fingers raced over the controls beneath the screen, desperately trying to restore the image, but the monitor remained blank.

"I am sorry, Bethany," HOMER's disembodied voice replied. "The transmission has terminated itself."

"Did you manage to locate its origin?"

"Unfortunately, no. As I mentioned before, the transmission was concealed amidst a number of incoming data streams. It did not evolve into a coherent form until it had already entered our internal network. At the end, the transmission was not truly cut off at its source; instead, it self-destructed according to a preprogrammed command."

"In other words," Abe Zimmer translated. "They didn't want a dialogue with us. They just wanted to get their message across."

"Well, they sure succeeded there," Felix stated. He looked at the others' stunned faces. "We have their demands. Now what do we do? I'm assuming, of course, that this is not for public consumption.''

Bethany's mind was racing. She paced restlessly across the office. She'd have to notify S.H.I.E.L.D. and the other law enforcement agencies about Madame Masque's involvement, not that that was likely to do much good. This new Madame Masque had gone underground after Whitney Frost's murder and had successfully eluded capture ever since. Madame Masque could be anywhere in the world. Bethany could have HOMER trace that other transmission Madame Masque mentioned, the one with the coordinates of the A.I.M. lab, but she doubted that would be any more productive. Madame Masque had obviously gone to great pains to cover her tracks; she'd probably been working on this plot ever since her disappearance a few years back.

We have to get the chip, Bethany realized, *if only to buy time for Tony.* But there was one thing she knew, and that Whitney Frost had known, that this Madame Masque clearly did not: Iron Man couldn't ransom Stark because Iron Man *was* Stark. Bethany could hardly send Iron Man after the chip when the real Iron Man was already a prisoner of the Maggia. Nor was this something she wanted to explain to Madame Masque. *Thank God,* she thought, *Whitney never revealed Tony's secret before she died.*

For a moment, Bethany recalled the suitcase her men had recovered from the yacht. Her hand brushed over the brown leather exterior of the case. With

HOMER's help, she could eventually find the combination of the lock and get the case open, but was it worth the effort? Both she and Happy had donned the armor in emergencies, most recently during that big battle against Ultimo, but neither of them had the skill or experience they needed to really replace Iron Man. There was only one man who was truly Tony's equal as a fully-powered armored warrior.

"Okay, everybody," she announced loudly. "I think I know what to do. This is a security matter; the rest of you go and hold this company together until Tony gets back. I need to make a private call."

"But . . ." Felix began, as she hustled the others towards the door. "You have to tell me something. I need to say *something* to the staff . . . !"

"Tell everyone I have things under control," Bethany said. She caught Happy Hogan's eye. He nodded and took Felix by the arm. The former boxer gently but firmly edged Stark's top lawyer out of the briefing room. Mrs. Arbogast gave Bethany a penetrating stare that made the younger woman feel like she was being sliced, diced, and examined under a microscope. Then, apparently satisfied, Mrs. Arbogast pushed Drs. Sondheim and Zimmer into the hallway.

"You'd better know what you're doing, dear," Mrs. Arbogast said as she pulled the door shut behind her. Bethany swallowed hard. *I swear,* she thought, *I'd rather fight a battalion of Maggia dreadnaughts than cross that tough old lady.*

Hopefully, she wouldn't have to do either. "HO-

MER," she said, alone at last except for the bodiless presence of the artificial mind. "Put me through to Jim Rhodes. Immediately."

This was the only option left, Bethany decided. With Iron Man out of commission, it was time to call on War Machine.

CHAPTER 5

Tony awoke hungry. After several exhausting hours working at the computer station, trying to look productive without really accomplishing anything, he had collapsed onto the cot in search of sleep. *Sleep,* he had thought; there was another good way to stall for time. His unseen jailer, whom had Tony had begun to think of, sarcastically, as Blank Screen, could hardly expect him to work without sleep, could he? And the more he slept, the longer he could keep Blank Screen from the secrets of his armor. *I wonder if I could convince him that I'm a narcoleptic,* Tony thought. *God knows I've had enough other ailments.*

Lying on his side beneath the thin sheets, he kept his eyes closed. He didn't know for sure that he was being observed, but it seemed like a likely prospect. There were no cameras visible, but that meant nothing; Allen Funt had proved that years ago with his old *Candid Camera* program . . . and the technology had only improved since the 1960s. These days, ordinary citizens could buy sophisticated surveillance systems for their homes and offices, never mind what was available to international intelligence agencies. For all Tony knew, Blank Screen could be watching him from a satellite miles overhead. Modern science had rendered total privacy an obsolete notion . . . for better or for worse.

I wonder if anyone has noticed our absence yet? Tony thought. Surely, the abrupt disappearance of a billionaire *and* a world-famous supermodel could not go unremarked this long. Chances are, *The National*

Enquirer would be on the case even before the FBI. Had someone found *Athena* adrift and abandoned, like a modern-day *Marie Celeste*, or had his kidnappers been ruthless enough to sink the yacht after they captured Ana? Obviously, Blank Screen and his minions had not discovered the attaché case containing his Iron Man armor, or they would hardly be forcing him to design a new suit. *Thank heaven for small favors,* Tony thought, relieved that the crisis was not worse than it already was.

With any luck, he realized, *rescue parties are already searching for us.* Bethany Cabe was a professional. The minute she knew he was missing, she'd sift through every drop of water in the Gulf of Mexico to find him. *Unfortunately*, he conceded reluctantly, *that may not be enough.* Every minute he stalled gave any would-be rescuers more time to come to his and Anastasia's aid, but he knew there were no guarantees that help was on its way. *I don't even know where I am, so how am I supposed to guess if someone else will find me?* He had tremendous faith in his friends and colleagues, not to mention his super-powered friends like Captain America and Thor, but he couldn't count on the cavalry riding over the hill at the last minute. *Better if I work on the assumption that I'm on my own for the time being,* he concluded, *and concentrate on getting me and Ana out of this place as soon as humanly possible.*

And if the Avengers or S.H.I.E.L.D. happen to save the day before I can free us myself . . . Well, he'd just have to live with that. Amused by the thought, Tony rolled over onto his back and tried to get some more sleep. His pillow felt like a big chunk of foam rubber. The sheets barely reached his shoulders. *I've slept in better beds than this,* he thought, *and with a lot more entertaining company.*

His growling stomach drove him from dreamland eventually. Did it want breakfast? Dinner? In this white, windowless cubicle it was impossible to tell what time it was, or even exactly how much time had passed. It felt like he'd been here for at least a day or so, though. He ran a hand over his chin, surprised at the lack of stubble. *Funny,* he thought, *you'd think I'd be halfway to a beard by now.* He sniffed the sleeve of his white shirt; the clothing still seemed fresh enough. *How time flies when you're having fun,* he thought sarcastically; he could have sworn he'd been here long enough to need a change of clothes. He contemplated the sterile confines of his prison. White walls everywhere; it was like being trapped in a sensory deprivation tank. *Poor Ana,* he thought grimly. *At least I have my work to occupy me. How ever is she coping with this endless, empty whiteness?* Tony felt his blood pressure rise just thinking about it. He had to get Ana out of here!

Acid churned in his belly. Reluctantly, he opened his eyes and sat up in the cot. To his surprise, and genuine delight, he saw a platter of food resting on the floor. Pulling on his shirt and trousers, he investigated the contents of the platter. He found a bowl of oatmeal, a few slices of bread (no butter), and a plastic cup. Simple fare, but sufficient; his mouth watered in expectation. He couldn't remember the last time he'd eaten.

Once more, his eyes scanned the chamber, looking in vain for so much as a doggie door. The walls appeared as impermeable as ever, so where in the world had this food come from? The mystery tormented Tony, but his hunger could not be denied. He took a large bite out of a slice of a bread, then dug into the food with enthusiasm.

The meal was bland and tasteless; even the juice just tasted like flavored water. Still, he felt better afterwards, and strong enough to face the computer again. The steady glow from the monitor cast shadows on his face. *What,* he thought sardonically, *no screensaver?* His work was as he left it; he'd set up an *xyz* grid on the screen in order to draw a 3-D diagram of the schematics for Iron Man's helmet. A label ran along the top of the screen:

IRON MAN ARMORED EXOSKELETON. DIAGRAM 1.1.

MAJOR HEAD SUB-ASSEMBLY.

He used the mouse to add a few more lines to a sketch of the neck assembly, then started typing in the specs for each of the various components of the helmet: face piece, vocal harmonizer/changer, super orbicularis oris padding, optical cluster, frontal orbital padding, parietal padding, cybernetic antenna array, electronic transpiration control layer, temporomandibular padding, subroutine processor, transducer array, occipito-mastoid padding, audio pickup and processing, flat mesh-type neural-net processor with storage, rear headpiece, starboard top outer head casing. . . .

It was a good computer, quick, responsive, and equipped with all the software he needed for his task. There was just one thing it couldn't do, as he had discovered almost immediately the first time he sat down to work; he could not use this computer to contact the outside world. He had tried, of course, but despite several minutes of determined hacking, he was unable to hook up with the Internet or any other system. On the great, interconnected web that was the information superhighway, this terminal was an off-ramp to nowhere. Not too surprising, under the circumstances, but he'd hoped that maybe his captors had overlooked the obvious. No such luck.

On and on he worked, never budging from his seat upon the stool. He slid the mouse back and forth over the small tabletop. His fingers tapped regularly at the keyboard. After relying on HOMER for so long, he was surprised at how fast it came back to him. There was something almost too satisfying about designing a suit from scratch once more, without artificial assistance. *Remember,* he kept telling himself, *you don't want to work too quickly.* The idea was to stall for time, to keep the full armor designs from Blank Screen for as long as it took to figure out a way out of this trap. Not unlike *The Bridge on the*

River Kwai, he recalled. In that film, a British army officer held captive by the Japanese during World War II was forced to construct a massive bridge. The officer got so caught up in the challenge of his engineering project that he eventually forgot that he was actually assisting the enemy, and he died trying to protect the bridge from his own allies.

I mustn't let that happen to me, he resolved, chilled by the very thought. Even trapped in this barren cell with nothing to do but create, he couldn't ever let his enemy possess the power of Iron Man. No matter what it cost him.

He inspected the audio processing controls, made an adjustment to the circuitry, then digitally cut-and-pasted the audio design into the total helmet schematics. There was a reason he had started at the top of armor, with Iron Man's helmet; most of the headpiece consisted of padding, protection, and sensory equipment, all state-of-the-art to be sure, but not exactly dangerous in the wrong hands. The bulk of Iron Man's serious weaponry resided in his chestplate and gauntlets, as well as in supplementary modules that he attached to his armor as needed. Without the rest of the armor, the headpiece was only the world's most incredibly sophisticated crash helmet.

But there was no reason to explain that to Blank Screen. Let him (or her) think he (or she) was halfway to conquering the world already.

Tony contemplated the blueprints on the screen. A sense of weariness and *déjà vu* came over him. He felt the walls of his cell closing in on him. *In a very real way,* he thought, *this was exactly how Iron Man began. . . .*

Vietnam. The trap was green, not white, and very, very hot. He came to the verdant jungles of that war-torn land to assist the United States military in a war that seemed to be dragging on and on. He'd hoped that his inventions, his powerful transistors and magnetic rays, would help end the bloody conflict, saving both American and Vietnamese lives. And also, to be honest, enhance the reputation of an ambitious young weapons designer and munitions manufacturer named Tony Stark. His parents had died a few years before, and he was anxious, even driven to make his mark upon the world.

Then, one hot and humid afternoon, he was out testing his equipment in the field . . . and his life changed forever. One minute he was strolling confidently through the underbrush, extolling the virtues of Stark technology to a small squad of impressed G.I.'s, the next he had stumbled over a concealed trip-wire. The booby-trap went off instantly. He experienced only a flash of sheer terror, followed by a heartbeat of flesh-rending pain, before the force of the explosion rendered him unconscious.

The pain still tore at his chest when he awoke to find himself the captive of Wong-Chu, a guerilla leader of legendary ruthlessness. Years later, an older and wiser Tony Stark would come to realize that the political situation in Vietnam was more complicated and morally ambiguous than it had seemed back then, and that the enemy Vietcong were not entirely the black-hearted demons our leaders claimed they were. Wong-Chu was in a class all his own, though; politics notwithstanding, he was as bad as they came: a power-hungry bully who delighted in lording over anyone weaker than himself.

As a prisoner of war, Tony found his illustrious reputation worked against him. Wong-Chu demanded that Stark, the famous American inventor, construct an all-new weapon of destruction for his men. But that was not the worst news Tony received; shrapnel from the land mine had seriously damaged his heart. He had only days to live, and Wong-Chu intended that he spend his final hours devising a superweapon for the Vietcong.

Despair gripped Tony's damaged heart, but he refused to abandon hope. He vowed to turn Wong-Chu's evil plans against the petty tyrant, even if it was the last thing he did. "This I promise you," he told Wong-Chu, feigning capitulation to the Red's decree, "I shall build the most fantastic weapon of all time!"

In an isolated village under the control of Wong-Chu, Tony was confined to a makeshift lab full of tools and scrap iron. Every tick of the clock brought the deadly shrapnel closer to his heart, but Tony toiled ceaselessly, despite his growing weakness and agony.

Even then an idea had consumed him, a vision of a mighty suit of iron that could destroy Wong-Chu—and perhaps save Tony's life. In theory, the transistors in the armor's chestplate would provide the power to keep Tony's fading heart beating even after the shrapnel completed its lethal work, if only he could complete the suit in time . . . !

With the ultimate deadline coming up fast, salvation arrived in the frail form of another prisoner. Professor Yinsen had once been acclaimed as Asia's greatest physicist. Long believed dead, the wizened old man had in fact fallen into the cruel custody of Wong-Chu. Yinsen shared Tony's hatred of Wong-Chu, and Tony badly needed assistance in finishing the armor. Taking a calculated risk, he took the elderly scientist into his confidence, revealing the nature of his mysterious project.

"An iron man!?" Yinsen said, intrigued by Tony's plans. "Fantastic! Think what a creature we could create! What wonders he shall perform!"

Together, the two men worked against the clock—and under the baleful gaze of Wong-Chu. The pressure in Tony's chest grew greater with each passing hour; it felt like a vise was slowly squeezing his heart to a pulp. The unrelenting pain made it difficult to concentrate, but Tony forced himself to ignore his torment and continued assembling the armor out of the crude materials Wong-Chu had provided. With no ventilation or air conditioning, not even an electric fan, the heat of Southeast Asia turned the cramped, closed lab into an inferno. Sweat dripped from Tony's body. Tiny winged insects buzzed about him constantly; he had to keep brushing them away from his eyes and skin. *Boy, could I use a drink,* he thought more than once, but Wong-Chu fed them only water and army rations.

Soon, he could no longer work on his own, or even support his own weight. His legs felt like limp noodles; his breath came in ragged gasps. He wanted to cut his aching heart from his chest, just to stop the pain for a single moment. Propped up against the lab bench, his hands holding on to the benchtop for dear life, he whispered hoarse instructions to Yinsen as the grey-bearded old scientist hastily struggled to complete the armor that might yet preserve Tony's life.

But the end was near. Tony felt his life slipping away; his heart seemed ready to explode. "Hurry," he groaned to Yinsen, who was making a few, final adjustments to the armor's self-lubrication system. At the last minute, Yinsen clamped the massive chestplate onto Tony's shaking body. Piece by piece, he assembled the complete suit around his young colleague, until only Tony's eyes could be seen through the slits in his cast-iron mask.

Trapped inside the heavy armor for the first time, Tony experienced a brief attack of claustrophobia. He couldn't move. He couldn't even sit up! He lay on his back on a large operating table, like a man-made monster in some old Karloff film. All he could see was the bamboo roof of the lab, as Yinsen hurriedly ran an electrical cord between the lifeless armor and their portable generator. "Have patience," he called out to Tony. "The generator will soon build up enough energy to furnish all the power you'll need to move."

True enough, the armor began to hum to life all around Tony. The life-giving heart of the suit kicked in first; for the first time in days he felt the awful pressure upon his heart start to recede. He still couldn't move his massive, mechanical limbs, but he could breathe again. *Thank God,* Tony thought. His desperate scheme was working after all.

Just then, however, he heard Wong-Chu approaching. A crimson warning light that he and Yinsen had secretly installed flashed ominously at the edge of his vision. *No,* he thought, *not now!* All he needed was a few more minutes. . . .

Paralyzed as he was, Tony was never entirely sure what happened next. He heard Professor Yinsen run out of the lab, listened in horror as the old man loudly denounced their enemy. "Death to Wong-Chu!" Yinsen shouted. "Death to the evil tyrant!"

The ringing report of a single gunshot ended the noble scientist's defiance forever, and Tony realized that his comrade had sacrificed his own life to buy Tony the precious minutes he needed.

You will not have died in vain, my friend, Tony thought fervently, even as system after system came to life in the armor. His heartbeat had become strong and regular; for the first time since the bomb exploded under his feet, he felt like his old self again. Experimentally, he tried to lift his finger. Responding directly to his brainwaves, the transistors in his right gauntlet activated countless tiny gears and levers, perfectly duplicating the action of his finger. *Yes!* he thought, exultant. Tony sat up, stepped off the table, and, for the very first time, Iron Man walked the Earth.

That prototype armor was a primitive and graceless thing compared to his later models. The original Iron Man looked like what he was: a man-shaped metal box. The armor was a uniform dull grey, and as bulky as a refrigerator on legs. A radio antenna protruded awkwardly from his left shoulder. But cosmetic concerns did not trouble Iron Man as he took his first clumsy steps in that distant jungle village. He lived! He walked! He conquered!

Wong-Chu and his guerrillas proved no match for Iron Man. Crude as that early armor was, Tony and Yinsen had equipped Iron Man with enough high-tech equipment to take on an army: air pressure jets in his boots to allow him to soar into the air; a magnetic turbo-insulator to repel bullets and grenades; a miniature buzzsaw inside his index finger, capable of cutting through a heavy wooden door in less than a minute; a loudspeaker; suction clamps; and, of course, the transistor-amplified strength of his mechanical limbs. Wong-Chu himself perished when Iron Man used a miniature flame thrower to ignite the Communist leader's own ammunition dump. Thus was Professor Yinsen avenged . . . and Iron Man born.

And here I am, Tony thought, *back where I started.* A prisoner once more, again forced against his will to design a weapon for his enemy. If anything, the situation was even more challenging this time. Blank Screen only wanted the specs for Iron Man, not the actual equipment. Tony could hardly construct a working suit of armor out of a cot, a toilet, and a compact home computer. True, he wasn't mortally wounded anymore; after years of heart problems, he'd finally replaced his injured ticker with a working transplant. Then, of course, a jealous girlfriend had shot him in the spine, setting off a new cycle of medical emergencies, but that wasn't his problem now. Ana was. *Her* life was in danger this time around, which raised the stakes dramatically.

How much longer could he stall Blank Screen before this modern-day Wong-Chu demanded results?

Tony's eyes watered from staring at the monitor. *I wonder if I'd be permitted another nap,* he thought. He glanced towards the cot, and discovered with a shock that the remains of his breakfast had disappeared. The platter, the empty bowl and cup . . . they had all vanished as though they had never existed. Tony hopped off the stool and ran towards the spot on the floor where he'd left the platter. He stomped heavily upon the floor, which seemed just as solid as before. *I don't understand,* he thought. *I didn't hear a thing.* Admittedly, he'd been lost in thought, but the platter had only been a few feet away. "How the hell did they do that?" he asked aloud.

The bare white walls refused to answer him. Confused and dejected, Tony sat down at the edge of the cot. His eyes took in the austere emptiness of his cell. Maybe it was just foolish nostalgia, but that long-ago jungle in Vietnam was starting to sound better and better.

No, he thought emphatically. *I didn't give up then, and I'm not going to surrender now.* Professor Yinsen had not died in vain, not as long as Iron Man lived. There was a way out of this cell, somewhere, and he was going to find it. For Ana's sake.

Gently humming the theme from *The Bridge on the River Kwai*, Tony Stark went back to work.

FRIDAY. 1:50 PM. PACIFIC COAST TIME.

James Rhodes had come a long way from the Philadelphia slums where he'd grown up. When he looked in the mirror, he didn't see the scrawny little street kid he had once been. Instead, as he straightened his imported silk tie in the executive washroom of WorldWatch Incorporated, he saw an imposing-looking man clad in a fine grey business suit. Penetrating brown eyes met their reflection, above a freshly trimmed mustache and beard that covered his dark skin. *Not bad for an ex-helicopter pilot,* he thought approvingly. Still, the suit and other trappings were just a costume, he reminded himself, that helped him convince others of his abilities to accomplish his goals. *Just like my other suit,* he thought, *is useful in more direct ways.*

Jim stepped out of his private washroom into his twelfth-floor office. Golden sunshine poured through the picture windows behind his walnut desk. Glancing out the window, he saw Los Angeles spread out for miles and miles beneath him. Raised in the overcrowded confines of the East Coast, the sheer spaciousness of L.A.'s urban sprawl never ceased to amaze him. You could drop all of Philly on top of L.A. and there would still be miles of freeways left.

The city looked peaceful enough this afternoon, but Jim knew appearances could be deceiving. As Executive Director of WorldWatch, Jim was responsible for monitoring—and responding to—human rights violations all over the world. There were always atrocities going on somewhere, he'd learned. Sometimes they were too obvious to be missed, like a bloody civil war or village massacre, but often the basic human rights of innocent men and women were callously ignored under the cover of darkness—or behind a fog of government misinformation and denials. Under Jim's administration, WorldWatch attempted to document and identify abuses from Los Angeles to Latvia. And WorldWatch did more than just watch and record crimes against humanity; they assisted relief agencies in humanitarian projects, and lobbied foreign and domestic governments in order to bring pressure to bear on the situations that most needed it.

And occasionally, when political and diplomatic efforts proved futile, a certain high-powered War Machine took matters into his own hands.

A knock on the door interrupted his reverie. "Come in," he said, seating himself behind the desk.

Sheva Joseph entered the office. Until recently, the raven-haired Israeli woman had served as one of Nick Fury's top agents. When she resigned from S.H.I.E.L.D. over a policy dispute, Jim had snatched her up as quickly as possible. Now she handled security for WorldWatch, a full-time job given that WorldWatch's mission practically guaranteed retaliation from the terrorists and dictators they worked so hard to expose. "I have an urgent message from Bethany Cabe," she announced. "On the priority channel."

"This business with Tony?" he asked her. Rumors concerning Tony Stark's mysterious disappearance had been all over the news for hours, preempting regularly scheduled programming. Katie Couric had even managed an exclusive interview with Fury, during which the grizzled war hero had divulged absolutely nothing. On another channel, Oliver Stone insisted to Geraldo that the "real Tony Stark" had vanished years ago, and that Kathy Dare, the jealous girlfriend who once shot Tony, had been trained by the CIA. Jim knew better; he'd been half-expecting this call all day. *Oh, Tony,* he thought, *what sort of mess have you gotten into now?*

Sheva nodded grimly. "Shall I have Paula put the call through?" she asked, referring to Jim's assistant, Paula Lin.

"Of course," he replied. "Thanks, Sheva. I'll let you know if I need you." As soon as she left the room, Jim pressed a button on the underside of the desk. A walnut panel slid away, exposing a square video screen beneath the desktop. The latest in Stark technology, he noted; WorldWatch used only the best equipment.

Bethany Cabe appeared on the screen. Before taking over WorldWatch, Jim had worked for Stark Enterprises for many years; he and Bethany were old friends. To be honest, one of the reasons he had hired Sheva was because she reminded him of Bethany Cabe; they were both tough but caring women who knew how to handle themselves when the going got rough. Just looking at Bethany now, he could see the tension in her face. *This is bad news,* he realized instantly, before Bethany even opened her mouth.

She quickly filled him on the whole story: the commando raid on *Athena*, Tony's abduction, the coded message from Madame Masque. "What do you make of it, Jim?" she asked when she was finished.

Jim scratched his chin, scraping the stiff bristles of his beard. "I don't know, Beth. Madame Masque, huh? She's been keeping a low profile for the last few years. Why this, why now?"

"Hell if I know," Bethany said. "And then there's this A.I.M. connection."

WorldWatch had a file on Advanced Idea Mechanics two inches thick. They were a secret society of corrupt technocrats dedicated to expanding their power and profits through scientific means. Every member of A.I.M. was a scientist of genius caliber; they were sort of like an evil Mensa. A.I.M. had started out as the Research and Development branch of Hydra, before declaring independence and striking out on their own. Iron Man, Jim recalled, had clashed with A.I.M. on numerous occasions.

"Well, that sort of makes sense," he observed. "The last time Madame Masque showed that gold-plated kisser of hers—*this* Madame Masque, I mean—she had hooked up with a bunch of rogue FBI agents to launch a gang war against both A.I.M. and Hydra. The Maggia wanted to eliminate the competition, I guess. Iron Man nipped that scheme in the bud, but Madame Masque slipped away in the confusion." A stray memory popped into his head. "Say, didn't I hear something about ShellHead knocking a Hydra goon off the Golden Gate this morning?"

"That's right," she confirmed. "As nearly as I can tell, that was about a half hour before *Athena* was attacked. According to HOMER, Tony was testing a new remote-controlled unit at the time. I've spoken to Nick Fury as well. His people fished the deceased perp out of the bay, but they haven't got a positive I.D. yet. He may or may not be connected to all this."

"Christ," Jim groaned. "A.I.M. The Maggia. Hydra. This is turning into a Robert Ludlum novel."

"I know what you mean," Bethany said. On the screen, she brushed her red hair out of her eyes. Jim wondered whether she'd eaten or rested since this crisis began. "I think for now we have to take Masque at her word, and get our hands on that chip."

Jim scowled. "You sure that's wise?"

"I can't think of a better option," she said. "With the chip we can bargain for Tony's freedom. Right now she's holding all the cards. We need something she wants."

"But if the chip is as powerful as she says," Jim pointed out, "do we really want the Maggia getting hold of it?"

Bethany shrugged. "Would you rather leave it with A.I.M.?" she countered. "It's a no-win situation, Jim, unless *we* have the chip."

In other words, Jim thought, *we'll cross that bridge when we burn it.* Well, he knew better than to waste time arguing with Bethany Cabe. She had a way of getting what she wanted. Once, before the collapse of the Berlin Wall, she'd broken into an East German maximum security installation to rescue her husband. How a smart woman like Bethany had let herself get hitched up to a junkie like Alex Van Tilburg was something that he'd never understand. *Then again,* he reminded himself, *I've fallen hard for the wrong person myself sometimes.*

"Will you do it, Jim?" she pressed him. "For Tony?"

That hit a nerve all right. He and Tony Stark had a lot of history between them, most of it good. They'd met in 'Nam, saving each other's lives in the hair-raising days right after Tony put on that ugly grey suit. Following the war, Jim had come to work for Stark Enterprises, eventually rising from pilot and all-purpose sidekick to director of the entire company after Tony "died" from his neurological problems. He'd filled in for Tony Stark in other ways, too. More than once, when Tony was down for the count, James Rhodes had become Iron Man, sometimes for months at a time. He'd fought every foe Stark had, from the Mandarin to Fin Fang Foom, and come back swinging. It was a good feeling, one he'd never wanted to give up.

But there was a time, not so long ago, when he might have hesitated before coming to Tony Stark's aid. Their relationship had grown strained after Tony returned from cryogenic suspension to take control once more of Stark Enterprises. Jim felt betrayed, partly because, as War Machine, he had put his life on the line by taking Iron Man's place with the Avengers' west coast branch, mainly because the man Jim considered closer than a brother had not trusted Jim with the true facts behind his apparent death. Tony had his reasons, of course, but it was a bad time for both of them, one that led to Jim Rhodes finally leaving Stark Enterprises once and for all.

Still, that was then. The two proud, stubborn men had finally buried the hatchet. Rescue Tony one more time? Jim smiled at Bethany. He didn't need to think about it very long.

"Sure," he told Bethany. "I'm with you. Tell me where to go."

Bethany let out a sigh of relief. "Thanks, Jim. I really appreciate this. I'll have the coordinates Masque sent us transmitted to you. The usual frequency?"

Jim nodded. "The sooner the better, Beth. From what you told me, every minute counts." He checked his wristwatch. It was two PM. They had less than a day to pry that chip out of A.I.M.—and to spring Tony before Madame Masque could carry out her threat. He didn't doubt that she capable of murder; Whitney Frost had found that out.

Bethany signed off and the viewscreen receded into the interior of the desk. Jim walked over and locked the door of his office. *Time to change suits,* he thought, tugging his tie loose. He dropped his briefcase onto the desktop and keyed a private four-letter code into its digital lock: D-O-I-T. The briefcase lid sprang open. Inside a mask of burnished white metal faced upwards, surrounded by several black-and-white flexmetal components. He lifted the mask from its setting. Accordion-like, the flattened mask instantly expanded into a three-dimensional head-piece. Like Hamlet contemplating the skull of Yorick, Jim Rhodes hefted the helmet with one hand and gazed at his other face.

There's a time for negotiation, he thought, *and there's a time for action.*

The armor was designed to be donned quickly, and Jim had the process down to an art. Less than five minutes after saying good-bye to Bethany, Jim Rhodes paused in front of his plate-glass windows and inspected his reflection once more. The respect-able-looking executive/activist was gone. In his place the War Machine now stood.

The basic design of the armor resembled Iron Man's, which was unsurprising since Tony Stark had devised both suits. But more distinguished this suit than just its striking black-on-white color scheme; the War Machine armor had been created especially for high-intensity combat situations. This armor had more sheer firepower than any of its predecessors, including offensive weapons such as repulsor rays, a uni-beam, pulse bolts, a shoulder-mounted Gatling gun assembly, a wrist-mounted laser blade, a shoulder-mounted micro-rocket launcher, and a wrist-mounted particle beam discharger. Jim checked his ammunition; the shoulder-mounted weaponry came with many different forms of ammo which he could select at will during a fight. His options included spent-uranium armor-piercing, high-explosive, concussion-type, high-temperature thermite, tear gas, tracer, flare, and smoke. They were all in place.

Okay, Jim thought, satisfied. *I am loaded for bear.* He sauntered over to a private elevator that took him to WorldWatch's roof. The elevator brought him up in less than thirty seconds. A gust of fresh air blew in as the door opened.

He and Tony Stark had a lot of history, that was true. And when Jim Rhodes ultimately decided to go his own way and left Stark Enterprises he took something with him, besides Tony's blessing: a suit of armor, a mission, and a name to go with them. Whatever WorldWatch couldn't handle, War Machine could.

He activated the built-in communications array in his helmet and accessed an intercom right outside his office. "Paula," he said. "Hold all my calls. I'm going to be busy for awhile."

He stepped to the edge of the roof, overlooking what passed for a Los Angeles skyline. His boot jets flared. Achieving liftoff, War Machine rocketed into the smoggy sky.

This one's for you, Tony.

Blank Screen was running out of patience. After several hours, Tony had only just completed the helmet specs and started work on the armor's excess heat radiators. The latter were certainly important; without these devices to shed excess heat, anyone wearing the suit would end up simmering in their own juices. Even with the electronic cooling and moisture venting systems throughout the armor, the heat had to go somewhere. Still, like the helmet, the radiators revealed little or nothing about Iron Man's offensive capabilities. Evidently, Blank Screen was all too aware of this.

A few minutes ago, the diagrams on the screen blinked out. Alarmed, Tony hastily entered a "Save" command, although he suspected the machine wouldn't let him erase any data even if he wanted to. Blank Screen's characteristic blood-red background replaced Tony's recent work on the monitor, along with a printed warning:

YOUR WORK IS TOO SLOW. STALLING WILL NOT BE TOLERATED.

"But I'm working as fast as I can," Tony lied. "This is no toaster I'm designing. Iron Man is one of the most complicated and sophisticated pieces of machinery on this planet. You can't just order up a suit of his armor like you would a new VCR!"

YOU WASTE TIME WITH FOOLISH DETAILS.

"The devil is in the details!" Tony shouted, venting his rage. "These are integrated systems; one small design flaw can cripple the entire suit." It was true.

Once a single speck of dirt, lodged in one tiny silicon chip, had caused a near-fatal misalignment in his right palm repulsor. Of course, that was a construction error, not a design flaw, but why explain that to Blank Screen?

DO NOT THINK YOU CAN FOOL ME. YOUR WORK IS BEING CAREFULLY REVIEWED BY EXPERTS. WE CAN RECOGNIZE TRIVIA . . . AND SABOTAGE.

Uh-oh, Tony thought. As an experiment, he had tried to introduce a subtle error into the specs. Specifically, he'd skewed the chemical composition of the golden alloy used in the heat radiators to lower the safety tolerances by a few crucial percentages. Under full flight conditions, the hot exhaust gasses from the microturbines in the armor's boots would have melted the exterior coating of the heat radiators on the boots, giving the armor's wearer a literal ''Achilles' heel.'' The vital difference between the right and the wrong composition was less than one-tenth of one percent, mere picograms in terms of actual materials, but in an actual combat situation it could mean victory or defeat. *Just in case Blank Screen manages to coerce a working suit out of me.*

But he had entered the false data less than half an hour ago. Surely Blank Screen couldn't have caught on to his ruse so soon? ''I don't know what you mean,'' Tony said.

I THINK YOU DO. NOTHING BUT YOUR BEST WORK WILL DO.

What did that mean? Had Blank Screen seen through his tricks, or was this only bluff and bluster? Without conceding anything, Tony assumed the worst. "Look, maybe I made a mistake. I don't know. I'm tired, I'm thirsty. . . ." *I hope I sound as pathetic as I feel,* Tony thought.

To be honest, he felt like a wreck. His neck ached from slaving over the keyboard all day, and his watery eyes felt like marbles rolling around in his sockets. His head throbbed, and he would have killed for an aspirin or two. Trapped away in this sterile dungeon, he felt like the imprisoned hero of some old melodrama. *The Count of Monte Cristo,* maybe, or *The Man in the Iron Mask.* Tony smiled grimly at the thought. If only he had his own iron mask right now. . . .

WORK AND YOU WILL HAVE WATER. LOOK BEHIND YOU.

Seated at the computer console, Tony glanced over his shoulder. Sure enough, he noted with less surprise than before, a black plastic pitcher and cup had mysteriously materialized while his back had turned. Both objects were lined up against the opposite wall, several feet away from where the breakfast platter had come and gone. *So much for the trapdoor theory,* he thought. "Okay," he said to the screen. "I'm impressed. How do you do that?"

THAT IS IRRELEVANT. FINISH THE ARMOR.

Retrieving the cup and pitcher from the floor, after filling it two-thirds full with fresh water, Tony wondered who was behind the red screen. As both Iron Man and Tony Stark, he had acquired far too many enemies over the years. His mind swiftly ran through some of the major suspects.

The Mandarin? The diabolical Chinese mastermind was far and away his most deadly foe, and once he would have been Tony's prime candidate for the insidious architect of this elaborate plot . . . but not any more. The high-tech trappings of the operation—the armored wetsuits and computerized cellblock—didn't fit the Mandarin's recent pattern. Where once he had sought power through super-science, the Mandarin had undergone some sort of religious conversion after a near-brush with death in the form of an ancient alien dragon. Now he preferred magic and mysticism to technology, employing demons and sorcery in his latest crusades to destroy Western civilization. If Tony's current predicament was the Mandarin's doing, then his old enemy must have reversed himself once more. Possible, Tony concluded, but unlikely. The Mandarin had renounced science with the same fervent fanaticism that had fueled his endless campaigns for world domination.

So who else was there?

Justin Hammer was another likely suspect. As Tony Stark's most unscrupulous business rival, he was certainly capable of this sort of industrial espionage and extortion. Hammer had also been known to employ out-and-out super-villains such as Blizzard and Blacklash to carry out his schemes and expand his financial empire. Yes, this was just like one of Hammer's more unsavory projects, except that Hammer would probably want more from Stark than just his technical know-how. So far, Blank Screen had shown no interest in Stark's considerable stocks and properties. Of course, just kidnapping Stark was probably playing hell with SE's finances, so he couldn't completely discount Hammer, either.

Who was Blank Screen? The more Tony thought about it, the more possibilities came to mind. Spymaster specialized in stealing corporate secrets, but kidnapping seemed too out-and-out aggressive for him; he was a skulker, not a raider. The Ghost wanted to destroy Stark Enterprises, but, for him, a mere kidnapping wasn't aggressive enough. He craved revenge, not information. Obadiah Stane was dead. Madame Masque hadn't been heard from in years. *Thank God the Cold War is over*, Tony thought, *or I'd have a whole other category of spies to consider.*

And then there was Hydra. Tony recalled his "virtual" experience at the Golden Gate Bridge. Was that days or only hours ago? He'd lost all sense of time. God knows Hydra had tried to poach Stark's secrets before; that was why Tony had persuaded the President to create S.H.I.E.L.D. in the first place. Later, after Baron Wolfgang Von Strucker apparently died in a battle with Nick Fury, Hydra fell under the control of leaders less diabolically inspired than Strucker, and the organization entered a long period of inactivity and internal dissension, becoming much less of a threat to humanity. Recently, however, an unholy experiment had brought Strucker back to life. Seizing control of his creation, the revived Baron had made Hydra once more a force to be reckoned with, and feared. According to Nick Fury, Hydra was back in a big way these days, yet Tony couldn't convince himself that that crazed loser on the Bridge could have had anything to do with an operation this slick. Justin Hammer still struck Tony as a more likely prospect, but even Hammer was only one of dozens of powerful and remorseless adversaries with old grudges against Iron Man or Stark: MODAM, A.I.M., the Controller, the Grey Gargoyle, Dread Knight, Whirlwind, Roxxon Oil, Sunturion, Radioactive Man, Crimson Dynamo, the Living Laser, Dr. Doom, Ultron, D.A.N.T.E., the Deviants, Master Pandemonium, Quasimodo, the Mad Thinker, Maximus the Inhuman, the Sons of the Serpent, Doctor Demonicus, Blizzard, Blacklash, the Avatars, Kang, Immortus, Thanos, the Supreme Intelligence, the Fixer, Mentallo, Baron Strucker, the Masters of Evil. . . . The list was endless.

Frustrated, Tony realized that he couldn't rule anyone out; hard experience had taught him that even enemies long believed dead could turn up alive after all, usually at the worst possible moment. Blank Screen remained a mystery, and he (or she) still wanted more information.

Tony turned his mind instead to the problem of his meals' sudden appearances and disappearances.

Matter teleportation was one explanation, as in "Beam me up, Scotty." Both the Mandarin and another old foe, the solar-powered Sunturion, could teleport, but the theory rang false. Anyone who could master matter transmission didn't need his engineering secrets. The Ghost, on the other hand, could walk through walls and turn other objects intangible as well. He could also make himself invisible, which might explain why Tony never saw anything. *Hmmm,* he mused, *could Blank Screen be the Ghost?*

"Who are you?" Tony asked, sitting down upon the stool. What the hell, it couldn't hurt to ask. Some super-villains could never resist bragging.

IRRELEVANT. FINISH THE ARMOR.

Just my luck, Tony thought grimly. *I would get taken hostage by the one criminal overlord who doesn't like to make long speeches about his personal invincibility and the brilliance of his plans. Where is Doctor Doom now that I need him?*

He had to appreciate the water, though. Designing could be thirsty work. He sipped the lukewarm water, refilled his cup, then placed the pitcher down on the surface of the work station, only a few inches away from the keyboard. That looked risky to him, so he reached to move it further away.

His hand froze. On the other hand, it suddenly occurred to him, why not? There were simpler ways to gum up the works than by tinkering with composite polyalloys.

"Oops," Tony said loudly, as he "accidentally"

knocked over the pitcher with the back of his hand. Clear liquid poured over the keyboard, seeping into the empty spaces between the keys. Feigning agitation, Stark clumsily mopped at the spill with the hem of his shirt. A few seconds later, he lifted the keyboard and tipped it on its side. What looked like several pints of water drained out of the flooded keyboard, forming a large puddle on the tile floor. Tony moved his bare feet out of the way.

"Sorry," he said sheepishly. "I can't believe I did that!" He struggled to keep from grinning. *I should have thought of this at breakfast,* he thought. *Wonder how long it will take Blank Screen to repair or replace the keyboard? And will it go the same way my meals go, even if I keep my eye on it?* Tony vowed to watch the entire computer setup like a hawk. There *had* to be a way out of here!

His staged mishap provoked an angry response from Blank Screen, but not the one Tony had expected. His spirits dropped as he read the message that flashed onto the monitor.

THAT WAS CHILDISH, MR. STARK, AND FUTILE. THE EQUIPMENT IS UNHARMED.

That made no sense, Tony thought. He eyed the soaking-wet keyboard. *I practically drowned the blasted thing,* he thought angrily. It couldn't still be working. Stark hardware was good, but it wasn't *that* good. Experimentally, he pressed the ESCAPE key. (*Hah,* he reflected bitterly. *If only true escape could be as easy as the push of a button.*) With any luck, the computer would not respond at all.

To his surprise, and fury, the crimson background vanished the minute his finger tapped the key. But his interrupted work did not reappear. Anastasia did.

He saw her on his monitor, in living color. Frantic, she pounded on the white walls with her fists. He saw blood on her knuckles and on her blouse. The gruesome stain over her wounded shoulder had grown since the last time he'd seen her; now one entire sleeve of the blouse looked soaked in gore. The blood was fresh, too, red and wet, not the dingy brown of dried blood. No sound accompanied the picture, but Ana's mouth gaped open in a silent scream. Her long legs, still clad in the dull white trousers, crumpled beneath her as Ana sank down onto her knees, still shrieking and hammering uselessly against the unyielding wall. Tony felt his blood boil watching her.

"Blast it!" he shouted at the no longer blank screen. "What have you done to her?"

Below the heartrending image, a subtitle responded to Tony's cry: NOTHING YET. WATCH . . . AND LEARN .

Suddenly, Ana sprang to her feet once more. Her eyes grew wide in panic. Her pale, white skin grew paler yet. Bolts of electricity burst from the floor, striking her hands, her feet, her body. The flickering lightning left scorch marks on her clothes and flesh, and Ana thrashed about like a marionette in a storm, her motions jerky and graceless. Her hair stood on end, turning her elegant pageboy coiffure into a spiky gold jungle. Flailing madly with her arms, she made sporadic efforts to protect her face and eyes, but she had little control of her limbs. Grey tendrils of smoke rose from her clothing as blood turned into steam; the noxious fumes left Ana choking and gasping.

"Stop it!" Tony yelled, his nails digging into his palms as he clench his fist in helpless rage. "Stop it right now!"

I DEMAND YOUR TOTAL COOPERATION.

"Yes! Yes!" Tony shouted. He couldn't stand to see Ana suffer like this. This was his fight, blast it! She was innocent. "Anything you want, just leave her alone!"

But the torture went on and on, as Ana danced madly in an electrical storm of his enemy's making, tears streaming from her eyes. *If I had my armor,* Tony thought, *I'd reduce this entire hellhole to atoms!* Finally, a coruscating blast of white-hot energy struck Ana at the base of her skull, and she dropped to the floor. *My God,* Tony thought, *they've killed her!* An overpowering sense of guilt gripped him. He had barely known her, and now she was dead—and it was all his fault. If only he could have saved her somehow. . . .

But wait! Maybe she wasn't dead after all. Looking closely, Tony saw that her prone body twitched feebly upon the floor. He watched her chest fitfully rise and fall. The unbloodied side of her blouse slid down, exposing the ivory slope of one shoulder and the curve of her breast. Tony breathed a heavy sigh of relief, then looked again at the pitiful image in front of his eyes.

Hold on, he thought abruptly. *Something's wrong.* Brows furrowed, Tony squinted at the monitor. Like an itch at the back of mind, his unconscious had alerted him to a problem he didn't fully recognize yet. Part of him was happy enough that Ana was still alive, that he still had a chance to save her. Why look a gift horse in the mouth? But another part of him, cooler and more objective, had noticed something else, some nagging detail that preyed on his mind even though he couldn't quite put a name to it. There was Ana: pale, wounded, but still alive. *What's wrong with this picture?*

Another subtitle flashed beneath the image: THIS IS YOUR FINAL WARNING .

You bet it is, Tony thought fervently. He couldn't let Ana come this close to death again. He had to beat Blank Screen and soon, while there was still hope for Ana. Ana who still looked beautiful despite her long ordeal, with her pale white skin and ivory curves. . . .

Pale?

Like a splash of cold water in his face, the realization hit him with such force that he almost toppled off the stool. More threats from Blank Screen were running along the bottom of the screen, but Tony barely noticed them. Eyes wide, he stared at the unconscious woman in the desolate cell. Not too long ago, less than a day or two, that same woman had been sunning herself on the deck of his yacht.

So what happened to her tan? When Tony last saw Anastasia Swift in the flesh, that flesh had been toasted to a luscious dark brown. Even allowing for a couple of very stressful days in solitary confinement, Anastasia could not have possibly lost her tan by now, could she?

The image—Blank Screen's "final warning"—disappeared. Tony found himself staring at his own detailed diagram of Iron Man's heat venting system. He noticed that his notes on the gold alloy involved had been amended by another hand. *So Blank Screen did catch my bug,* he thought without too much concern; he had more important questions on his mind. Apparently, Blank Screen (like the Ghost) was no technological slouch, or else he hired good people to do his/her scientific dirty work (like Justin Hammer). Come to think of it, didn't Blank Screen mention something about a team of experts before? Interesting, but not as much as the Strange Case of the Vanishing Tan.

He wasn't sure what it meant, but he knew one thing already: Things were not what they appeared.

FRIDAY. 4:15 PM. PACIFIC COAST TIME.

Seven thousand feet above the coast of Southern California, a flock of birds flew into War Machine's flight path. His forward laser scan alerted him to the oncoming threat, and he automatically made a minute adjustment to his trajectory. Travelling at Mach 1.5, the entire procedure took less than a second. War Machine barely noticed; after years in an armored suit, such a maneuver had become second nature to him.

When in flight, he had learned to remain fairly rigid to maintain his most aerodynamic posture: arms outstretched in front of him, his legs locked together. Meanwhile, he scanned his surroundings on various visual and electromagnetic frequencies. LED displays on the interior of his mask kept him up to date on the power levels of each of the armor's individual systems, appearing as lighted screens at the bottom of his point of view. Cybernetic commands allowed him to access other displays at will, including an online location finder. Micro-TV projectors in the eyepieces projected the graphs and other read-outs so that the images seemed to float in front of his face.

He watched the birds pass safely beneath him. It wasn't just concern for the birds that motivated his change of course. Even with numerous jets in his boots, each with automated restart, a few feathers sucked in by the microturbines could end his flight quickly. He glanced down at the coastline; at this height, the landscape resembled an immense quilt, crisscrossed by thin intersecting lines that War Machine knew were actually roads and freeways. It all looked surprisingly artificial; did people ever realize how much humanity had changed the very physical appearance of the planet?

I'm a fine one to talk, War Machine thought. *Look at me: spending half my life in a computerized shell.* Jim Rhodes had spent more time in Iron Man armor or Iron Man–like armor than anyone except Tony Stark himself, and now he had a full-time career as War Machine. Jim was determined to use his automated power to make the world a better place. As a rule, he preferred social activism to mainstream super heroing; given a choice, he'd rather topple a corrupt political regime than trade death rays with some costumed megalomaniac like the Red Skull or Kang the Conqueror. This time around, though, he'd make an exception. If beating up on A.I.M. would help free Tony from the Maggia, then Advanced Idea Mechanics was in for a bad day.

If only he didn't feel like Madame Masque's goddamn errand boy!

Rising above the cloud cover, to fifteen thousand feet and climbing, he activated his autonavigator. According to the location finder, the coordinates Bethany had beamed to him were for a stretch of ocean off the coast of Miami. That was a long way to fly, even at full speed, and the clock was ticking as far as Tony's safety was concerned. Fortunately, he knew a good shortcut, or rather his computer did. He mentally keyed the coordinates into the autonavigator, then kicked his jets into full liftoff mode. A powerful blast of ignited liquid oxygen sent him rocketing above the clouds. Veering upwards, he flew perpendicular to the surface of the Earth, rising higher and higher until the planet itself resembled a huge blue dome beneath him. War Machine came to a halt, hovering over the Earth at an altitude few human beings had ever attained. Speckled with starlight, the black vastness of space expanded infinitely above him. A low-flying satellite drifted not far away. Automatic sensors scanned the satellite and calculated its orbit before judging it no threat. Meanwhile, War Machine gazed in wonder at the awe-inspiring vista before his eyes. Was this what the very first astronauts saw? *Guess I've got the right stuff now,* he thought with a smile.

Tony called this trick a suborbital parabolic maneuver. Basically, you hang over the earth until your destination's below you, then you drop right down on the site and, bingo, a transcontinental flight completed in less than an hour. Floating in zero-gravity, War Machine watched the Earth slowly spin around, waiting for the autonavigator to give him his cue. He took advantage of the delay to contact Sheva back at the office. His antenna array bounced a signal off a communications satellite to establish a link with WorldWatch. Sheva picked up immediately. *She must have been waiting by the comm,* he guessed.

"Yes, Jim?" she asked. The Israeli woman was one of the executive staff at WorldWatch, who all knew that James Rhodes was also War Machine. She had learned his secret when they'd teamed up to restore democracy to the oppressed people of the African nation of Imaya. That mission led to Sheva resigning her position at S.H.I.E.L.D., and brought Jim a valued friend and employee. Now he updated her on his status and location, just in case something went wrong.

"I can't talk long," he concluded. "Anything I should know?"

Sheva's voice crackled in his headset. *Damn,* he thought. *Must have a bad connection.* "No new information on Stark," she said, "but Bethany has contacted Interpol. She may have a lead on Madame Masque."

Good, he thought. There was no reason that gold-plated witch should hold all the cards. "Keep me posted," he told her. A warning light flashed at the edge of his vision. Shifting his gaze, he watched an LED display start a countdown to reentry: *10 . . . 9 . . . 8 . . .* "Gotta go," he said. "Wish me luck."

"Shalom," Sheva said before signing off. War Machine assumed reentry position, his head pointed downwards at a right angle to the atmosphere.

7 . . . 6 . . . 5 . . . 4 . . .

Despite the armor's cooling system, a bead of sweat trickled down Jim's forehead. *Damn,* he thought, *I hate this part.* A few years ago, he had been forced to descend through the Earth's atmosphere in a suit of badly damaged Iron Man armor.

Burning up in reentry, as the suit's defenses failed, had been one of the most frightening and painful experiences in his life. He had survived, with Tony's help, but only barely; severe burns all over his body had left him bedridden for months—and ended his first term of duty as Iron Man in the worst possible manner. He still got the shakes when he thought about it.

3 . . . 2 . . . 1 . . .

Jim shook off his trepidation. That was then and this is now, he told himself, and his new-and-improved War Machine armor had proved itself a hundred times over. As the countdown reached its climax, his afterburners surged to life and War Machine blasted forward, diving headfirst into the dome of heaven. His armor glowed red, then white, but inside the insulated suit Jim remained cool if not comfortable. He forced himself to breath regularly. To steady his racing heart, he mentally counted all the layers between his flesh and the white-hot exterior of the armor, starting from the outside: expitaxially deposited diamond, high-temperature enamel, crystallized iron, heat-exchange piping, and many other layers all the way down to the cushioned padding pressing against his bare skin. Each individual tile that made up the flexible "chain mail" of his armor was actually a three-dimensionally tessellated sandwich of exotic materials held together by small but collectively powerful magnetic fields—or so Tony had explained it to him. Jim just hoped it all held together one more time.

He plummeted towards the Earth like a blazing meteor, using his jets for guidance only; gravity provided all the propulsion he needed. The glow around him grew to an incandescent peak, then quickly dissipated. He tore through blue sky and clouds until, almost as soon as it had begun, his headlong descent came to a gradual halt. War Machine leveled off about twenty feet above an empty stretch of turquoise water. *Hello, Atlantic Ocean*, he thought, breathing a sigh of relief.

The sun was a bright red orb sinking towards the horizon. Twilight approached, reminding War Machine of the three-hour time difference between California and Florida. Switching on the tri-beam projector on his chestplate, he illuminated the face of the waters with a powerful searchlight. The beam raced over the shimmering waves like the fairy-glow of some mythical sea-spirit, but all the light revealed was an occasional school of fish swimming near the surface of the sea. He had expected to find a small, uncharted island at these coordinates, yet there seemed to be nothing here but ocean.

War Machine established an uplink with the tracking satellite overhead. According to the location finder, he was in the right place, so where was A.I.M.'s secret lab? Had Madame Masque sent him on a wild goose chase and, if so, why? Was there even an energy chip at all, or was that, too, a devious fabrication of the Maggia leader? Beneath his mask, Jim frowned. Too much about this entire business didn't make sense.

If there was a lab here, he realized, it had to be underwater, *deep* underwater. *Only one way to find out,* he thought, switching from visual reconnaissance to ultrasound imaging. An optical display replaced his ordinary P.O.V. with a topographical map of the ocean floor, rendered in glowing lines of orange, green, and blue. The picture reminded him of a child's Light-Bright toy. At first, his ultrasonic probing bounced off only coral reefs, undersea chasms, and the rotted hull of a long-forgotten shipwreck. "Hmmm," he said, thoughtfully; if WorldWatch ever ran low on cash, deep-sea scavenging might make a hell of a fundraiser. But that was a thought for another day. War Machine continued to scan the ocean, flying slowly only a foot or two above the waves. The sky grew darker by the minute, as a moonless night descended over the Atlantic, turning the green water black as a buccaneer's soul. War Machine was ready to give up and call Bethany, to tell her that Madame Masque had played them all for fools, when the ultrasound suddenly turned up something far from ordinary.

On the optical display, it looked like a fluorescent crayon drawing of the Houston Astrodome: a smooth, unbroken hemisphere the size of a suburban mall. For a moment, War Machine recalled Prince Namor, the Sub-Mariner, and his undersea kingdom of Atlantis, but, no, that was hundreds of miles from here. This *had* to be what he was looking for. Hovering above the water, he directed all his sensors at the domed structure, but the ultrasound proved unable to penetrate the dome's outer shell, as did the infrared. *Big deal*, he thought. This was the place. *Energy chip, here I come.*

He checked his air supply before going further. The tanks were still two-thirds full; he had a good forty-five minutes' worth of breathable air. Tony had built, he knew, a suit of armor specifically designed for deep-sea diving, but that suit was probably back in one of Tony's labs in California. Besides, if A.I.M.'s defenses were as formidable as Madame Masque claimed, he was going to need firepower more than air, and no armor on Earth had more blast for the buck than the one he was wearing. The way he figured it, there had to be air in that dome; those brainy A.I.M. types had to breathe too, right?

He closed the vents in his mask, and inhaled canned air once more. "Let's rock and roll," he said, and dived into the black and beckoning waters.

Steam rose from his armor, still hot from its trip through the atmosphere, as he coursed through the briny depths, his searchlight cutting a swath through the murky darkness. A school of yellow-tail snappers, startled by the sight of a mechanical man zipping through the water like gleaming torpedo, dispersed in all directions. *Welcome to The Undersea World of James Rhodes,* he thought, amused despite the urgency of his situation. *I should have brought along a camera crew from PBS.*

A hammerhead shark circled him warily, apparently unsure whether War Machine was fit prey or not. *Can he smell the human meat inside this tin can?* Jim wondered, contemplating the shark's dead black eyes and rows of serrated teeth. *Probably not*, he decided, but he gave the shark a very mild zap from his left palm repulsor anyway. The yellow beam hit the shark lightly on its nose, flipping it over backwards. Discouraged, the shark righted itself and swam away in the opposite direction, its powerful tail churning the water behind it.

Good, he thought. His repulsor ray actually consisted of a beam of accelerated neutrons traveling through a blast of ionized air. When the neutrons collided with the surface of any solid object, the resulting subatomic explosions produced the "repulsing" effect. He'd been unsure how well the rays would function underwater. It was one thing to punch a shaft of ionized air through an ordinary atmosphere, or even the vacuum of space, another to shoot it through several cubic meters of water. Without that column of air, the neutrons produced by the lasers in his gauntlets and chestplate would have no means of transmission. Judging from the shark's retreat, his repulsors still packed a punch even when submerged, but that, he reminded himself, had been at reasonably close range. Would all this water cut down on the ray's strength over distance? Jim was a soldier, not a scientist, but it seemed logical that it would. Ordinarily, the beams took several dozen yards to disperse, but under the sea? This was Namor's home turf, not War Machine's.

Well, I guess I'll find out soon enough. Jim smiled grimly beneath War Machine's forbidding countenance. Unlike Iron Man, War Machine's faceplate came in two overlapping segments; in a pinch, the upper plate could lift away from the lower jaw. The two-part construction gave War Machine a permanent metal scowl that generally put the fear of God into all but the most arrogant of adversaries. Armor with attitude, or so Jim believed.

He scooted above the sandy ocean floor, his ultrasonic sensors leading the way. A large black manta ray glided beneath him, its whip-like tail stirring the sand as it noiselessly flapped along like a deep-sea vampire bat. War Machine quickly left it behind. So far, the armor had easily withstood the pressures of the deep; checking another display, Jim saw that armor's structural integrity remained rated at one hundred percent. Countless fathoms beneath the sea, he was warm and dry inside his iron suit.

Soon, the searchlight showed him a glimpse of the dome in the distance. He deactivated the ultrasound display, reverting to regular vision. Aside from a flashing blue beacon at the top of the dome, the structure was grey and opaque. A.I.M.'s hidden underwater lab, if that's what this really was, sure wasn't designed to attract visitors. *Tough luck*, he thought. *War Machine's come calling, whether they like it or not.* The base of the dome was about two hundred yards away. War Machine jetted towards the bleak grey barrier, looking for an airlock or porthole. He checked his air supply: not even half empty yet. *So far, so good,* he thought. *Maybe this is going to be easier than I thought.*

Suddenly, the ocean bed erupted in front of him. Sand and muck swirled madly as they were tossed aside by the several massive objects emerging rapidly from underneath the sand. Through the roiling slurry, War Machine beheld heavy mesh netting being peeled back to reveal huge mechanized monsters rising up from a rocky chasm between him and the dome. *Camouflage,* he realized instantly. The sandy ocean floor had hidden what now looked like a veritable underwater armada.

Sleek silver submarines the size of stretch limos rose from the watery abyss. War Machine counted at least six of them, maybe more. In design, they resembled immense steel versions of the hungry shark he'd repelled earlier. Twin searchlights protruded from each sub like the eyes of a shark. Rows of forward torpedo tubes took the place of the hammerhead's voracious jaws. Hovering above the subs were three more vehicles that looked like the offspring of a bathysphere and a helicopter; they were bright yellow spheres of steel large enough to hold one or two passengers, propelled by rotors jutting out from the top and bottom of the globe. Large mechanical arms, with pincers like a giant crab's, surrounded the vehicle's equator. Each sphere had four sets of steel pincers. Jim didn't like the look of them.

Then again, he reminded himself, he'd been warned of heavy defenses. That's why Madame Masque had wanted Iron Man—and got War Machine. *Seems like a fair exchange,* he thought. *Now we find out if she got a bargain or not.*

Flanking each other, the subs lined up in front of the dome, blocking his path. The "crabs" waited several yards above and behind the subs. There was no way to go around them, and they didn't wait for War Machine to make the first move. With a rush of bubbles from its forward tube, the central sub fired a torpedo at the oncoming intruder.

His sonar alerted him to the torpedo an instant before he saw the bubbles. He found himself on a head-on collision course with the torpedo. Instantly, he took evasive action, veering up and away from the blockade of subs. He hoped the torpedo would continue on a straight path towards his former location, but no such luck; the torpedo corrected its course almost immediately. Jim wasn't too surprised. A.I.M. was known for the quality of its destructive hardware; they were, after all, the only terrorist organization in the world that was run exclusively by scientists and engineers. *Let's hear it for the revenge of the nerds,* he thought bitterly. Rear sensors warned him that the torpedo was trailing him, and gaining fast. *Naturally,* he realized. *The damn thing was built to accelerate underwater.*

The torpedo ate up the distance between them. War Machine suspected his armor could survive a direct hit, but he didn't want to find out. One breach in the suit's integrity and he'd drown in his own armor. He risked a glance over his shoulder. The torpedo was nipping at his heels, a trail of bubbling white foam streaming behind it. He couldn't outrace the thing, obviously, so he'd have to blow it away before it caught up to him.

His own missile launcher remained stowed in its standby position on his back, as was the minigun. The flamethrower wasn't likely to function underwater, and he still had his doubts about the repulsor rays; it was one thing to bonk a shark on the snoot, something else entirely to blast a torpedo out of existence. And he didn't want the torpedo close enough that he could use the laser against it.

That left the minicannon in his right gauntlet. Without turning around, he pointed his right fist at the onrushing torpedo. The twin muzzles of the retractable cannon protruded from their housing on his wrist. *The explosive cartridges,* he selected. A continuous belt-feed mechanism instantly loaded the correct ammo into the firing breech. Aiming quickly but carefully, so as not to shoot himself in the foot, he fired an entire round of 3.9mm explosive bullets.

He felt, but did not hear, the shock waves as the ammo detonated against the torpedo. *That's the prob-*

lem with underwater battles, he thought, slowing to watch his shot's effect on the torpedo. *They're too damn quiet.* He remembered the big underwater battle at the end of *Thunderball.* Not his favorite James Bond flick—the remake was much better—but all those scuba divers blasting each other with spearguns had been cool to watch *and* listen to.

The explosive bullets halted the torpedo, but, as the flash of the explosions and the frothing water both cleared, he was amazed to see that the torpedo was still intact. What's more, it didn't even look scratched. A.I.M. deserved its reputation for excellence, he conceded reluctantly. *What was the stupid thing made out of anyway?*

He floated several yards away from the inert torpedo, facing it. To his shock, he watched the shiny, silver projectile sputter back to life. The torpedo spun randomly for a second or two, then its head swung around to point directly at War Machine. A seething plume of exhaust jetted from its tail as the torpedo headed straight for his chest.

Armor-piercing, he thought desperately even as he hastily aimed the cannon at the incoming torpedo. The gun instantly switched ammunition. He fired off another round, and watched with wide-open eyes as the armor-piercing ammo, with their ultra-dense, spent-uranium cores, tore into the torpedo, ripping through its armored casing only heartbeats before the torpedo would have impacted with his armor. The torpedo disintegrated beneath a hail of bullets.

Hah, he thought joyously. *Take that, you heat-seeking barracuda!* Stark technology was at least a match for the bloodthirsty ingenuity of Advanced Idea Mechanics. But there was no time to bask in his victory. Suddenly, his warning systems went crazy, simultaneously alerting him to more potential threats than he could count. He turned rapidly to confront the forces guarding the dome—and saw easily a dozen torpedoes stampeding towards him.

The first torpedo had only been a test of his abilities, he guessed. A.I.M. had plenty more to spare. *No way to outrun them,* he knew. *Nothing to do but stand and fight.* Fine, he thought, that was just how he liked it.

Retreating was not an option, not with Tony's life at stake. Anyway, A.I.M. wasn't going to let anyone see their secret lair and live. *Dead men tell no tales.* Some Caribbean traditions never changed. . . .

He fired the minicannon continuously, sweeping the water with armor-piercing gunfire. The shots intercepted the path of the torpedoes, shredding some but not all of the torpedoes. At least of a third of the salvo got through. He tried the repulsors in his other palm, but, as he'd feared, the beam seemed weak and diffuse underwater. Maybe the repulsors slowed a couple torpedoes, but that was all. He switched to laser mode instead. A laser blade, long and neon-red, appeared out of his left gauntlet, slicing through the shadowy water as though it were open air.

Batter up, he thought, swinging his arm to block

a rushing torpedo with the blade. Coherent light cut through armor plating, bisecting the torpedo only a few feet away from War Machine's face. Using his backhand, the laser caught another torpedo on its tip, apparently disabling the tracking mechanism. The crippled torpedo went spiraling off, its exhaust trail forming a pinwheel in the water.

Still the torpedoes kept on coming. While batting away one, two, three more torpedoes, War Machine saw another salvo coming from the direction of the subs. He fired his cannon at the new assault, while, with his other hand, he slashed away with his laser sword at the stragglers from the first batch. Or was this the third salvo already? He'd lost track in the moment-by-moment struggle to keep the hunter torpedoes at bay.

Then it happened: one of them got through. He swung the laser at two torpedoes at once, hoping to stop both attacks with a single blow. The blade connected soundly with the first torpedo, decapitating it, but the second came in under his arm and exploded against his chestplate.

The impact left him reeling, but intact. *Strike one,* he conceded, hoping he still had two more to spare. He waited anxiously for the first sign of a fatal leak, but no emergency warning flashed. Power levels were dropping, though, and so was his air supply. He had about twenty minutes of air left.

Another torpedo raced at his head. He chopped at it frantically; he couldn't afford to take another hit.

He was clumsy and slow. It took three strokes to stop the projectile, but he destroyed it eventually, even as he fired at an oncoming wall of torpedoes with his other gauntlet.

All at once, the shells stopped. He'd run out of armor-piercing ammunition, and there was no time to reload with the extra dispenser mats on his belt. Running low on options as well, he switched to concussion-type ammo, but these fared no better than the high-explosive versions had. Still more torpedoes got through his hail of gunfire. He found himself losing ground (or ocean), retreating from the torpedoes while he hacked away at them with growing desperation.

Firing his boot jets, he shot out of the path of the latest of the damned heat-seeking torpedoes. It passed between his legs, dodging his blade, then doubled back and headed for him again.

Heat-seeking. . . .

Was that the answer? A wild idea occurred to him. It was his last chance, but, in theory, it should work. Abandoning the useless concussive shells, he switched ammo once more . . . to high-temperature thermite charges. The torpedo was less than six meters away when he fired again, not at the incoming missile but at its source: the A.I.M. subs. Another volley of torpedoes, he observed, was already on its way. His cannon's deadly fruit passed by the new torpedoes in the churning water, the thermite ammo tearing through the water, even as the earlier torpedo raced at War Machine. Laser blade ready, he watched the persistent projectile approach. There was no way, he realized, his thermite charges were going to reach their targets before this torpedo finally zeroed in on him. He was going to have to dispose of this one the hard way, by hand.

The silver torpedo climbed towards him at a forty-five degree angle. Calculating its speed and trajectory, he parried with his laser blade . . . and missed. The torpedo, moving like a living thing, ducked out of the laser's path. *My God,* he thought, appalled. *Do these things actually have learning capacity?* If so, he was in more trouble than he thought.

With no other option, he instinctively fired his right palm repulsor at the torpedo. At close range, the neutron beam worked its usual magic, halting the torpedo in its path, then sending it spinning backward. The repulsor made the torpedo an easy target for the laser emitted by War Machine's other gauntlet. He ran the sabre through the torpedo, spearing it on his laser blade—and lobotomizing its tracking mechanism in the process. When he withdrew the blade, the torpedo, effectively neutralized, began a slow descent to the ocean floor.

About time, War Machine thought. He swiveled in the water to face the next threat. More "smart" torpedoes cruised towards him, gaining speed and momentum with every heartbeat, but what about his own thermite salvo? The searchlight on his chest focused on the distant subs. He watched with satisfaction as the ammo detonated against the argentine steel hulls of the subs. White-hot flames, capable of burning for short periods even underwater, blazed suddenly every time his bullets hit home. Currents of fire washed over the subs, turning the chilly brine to steam.

War Machine waited expectantly, one eye on the inferno he had created and the other on the latest wave of torpedoes. *Now,* he thought, *let's see if I've got those bombs psyched out or not.* For a few breathless seconds, he tracked the incoming torpedoes. His laser blade remained drawn, just in case his brilliant stratagem proved less than effective. His right repulsor targeted the lead torpedo.

Then, as he'd hoped, the entire pack of torpedoes reacted in unison, changing their course before his grateful eyes. The torpedoes executed a tight U-turn in the murky water, heading back towards the burning subs, drawn by the crackling flames. *Way to go, heatseekers,* Jim exulted as the torpedoes pounced eagerly on the fleet of subs. Massive explosions erupted from the onslaught. The shock waves buffeted War Machine where he floated, surveying the destruction. He nodded approvingly.

Jim Rhodes was not as reluctant when it came to killing as, say, Tony Stark. He did not enjoy being responsible for another person's death; indeed, he spent most of his professional life trying to preserve and enhance human life. But in the down-and-dirty world in which he operated, sometimes the only way to stop the bad guys was to blow them away. Every death preyed on his conscience, but the way he figured it, if protecting the innocent meant some sleepless nights on his part, then so be it. War Machine had chosen the greater good over his own personal misgivings. *That's just the way the game is played in this crummy world,* he thought. *And it's not like the bad guys don't bring it on themselves.* He contemplated the explosions rocking the subs. *Those who live by the heat-seeking torpedoes risk dying by the heat-seeking torpedoes.* A.I.M. had fired first, without even issuing a warning or requesting an explanation for War Machine's presence.

But as the explosions died down, and the billowing smoke and foam was washed away by undersea currents, he saw that his harsh rationalizations were more than a little premature. Advanced Idea Mechanics built its subs as well as its torpedoes. Although visibly battered, the compact subs remained intact. Their silver hides scarred and scorched, the subs still floated between War Machine and the dome. The steel crabs had weathered the storm even better; a single set of mechanical pincers now dangled limply, but only one of the crabs looked damaged at all. The other two appeared good as new.

Not as good as I hoped, War Machine concluded, *but not as bad as it could be.* At least, he'd finally gone on the offensive, instead of being chased around by a pack of hero-hungry torpedoes. Now to keep the pressure on the opposition, and in a big way. *Lock and load,* he thought.

The cybernetic controls in his armor responded instantly. The missile-box launcher stowed on his back slid up its high-speed positioning rail into its deployed position atop his left shoulder. Another rail brought his minigun, a sort of state-of-the-art Gatling gun, into place on his opposite shoulder. The laser target designator on the left side of his helmet established a link with the missile launcher; the minigun had its own laser-sight guiding system, mounted to the gun itself. Conveniently, the missile-box was already loaded with a full complement of six armor-piercing missiles. He fed another round of thermite charges into the cannon in his gauntlet, and decided he was ready.

Time to go to town, he thought. Briefly, he considered broadcasting a call for surrender on all available frequencies, then thought, *To hell with it. Why give the subs another chance to lob torpedoes at me?* Reversing their own torpedoes on them had given him a breather; he was determined to make the most of it.

Assuming full flying position, arms out front and boot jets blasting at close to top speed, he charged at A.I.M.'s aquatic armada. One man against at least ten armed and armored vessels seemed like suicide, but War Machine explosively demonstrated that he lived up to his name. Nearly every weapon at his command fired simultaneously, and the small armored figure rapidly made himself the center of a firestorm of destruction, fathoms beneath the waves. War Machine lashed out in all directions with the most lethal combination of high-tech armaments that the genius of Tony Stark had ever devised.

He targeted the subs with the missiles. About the size of road flares and each one finned like a shark, the missiles burst from their launcher, each propelled by a built-in solid-fuel rocket and guided by forward-looking sensors that were tuned to the laser target designator affixed to War Machine's helmet. He swept the laser over the subs and the missiles followed, accelerating underwater to almost Mach Two. Realizing their danger, the subs broke formation, spreading out beneath the ocean with admirable speed and efficiency. The scarred submersible vessels zipped by War Machine on all sides. The silver underbelly of one sub passed directly over him. His laser cut a deep gouge in its hull. He noted with satisfaction bubbles of air escaping through the wound.

Nor did the other subs escape so easily. *You're not the only one with smart bombs,* War Machine thought vindictively. Every one of his eight missiles responded to a different and distinct sequence of blinks from the targeting laser. By altering the blink-rate for every target, War Machine could send one missile after each of the enemy subs. Warheads tipped with spent-uranium cores penetrated the armored hull of first one sub, then another. Jim saw one ship, gushing air from a gaping hole in its side, crash nosefirst into a coral reef. Smoke, froth, and blood clouded the dimly lit water. His searchlight found drifting streaks of red diffusing into the green-black shadows.

But the rocketing missiles were but one part of the carnage emanating from War Machine. Mounted on his right shoulder, his 3.9 mm electric minigun fired at a rate of over seven hundred and fifty rounds per second. He could have fired faster—the gun's maximum speed was a full thousand rounds per second—but he wanted to save some ammo in case he encountered resistance within the dome itself. The spiral-feed ammunition cassette spun almost frictionlessly around the firing chamber; since the ammunition was caseless and electrically primed, there was no spent casing to eject and reloading was effectively instantaneous.

The attached laser aiming system directed the gun against the crab, and hit him with a barrage of 2-mm hollow-point shells. Each bullet contained a drop of restrained mercury which vaporized upon impact, transforming the dense, spent-uranium core into a jet of hot metal that could easily pierce all but the most indestructible of armors; the further nastiness of the mercury vapors added a little extra bite to every shot.

A dying Tony Stark had designed the War Machine armor when he thought his time was running out. Determined to end some old battles once and for all, he went further than he had ever permitted himself to go before—and War Machine was the result. Jim sometimes wondered if Tony, now that he had recovered from his close encounter with death, ever regretted creating such an incredibly destructive piece of equipment; certainly, he had passed the suit along to Jim as soon as humanly possible. Jim appreciated Tony's scruples; it had to be rough being a first-class weapons designer *and* a man of conscience. At times like this, though, when Jim found himself surrounded on all sides by no-good trash with more firepower than decency, he also appreciated every bit of War Machine's fabulous artillery.

The electric minigun emitted round after round. Undersea battles are fought in three dimensions, so War Machine spun like a top as he cruised through the water, firing above and below and sideways. Laser light flickered over the surface of the crabs. Armor-piercing bullets followed the lasers in steady streams. One of the crabs buzzed War Machine, its forward claws reaching out for him. Concentrated fire from the minigun hit the elbow of one of the crab's mechanical arms. The bullets ripped through the joint, severing the connection entirely. The upper arm, claw included, broke off completely from the rest of the craft and fell like an anchor towards War Machine, who deftly rolled on his side to avoid it. He fired again at the crab, whose body turned out to be more heavily armored than its limbs. His bullets blew out its searchlights, and left a rows of dents and dings in the armored exterior, but, as nearly as he could tell, they did not penetrate to the passenger area. He swatted at the crab with his laser, but, like the helicopter it vaguely resembled, the crab ascended vertically out of his reach.

He considered trying out a repulsor ray on the

crab's rotors, but he was too busy with other things. War Machine was the eye of a chaotic, mechanized hurricane, the target and destroyer of all of A.I.M.'s deep-sea defenses. His chest searchlight, which less than one hour ago had illuminated a scene of postcard prettiness above this very ocean, now darted over underwater pyrotechnics and twisted silver metal. Any fish or other sea life that may have inhabited these waters had wisely fled the vicinity. The only moving objects exposed in the strobe-like rovings of his searchlight were A.I.M. battleships, disabled or otherwise. He glimpsed one compact sub resting on its side on the ocean floor, its starboard side a steaming, bubbling ruin. There were going to be a lot more shipwrecks on the bottom of the ocean before this fight was over, War Machine realized, but there was no time to consider the salvage possibilities. A pack of killer torpedoes came at him from two o'clock; both barrels of his minicannon fired thermite charges to confuse the heat-seekers. War Machine saw the torpedoes jet off course, swerving upwards towards the crippled crab. Another powerful explosion stirred up the water.

Inside the armor, Jim Rhodes felt an adrenaline rush heighten his senses. His heart pounded and every blast of his weapons felt like an extension of his own body. *Keep cool,* he coached himself. *Make every shot count.*

One more torpedo, strafed by minigun fire, zigzagged through the depths, wildly out of control. It came straight for War Machine's face; he could see his iron mask reflected in its silver casing. Raising a hand in front of his face, he knocked it aside with his repulsor. Deflected onto another course, the torpedo zoomed away and rocketed through the water before detonating against an A.I.M. submarine two hundred yards away. Waving the bubbles from the torpedo's contrail away from his face, War Machine saw superior A.I.M. technology (in the form of the torpedo) destroy superior A.I.M. technology (in the now-devastated form of the sub). The wounded sub disappeared into the vast and gaping chasm from which all the ships had originally emerged. War Machine wondered just how deep the undersea canyon was.

And still he kept moving, swooping and rolling like a fighter plane in an aerial dogfight. His searchlight and laser sighting systems swept through the murky water like beacons of destruction, and, with laser and repulsors and gun and cannon and missiles all firing at once, he struck like an aquatic, one-man army. One of his missiles finally caught up with a sub that had been desperately trying to elude it. The entire back half of the sub, already battered by previous missiles and turncoat torpedoes, transformed into an immense burst of released oxygen as the warhead ignited. *Carly Simon was right*, he thought smugly, *nobody does it better*.

He paused for a second to watch the severed sub

sink towards the chasm. His boots sank up to his ankles in the sand covering the seabed. A solitary survivor ejected from the sub. He wore a bulky rubber diving suit with a single air tank. *Just be thankful I didn't use the nuke,* Jim thought, only half-joking. His supply of missiles included a sub-nuclear variety equivalent to 1.8 kilotons of TNT. So far, he'd never had to use it.

After several minutes of frenetic action and combat, the danger seemed to have abated. Surveying the eerie, aquatic landscape, War Machine detected no immediate threats. All his foes seemed defeated or on the run. He tried to take inventory of the fallen or crippled vessels, but he wasn't sure how many there were to begin with. *Maybe if I run a playback of the sensor readings for the last half hour . . . ?* The water was still muddy and clouded with all the silt, debris, and destroyed machinery thrown up by the battle, but the swiftly moving ocean currents were already washing it away, clearing the water around him. Soon, only the wreckage of various subs and crabs would remain to mark the site of the ferocious warfare that had just been waged here. He let the silence of the depths wash over him. It was surprisingly peaceful. His tense muscles relaxed, and his heartbeat slowed to normal. The twin barrels of his minicannon retracted into his right gauntlet. He kept both minigun and missile launcher in their deployed positions atop his shoulders, even though the melee appeared to be over. *I could get into this,* he thought, savoring the sudden tranquility of the ocean floor.

The surviving sub-mariner, *sans* flippers, kicked awkwardly through the water, trying to reach the dome. War Machine tracked the swimmer with his searchlight in the hopes that he could lead him to an entrance into the dome. He checked his air supply, and grimaced. The fight had taken more out of him than he'd thought. He had less than ten minutes of air left. *Uh-oh,* he thought. *I'd better get into that dome and soon.* He shook the sand from his boots, and started to lift off. If necessary, he'd scoop the swimmer up by his rubber collar and *make* the guy show him the way in.

Then, unexpectedly, something smashed into his chestplate. His searchlight winked out, leaving Jim in total darkness. He suddenly remembered a cave he had visited as a child on the East Coast. When the tour guide had turned off his flashlight, young Jim had experienced a blackness more complete and absolute than the darkest night he had ever witnessed on the surface. This blackness was like that: impenetrable and all-encompassing. He literally could not see the glove in front of his mask. War Machine tried to reactivate the searchlight, but the effort proved futile. The entire tri-beam apparatus was inoperative. *What the hell hit me?* he wondered, then gasped as he felt, all the way through his armor, the crushing impact of two heavy objects squeezing him around the waist. His arms were trapped against his sides by whatever had caught him, and was now trying to scissor him in two.

Like pincers, he realized instantly. One of the crabs must have survived the fracas intact and snuck up behind him. But how come his sonar hadn't alerted him to the mechanical monster's approach? Some sort of radar-reflecting force field, he guessed, like Tony built into the specialized "stealth" armor he uses on his most covert missions. *Damn,* he cursed himself, *I should have figured that A.I.M. would have something like that.*

The pressure around his waist increased steadily. A bright red optical display flashed before his eyes, warning of an imminent armor breach. The glowing red letters were the only light in his universe. *First the bastard blinds me*, he thought angrily, *then he tries to break me in half.* Jim found himself panting for breath. How much air did he have left? Not a heck of a lot, it seemed.

Fortunately, although blind as a bat, he had the resources of a bat as well. Abandoning normal vision, he reverted to ultrasound imaging. A full-color topographical display of his surroundings appeared, looking like a line drawing sketched out with glow-in-the-dark Magic Markers. The edge of the great chasm showed up less than three yards away from where he was standing. The ultrasonic sensors could not reach the bottom of the abyss; it appeared on the display as a hungry black hole, marked by a glowing green event horizon much too nearby.

The crab grabbing onto him from behind was definitely radar-shielded; it showed up on the ultrasound display as only a fuzzy, flickering shadow of white optical snow. That was okay. He didn't need to see it to feel the giant pincers crushing the life out of him. Compulsively, he checked his air supply again. Only five minutes left.

His weapons were no help this time. With his arms pinned, he couldn't bring any of the armaments in his gauntlets into play, and the minigun on his shoulder was pointed the wrong way. The missile launcher had the capacity to fire backwards, but first he'd have to reload it. He'd used the full complement of missiles to take out the subs. Now he wished he'd saved at least one rocket for the slimy weasel piloting this crab.

Instead, he'd have to rely on brute strength, of which, thankfully, he had quite a lot. His suit was more than merely a well-armored carrying case for plenty of high-tech gizmos; his transistorized exoskeleton amplified Jim's own muscle power by several orders of magnitude. He could bench press a tank without working up a sweat.

But could he break the hold of a robot crab monster before his lungs gave out? *Let's find out,* he thought.

War Machine struggled to raise his arms, straining both his biological and mechanical muscles to the utmost. Miniaturized servo-motors *whirred* frenziedly, and Jim felt like his arms were going to break, as he pressed against the force of the pincers. Beneath multiple layers of crystallized armor and microscopic circuitry, Jim's tendons bulged in his arms and shoulders. He clenched his jaw, sucking air through his teeth, and he refused to yield to the pincers's crushing grip. *Can't give up*, he grunted to himself. *Gotta break loose.*

The as-yet-immovable object that was War Machine contended against the irresistable force of the crab. For several seconds, the best War Machine could achieve, even exerting all his might, was a frustrating stalemate. The pressure squeezing him seemed to abate a bit, or at least he had halted its steady increase, but the crab-machine still held him fast. The pincers could not overwhelm his resistance, just as he couldn't yet break through the pincers trapping him. The heavy metal claws would not budge, no matter how hard he strained. Every muscle ached. He diverted most of his emergency power reserves into the servos driving his upper arms. Jim wasn't sure how much longer he could keep it up. His air supply felt thin and stale. He was starting to get light-headed. *I have to get free,* he thought passionately. *For Tony's sake.* He could see Tony Stark's face in his mind's eye, crying out for Jim's help. Other faces, other people, drifted up from the recesses of his memory: Rae Lacoste, his beautiful and accomplished girlfriend; Sheva Joseph, Dr. Jeffries, and the rest of the gang at WorldWatch; Vincent Cetewayo, the martyred African visionary whose dream had inspired Jim to take over WorldWatch; Nick Fury, Hawkeye, Deathlok, and all the other heroes and heroines he had so often fought beside; and many, many others. *I can't die here,* he resolved, *alone at the bottom of an overgrown pond. Too many people, living and dead, are depending on me.*

The crab wasn't giving an inch, though. *It must have its rotors on overdrive,* he guessed, *to hold its position despite my efforts.* Maybe that was the key, he thought. Forget the pincers, and go for the body of the ship. Still fighting to raise his arms, he bent at the knees as far as the armor would allow and fired his boot jets up at the floating crab. Fourteen microturbines ignited at once, jolting the crab with over four thousands pounds of thrust. On the optical display, he saw the blurry representation of the crab lurch forward, over War Machine's head. *Talk about a kick in the rear,* he gloated. *Bet you weren't expecting that, you crustacean wannabe!*

But, even out of control, the crab did not let go of War Machine. It tumbled onward, taking War Machine with it. Jim abruptly found himself upside down, then right side up again, as the crab and its armored captive somersaulted together above the seabed. Another warning light flashed before Jim's eyes. *Oh no,* he realized. *We're heading for the cliff!*

The undersea chasm waited for them, only a few feet away. War Machine couldn't tell how far down it went, and he didn't want to find out. Maybe the crab had been constructed to survive that kind of pressure, but he doubted his armor could withstand the full force of the lower depths, especially after the battering it had just taken. Too much pressure, too far down, and his armor would collapse like an eggshell in a gorilla's fist. His air gauge started flashing at him, too; only one minute left. *I know, I know,* he thought irritably. Every warning system in his armor seemed to be yelling at him.

It's now or never, he knew. The crab had reached the very brink of the abyss. He felt himself toppling over, helplessly locked in the mechanical monster's powerful pincers. Was it just his imagination, or had the crab's grip loosened during its headlong tumble? *I hope so*, he thought, putting everything he had into one last, convulsive thrust against the pincers. Adrenaline fueled Jim's muscles while solar power poured out of the armor's storage cells, transforming into kinetic energy and energizing the servos controlling his exoskeleton. All at once, the pincers shattered before his might. Free at last, War Machine darted away from the spinning crab, its remaining limbs flailing wildly as it plummeted into the darkness of the underwater canyon.

I must have done in its propellers with my boot jets, War Machine surmised. On his ultrasound display, the flickering white image of the crab grew smaller and smaller as the actual object descended into the chasm. Within seconds, it had passed completely beyond his sensor range. Jim wondered momentarily what would happen to the crab's pilots.

Knowing A.I.M., there was probably a genetically engineered sea monster living at the bottom of the moat. *That's their problem,* he decided. His only concern now was finding fresh air, and fast.

He definitely wasn't getting enough air. He felt faint and slightly nauseous. Dark spots speckled his vision. Everything seemed to be growing dimmer. . . .

Even if he tried for the surface, he knew he'd never reach it in time. That left the dome. Jim consulted the ultrasound display. The little man in the wetsuit had vanished during Jim's fight with the crab. Presumedly, he had reached an entrance to the dome. Jim would have to find his own way in, without benefit of a guide. He cruised over to the dome, flying above the abyss. The smooth, sloping wall offered no hint of an airlock or other passageway.

No time for subtlety, he decided. Fresh air waited inside the dome, not to mention the famous energy chip that might buy Tony Stark his freedom. After fighting subs, torpedoes, and a grabby crab to get this far, War Machine wasn't going to let some heavy masonry stop him now. Only fifteen seconds left, his air gauge reported. He cybernetically unsheathed his laser blade, and jabbed it straight into the wall. If A.I.M. wasn't going to open the front door for him, then he'd just have to make his own. The laser blade carved through the reinforced steel wall like a butcher knife through a Thanksgiving turkey. Electricity sparked and unknown gasses bubbled as he sliced through insulated cables and tubing. War Machine kept on cutting until finally the blade pierced the last layer of walling and came into contact with empty air. *Yes,* Jim thought exuberantly. He was almost there! He twisted the blade, expanding the hole he'd punched through the wall.

But the ocean, even more impatient than War Machine, could not wait any longer. Several cubic tons of water poured past him, gushing through the tiny opening he had made and tearing it larger. It was like standing in front of the world's biggest garden hose; War Machine was caught up in the flow and washed headfirst into the dome. He splashed helplessly in a torrential outpouring of brine. The waterfall hurled him to the floor of the dome, then washed him down a flat, polished surface. Slipping and sliding, War Machine could not regain his footing. His ultrasound display had been reduced to incoherence by the noisy tumult of the flood; all he could see was a wild, undecipherable jumble of colors and lines.

Then his back slammed into a bank of computers. He lifted his head above the rushing water, set the armor to take in ambient air, and took a long, deep breath. It tasted like heaven. *I will never complain about the smog in L.A. again,* he vowed. *I don't care if you can see it, as long as I can breathe it.* After a few more breaths, he scrambled to his feet and surveyed the scene before him, taking in every detail.

High-pitched alarms sounded noisily, the shrill sirens alerting everyone in earshot that the dome's integrity had been breached. *Sorry about that, gang,*

War Machine thought, without much sincerity. He stood on the floor of a one vast, coliseum-like chamber. Instead of the many compartments he had imagined, the entire dome had been given over to a single laboratory the size of a major sports stadium. The domed ceiling rose more than one hundred feet above War Machine's head. Row after row of elevated terraces and catwalks were affixed to the wall of the dome. From his vantage point on the floor, the various terraces looked like concentric circles staffed by increasingly smaller toy people. Rows of gleaming computers and monitors ran along the terraces. Everything appeared clean, unscratched, and state of the art—except for the bits soaked by the recent oceanic deluge. This is what Mission Control would look like, War Machine thought, if NASA had more money than God. *Too bad A.I.M. was more interested in power than in "peace for all mankind."*

Despite himself, War Machine was impressed by the wide-open spaciousness of the lab. Not even Stark Enterprises had ever devoted this much real estate to a single laboratory. It was awe-inspiring, in a cold futuristic sort of way, like the Krell laboratories in *Forbidden Planet* or the interior of the Death Star. Science fiction provided the only comparisons that made any sense; there was nothing like this in ordinary life, not even the extraordinary life of a super hero. Jim Rhodes had never seen a psychological personality profile of a typical A.I.M. technician, but at this moment he would have bet a week's paycheck that the word "Trekkie" fit in there somewhere. A bunch of messed-up science geeks obsessed with bringing their fantasies of technological omnipotence to life.

Hundreds of technicians populated the work areas above him, all wearing the same monochromatic uniform the color of fresh lemons. The sterile yellow outfits completely covered their bodies; not an inch of flesh was exposed. Their bulky, cylindrical headgear made them look like an army of beekeepers. A faceplate made of thick black mesh allowed them to see and breathe, but offered no hint of any person's race or features. Individuality, it appeared, was not something A.I.M. encouraged. War Machine glanced quickly at a row of work stations on the ground floor and noticed that each table and computer was identical to the one next to it. Unlike every other work environment he had ever seen, no attempt had been made to personalize the individual computer stations with photos, knickknacks, or souvenirs.

The only thing that ruined the perfect, breathtaking symmetry of the huge domed chamber was the newly created waterfall pouring down from a ragged gap in the dome about seventy-five feet up. *Did I fall all the way from there?* War Machine marveled. *No wonder I feel so sore.* The free-flowing torrent had already torn out great chunks of the terraces and cabled walkways directly below the source of the waterfall. Twisted and broken debris littered the floor of the dome, along with close to a dozen bodies in torn yellow uniforms. Some of the bodies were still moving. War Machine heard groans and screams of pain, and felt the burden of his guilt grow a little heavier. The sea continued to spout through the punctured dome. On the floor, the water was knee-deep and rising. Upon the various terraces, yellow figures abandoned their posts in fear, or stood in shock next to their seats, unsure what to do. War Machine saw a running technician slip and fall off a water-soaked catwalk; she dangled precariously above the surging maelstrom many feet below her, hanging on with one hand to a wet metal cable. War Machine considered flying to her rescue, then saw another technician pull her back to safety. The volume of the sirens grew to an ear-splitting level. The dome had obviously seen better days.

War Machine again opened the armor's air intakes; miniature pumps began refilling his air tanks from the ambient atmosphere. *Time to stock up*, he thought. He didn't intend to stay here forever, and it was a long way home.

"ATTENTION," an amplified voice shouted over the sirens. The voice came from a concealed public-address system. "STAND BY YOUR POSTS. THE SITUATION IS UNDER CONTROL. REPEAT: THE SITUATION IS UNDER CONTROL."

Turning his gaze upwards, War Machine saw that the deluge did indeed appear to be slowing. The dome's automatic sealing mechanisms were overcoming the press of the ocean. He wasn't too surprised by this development. A.I.M. would build a dome that could survive an accident or two. *If only,* he thought, *they could turn that genius to positive ends, like providing cheap energy or durable housing for the world's wretched masses, what a lot of good they could do for humanity.* It was a cliché, he knew, but it was true.

Only minutes had passed since he crashed into the floor of the dome. Jim spit salt water out of his mouth, grimacing at the foul taste of the stuff, and concentrated once more on his mission. *Now if I was the world's most powerful energy chip,* he thought, *where would I be?* The monomaniacal design of the lab made that question an easy one. Every bench, booth, and work station in the dome faced one central location at the exact center of the ground floor. Tearing his gaze away from the last dripping remains of the waterspout, War Machine contemplated the apparent focus of the entire complex's efforts and attention.

It rested a few inches above a stainless steel pedestal, about five feet tall, surrounded by an impressive array of scanners and monitors. An honor guard of A.I.M. security forces circled the intricate mass of machinery. About a hundred flashing lights and buttons covered the surface of the pedestal, and all manner of apparatus were directed at the tiny object floating over it, seemingly suspended by a column of shimmering blue energy: a translucent, crystalline chip about the size and shape of a postage stamp. War

Machine couldn't even begin to guess what half of the equipment surrounding the chip was for; he suspected you had to be a scientific genius on the order of Tony or Reed Richards of the Fantastic Four to identify the purpose of these gizmos by their appearance alone. It was more science fiction stuff as far as he was concerned. Still, he had to admit, it was nice of A.I.M. to point their entire multizillion dollar, super-scientific, deep-sea laboratory at the one small gadget he had come to find. Why not just erect a neon sign saying, *Here I am. Steal me.* For such smart guys, they had a lot to learn about good, old-fashioned sneakiness.

War Machine strode decisively towards the pedestal, only to be met by a battalion of armored guards. "INTRUDER ALERT! INTRUDER ALERT!" the unseen loudspeaker blared. "ALL PERSONNEL ARE COMMANDED TO PROTECT THE CHIP AT ALL COSTS!" Inside his mask, Jim sneered at the very thought. *Just try and stop me,* he thought derisively. After tackling submarines, giant crabs, and killer torpedoes to get this far, a bunch of goons the same color as Chiquita bananas seemed like no threat of all.

Then a crimson beam from an A.I.M. energy rifle knocked him off his feet. The beam struck him right between the eyes, and he felt the impact all the way through his armor. *Christ,* he thought, *that actually hurt.* Blood dripped down his forehead, clouding his vision. Jim blinked the blood away. His head smarted near his hairline. *Probably just a minor scalp wound,* he guessed. *Serves me right for getting cocky.* He tried to climb back onto his feet, but more beams came at him, continually knocking him off balance. He was a target in shooting gallery, beset from all sides. Every hit seemed to vibrate through his armor to rattle the tender flesh and bone inside. Bursts of heat penetrated the armor as well, stinging his skin wherever the beams struck home. Some sort of combination sonic and microwave weapon, Jim guessed as he thrashed beneath the onslaught of crimson beams. Shake and bake.

Okay, he thought, *no more Mister Nice Guy.* It was time for this target to start shooting back. Rolling like a log across the laboratory floor, he careened into the packed crowd of beam-blasting A.I.M. guards, firing his repulsors and minicannon simultaneously. War Machine crashed against the guards's legs, toppling them like bowling pins, while his offensive weapons wreaked havoc on everything that came within range: technicians and machinery. War Machine heard shouts and screams, as well as the crackle of severed power lines and the ear-splitting screech of tearing metal. *Careful,* he warned himself, *I don't want to blow apart the chip I've come to steal.*

The crowd was his protection, though. As long as he was in their midst, the A.I.M. guards had to worry about shooting each other, while War Machine could fire freely in any direction—and be pretty sure of hitting one or more of the bad guys. Taking advantage of the chaos, he clambered to his feet and regained his bearings. Countless figures in bright yellow suits had rushed onto the floor, with more streaming down from the walkways lining the interior of the dome. All of A.I.M. seemed determined to come between him and the precious chip. *Good,* he thought. Clenching his metal fists, he waded further into the press of saffron bodies.

Jim was a tall man, and his armor gave him an additional height advantage over the mob opposing him. He towered above them, peering over the flat-topped headgear to keep his gaze fixed on the crystal chip atop its supportive beam of light. A.I.M. guards and technicians swarmed over him, but War Machine marched inexorably through the pack that pushed and shoved against him, brandishing fists and weapons. A short man in a yellow suit thrust the muzzle of an energy weapon towards War Machine's armored face; the hero grabbed the A.I.M. guard with one gloved hand and flung him across the room. The man flew over the heads of many of his colleagues before smashing into the crowd, bowling over more A.I.M flunkies. Crimson rays crisscrossed the chamber, but few hit War Machine. Instead, he heard equipment sizzling and angry cries of rage and pain. With the battle reduced to hand-to-hand combat, he barely needed his own repulsors. His iron fists smacked into yellow padding, and collided satisfactorily against human chins and jaws. Discarded energy rifles crunched to pieces beneath his heavy tread. Like a walking tank, War Machine cut a path of destruction through the broken and battered bodies of all who served Advanced Idea Mechanics. "STOP THE INTRUDER! PROTECT THE CHIP! STOP HIM NOW!" shouted their leader's voice over the loudspeakers. Jim heard more than a hint of panic in his tone.

"Yeah, right!" he snarled. A.I.M. didn't stand a chance of stopping him now. He switched to nonlethal ammunition in his wrist cannon, firing alternate rounds of tear gas and smoke. The guards nearest him collapsed onto the floor, choking and gasping. One guard frantically ripped her headgear off her uniform, revealing the face of an attractive young black woman, roughly thirty or so years old. Tears streamed from her brown eyes, staining her cheeks. She sneezed and snuffled. Mucous ran from her nose. For one guilty moment, War Machine felt like offering her a tissue. *I think I liked it better when they kept their masks on,* he thought ruefully. Faceless hordes were easy to fire upon; it always hurt when he remembered that there were faces and individuals behind every cause, no matter how twisted. As he watched the young woman, and her uniformed companions, coughing and retching all around him, he couldn't help wondering what her story was, how she got mixed up with a psycho organization like A.I.M.

What's a nice girl like you doing in a hidden undersea laboratory like this? he thought. Then again, for all he knew, she was probably a specialist in bacterial warfare, calmly plotting the death of millions. Or a once decent person driven to terrible extremes by some heart-breaking tragedy in her past. Or both at the same time. There was no way for him to judge her, or any of them, fairly, not under these circumstances. That was the hell of it.

Marching forward, tossing men and women aside like an unstoppable iron juggernaut, he left the gassed woman behind him, vomiting onto the polished, spotless floor of the dome. Thick white smoke swirled about him, confusing his enemies. More saffron uniforms hurled themselves against him, but his mechanized muscles knocked them aside with ease. Maybe their hearts weren't in the fight anymore; he knew his wasn't. *Let's get this over with,* he thought. He'd had his fill of beating up stupid brainiacs, no matter what they'd done in the past.

The crystal chip, still resting upon its pillar of light, beckoned to him. The blue beam holding up the chip seemed to repel the heavy smoke, so that the chip sparkled in a pocket of clean air surrounded by smoke and fumes. *Like the eye of a hurricane,* War Machine thought soberly. A dark purple repulsor blast decked the last guard standing between him and his prize. His metal boots stamped up a small flight of steps, stepping over the fallen guard, until he stood before the pedestal. The chip, so vital to Tony's future, hovered before War Machine's eyes. He reached out for it, then felt a burning sensation at the back of his neck. The shock staggered him, and he stumbled clumsily against the pedestal, which shook beneath the impact of his massive armored form. To Jim's horror, he saw the blue force beam blink out suddenly, and the delicate-looking crystal chip fall towards the floor.

Oh shit, he thought suddenly. A terrifying vision, of the chip lying shattered at his feet, raced through his brain. Desperately, he grabbed for the falling chip. His heart skipped a beat, cold sweat broke out over his back, then the chip landed safely on the palm of his glove, directly over his dormant repulsor ray projector. Jim breathed a sigh of relief. Cautiously, carefully, he closed his fist around the chip. *At last,* he thought. He had the chip, and nobody but nobody was going to pry it out of his hand until Tony Stark was safe and sound.

Another beam hit him in the back of his head. The blast didn't even dent his helmet, but he felt the heat and vibration beneath his armor plating. *Who's shooting at me now?* he wondered angrily. He swiveled around to face the sniper, and found himself staring at the same woman he had gassed minutes before. Dried tears and snot stained her unmasked face, and she had to lean against a bank of computers for support, but crazed fury filled her brown eyes and she cradled a gleaming, high-tech rifle in her slender arms. "Die!" she cried at him. Her voice was hoarse from the effects of the gas. "Why don't you die?" A red glow suffused the muzzle of her rifle, casting hellish shadows upon her face, as she swung the weapon towards War Machine once more.

"Oh hell," he groaned. Clutching the chip in his right hand, he swiftly aimed his left palm at the woman. Before she could fire her own weapon, a violet bolt of lightning leaped from War Machine's glove, crossing the open space between them in less than a second, and striking the woman in the chest. The pure concussive force of the repulsor beam threw her backwards into the computer bank. Her head banged against the blinking apparatus, then drooped forward. A sense of depression washed over War Machine as he watched her unconscious body slowly slide onto the floor, to join the numerous other bodies he had left scattered over the base of the dome. Suddenly, he felt less like a super hero than like a housebreaker in the employ of Madame Masque and the Maggia.

Just remember, he consoled himself, *A.I.M. are the bad guys, too.* It wasn't as though he had attacked, say, Stark Enterprises. In time, A.I.M. would have invariably turned their chip against the general good of humanity, just as they had perverted all their other great discoveries, from the Cosmic Cube to the Mobile Organism Designed Only for Killing, better known as MODOK. By capturing the chip now, he had merely launched a preemptive strike against a future A.I.M. offensive.

So why did he feel so crummy?

War Machine took a last, long look at the carnage he had created. The smoke was beginning to die down, but the alarms and sirens were still wailing

away at full volume. The only A.I.M. personnel remaining on their feet seemed to be scurrying for
safety. Still, reinforcements were bound to arrive at
any time; the sooner he got out of the dome, the better. He gently placed the chip in an protective compartment on his belt. *All this violence over such a tiny
little chunk of crystal,* he thought. *I hope it's worth
it.*

Making sure he had a full tank of breathable air,
he raised his arms above his head and prepared to
blast off. *Good thing this dome's self-sealing,* he
thought, *because I don't think anyone's going to show
me the way out.* Sure enough, a fresh battalion of
A.I.M. guards suddenly erupted from trapdoors in the
floor of the dome. More yellow uniforms, brandishing
futuristic weapons, poured out into the gigantic
domed laboratory, apparently from subterranean
vaults carved out of the ocean floor. "STOP HIM!
STOP HIM AT ALL COSTS!" The voice on the
loudspeaker screamed hysterically. "STOP HIM . . .
OR DIE YOURSELVES!"

"Stop yourself," War Machine retorted. The afterburners in his boots surged to life, lifting him
above the casualty-strewn floor of the dome and sending him soaring aloft on a tower of heated exhaust.
Energy rays of every color of the rainbow pursued
him as he shot straight up at roof of the dome. The
beams intersected in the smoky air, forming a lethal
net of multicolored light. Sparks crackled and flashed

wherever beam met beam, but War Machine quickly left the slicing rays behind. His gauntlets slammed into the ceiling like twin piledrivers, drilling through layers of steel and concrete, and burst through the dome into the ocean itself: cold, dark, and silent. Seawater raced into the tunnel he'd formed, but War Machine was already long gone. Propelled by powerful jets, he shot towards the surface at full speed, leaving the plundered dome of A.I.M.'s secret lab far behind him. *Luckily the suit keeps me at atmospheric pressure*, he thought idly as he plowed upward through the sea, *so I don't have to worry about the bends.*

His mind raced ahead then, to his coming confrontation with Madame Masque, the enigmatic and ruthless godmother of the Maggia. *Okay, Masque,* he thought, *I've got your damn chip. Now what?* He wasn't entirely sure what was going to happen next. Hell, he'd been improvising, and racing the clock, ever since Bethany first told him about Tony being kidnapped. He checked the armor's internal chronometer. It was almost ten PM Florida time, which meant about seven PM back in California. Madame Masque wanted the chip by one o'clock on Saturday, so they had less than eighteen hours to try and find a way to turn the tables on Madame Masque herself. In theory, Bethany had been working on the problem while he was breaking A.I.M. heads. With luck, she had worked out a plan already.

At the moment, though, he was certain of only one thing: He wasn't just going to hand the chip over to the Maggia. There was no way he was doing that, he vowed.

No way in hell.

He could hear her screams now. They were deafeningly loud and heart-breakingly sad. Anastasia shrieked out loud, her mouth wide open, her face contorted with sheer agony. Her once-bronzed skin had faded to a deathly white; she looked like a vampire being tortured by the searing rays of the rising sun. Her pale flesh glowed with a harsh blue radiance, as though she was radioactive. Gray tendrils of smoke rose from her blond hair and sapphire eyes, while her pain-drenched howl grew more high-pitched and excruciating every moment. She was no longer merely a six-inch image on a computer screen. Tony could see her right in front of him, her torment as large as life. No sheet of glass separated them now. She was only inches away, yet Tony found himself unable to reach her. His arms reached out to hold her, to rescue her, but she always seemed just a fingertip away. He struggled to move closer, if only a few more inches, but he was frozen, paralyzed. He couldn't move a muscle, he could only watch as her anguished cries grew louder, and her golden tresses burst into flame, consuming Ana's entire face, then her body, until all that was left was a blazing torch that, impossibly, kept on screaming. . . .

Tossing and turning upon his cot, Tony Stark wrestled with the recurring nightmare. No matter how hard he tried to push it away, the same horrific vision kept intruding into his imagination. He slept fitfully, half aware that he was dreaming but unable to halt the relentless progress of the nightmare's terrible scenario. Other times, he lay awake, his eyes squeezed shut to block out the remorseless white light that suffused his cell every hour on the hour without respite. *There's still something not quite kosher about that last transmission,* he reminded himself. What *did* happen to her tan after all? Despite his suspicions, however, he could not forget or ignore the sight of Anastasia being so brutally and unjustly tortured. Those screams! He hadn't really heard them, not in real life, but he obviously could imagine them all too easily.

This can't go on, Tony decided. He had to see Ana in the flesh, find out how badly she'd been hurt. He must match Blank Screen's ultimatums with one of his own: no more work until he saw Ana in person. It was a dreadful risk; Blank Screen would surely threaten Ana again, if not do worse. Deep down inside, though, Tony could not simply observe Ana's peril from long distance anymore. Only by reuniting with her could he get to the bottom of this mystery, and perhaps save them both. The sole alternative was to watch his nightmare unfold again and again, for real this time, as Blank Screen continued to use Ana's suffering as a goad to force Tony to reveal ever more of Iron Man's secrets. Every time he balked, Blank Screen would escalate the violence against Anastasia—until it was too late to save her.

Eyes shut, Tony rested on the cot, working up the energy and courage to go and present his ultimatum to Blank Screen. It would be hard, knowing that Ana was even more at risk than he, but he had to learn the truth. *Blast it*, he thought, *for all I know they may have killed Ana days ago, and are simply showing me old footage recorded before her death.* He hoped it wasn't so, but every instinct he had told him something was fishy here. *Where the hell did her tan go?* He ran a hand over his cheek; he still couldn't feel any whiskers. *This simply doesn't make sense,* he thought, puzzled and frustrated. He felt like a character in a script by Rod Serling: *"Submitted for your approval: a confused industrialist and occasional super hero, trapped in a blank white room with no entrance and no exit, where food comes from nowhere and disappears the same way, where time and facial hair apparently stand still, but a supermodel's carefully constructed tan vanishes almost immediately. Meet Mr. Anthony Stark, alias the invincible Iron Man, condemned to solitary confinement in . . . The Twilight Zone."*

Tony sat up in the cot. He dropped his bare feet onto the floor. Enough stalling, he decided. No matter how surreal his situation, he still had to confront it as best he could. He walked over to the computer station and plopped down on the stool. On the monitor, his armor designs remained just as he'd left them. Tony glanced at a cutaway diagram of Iron Man's AC/DC Universal Power Connect Panel; automatically, he noted a transistor link that could be streamlined, and resisted the temptation to use the mouse to sketch in the correction on the screen. He took a deep breath, and wished, rather guiltily, for a stiff drink. *No more tinkering,* he scolded himself. It was time to confront Blank Screen, once and for all.

Then, mere seconds before he could speak, he heard something unexpected: a soft, sibilant *whoosh* of air. His gaze drawn by the sound, Tony gasped in surprise as a crack suddenly appeared in the unbroken plaster whiteness of the wall next to the computer station. Like his meals, the crack arrived from nowhere. It simply materialized, less than an inch long and razor-thin, midway up the wall to the right of where he now sat. He watched, eyes wide, as the crack, black as night against the dull white wall, grew quickly along a vertical line, stretching towards both the floor and ceiling. *This is impossible,* Tony thought. *I examined every inch of that wall. It was completely seamless.* Now, however, a thin black line connected the roof and the floor. Tony stood up hurriedly. His jaw dropped in amazement as the line rapidly grew thicker. Then he realized it wasn't the gap that was growing; instead, the entire right-hand section of the wall was sliding away, exposing an open doorway that led to a darkened corridor. Observing the action of the door, Tony could not figure the mechanism by which it worked, or how the hermetically sealed chamber could suddenly produce movable walls. *I hope it's not magic,* he thought. *I really hate magic and spells and all that sorcery stuff.* No matter the explanation, though, he stepped towards the portal, reluctant to look a gift exit in the mouth. He hesitated only a moment at the foot of the door, wondering if this miraculous portal could be a trap of some kind. *Probably,* he conceded, but it was also his best shot at escape. *Give it your best shot, Stark,* he thought. *You've beaten foolproof deathtraps before.*

Footsteps sounded outside his cell. Instantly wary, Tony peered past the open door and saw a shadowy figure hurrying down the dimly lit hall, heading for the cell. Footsteps clattered on the tile floor outside his prison. Tony glanced around the cell, looking for something, anything, he could use as a weapon to defend himself, but the room offered nothing remotely suitable. Even his plates and cutlery had disappeared long since. *As Iron Man,* he thought, *I could easily lift the entire cot and use that as a club. Of course, if I had my armor, I wouldn't need any weapon except my repulsors.*

Tony couldn't tell if the approaching figure had seen him yet. He darted to the side, pressing his back up against a blank stretch of wall next to the doorway. The footsteps grew louder as the other person neared the cell. Locking both fists together, he raised his arms above his head, ready to ambush his mysterious visitor the minute he stepped through the door. His muscles tensed in anticipation. He had to put everything he had into the first blow. He held his breath, afraid to make any noise that might alert the other. The steps sounded like they were just outside the door. A faint, indistinct shadow crossed the threshold, cast by the dim illumination in the hallway beyond. *Ready,* Tony thought. *Here goes nothing. . . .*

The figure stepped into the cell, and Tony lunged forward, swinging his fists down towards the intruder's skull. He got an instant glimpse of gleaming blonde hair, recognized a trim yet feminine figure, and felt a sudden jolt run through him as a pair of striking blue eyes turned towards him, their lush, voluptuous brows arching upwards in surprise and alarm. *Oh my God,* he thought. *Ana!*

Halting his savage blow in mid-swing, Tony froze in shock. His eyes gaped and his mouth dropped open as he stared at the woman before him. Anastasia stood on her own two feet, alive and well and apparently intact, less than two feet away. The sling that had once held her arm had vanished, and she had somehow exchanged her charred and blood-stained prison garb for a fresh, white, short-sleeved uniform, along with a pair of high black boots. Barefoot, Tony contemplated Ana's new boots with a certain degree of envy.

It was the automatic rifle she cradled in her arms, however, that really drew his attention. The massive blue-black steel weapon, complete with a full ammo clip, looked almost as large as Anastasia herself. Clutching the assault weapon confidently with both hands, her long and slender legs spread wide, the blonde supermodel looked a B-movie action heroine, ready to take on the world. *I was going to rescue* her? Tony thought, amused despite the seriousness of their situation. *I think I may have seriously underestimated this woman.*

Most of all, though, Tony was overcome with joy and relief at the sight of Anastasia, restored to him at last and without any visible injuries. Only a faint purple bruise on her pale forehead, left over from the energy bolt that had knocked her unconscious aboard *Athena,* testified to the ordeal she had endured since the attack on the yacht. The conspicuous absence of her tan still bothered him, but there would be time enough to ask her about that later. For now, the important thing was that she was here and alive. "Thank God!" he exclaimed. Arms outstretched, he rushed towards her. Ana shifted the gun out of the way and he wrapped his arms around her. Ana's body felt firm and strong, although slightly cool to the touch. He hugged her for maybe a minute or two, then she pulled away from him. A thousand questions, all regarding Ana's miraculous appearance in his cell, filled Tony's mind. "How . . . ?" he began.

"Not now," she shushed him, placing a finger over his lips. She held on to the rifle with her other hand. "We have to hurry, Tony. There's not a moment to lose." Her eyes met his; after his long captivity, seeing Ana only as a tormented image on his computer's small monitor, he'd forgotten how truly lovely she was. Taking him by the hand, she guided him towards the door. "This is our chance, darling," she whispered, "but we must move quickly."

"But how did you get free?" Tony asked her. "Where did you get that gun?"

Ana shook her head, sweeping her blonde bangs above her eyes. "I'll explain later." She tugged on his hand. "Come with me now."

"Okay," he agreed. Frankly, he couldn't wait to get out of this damn white room. First, though, there was something he absolutely had to do. "Hand me the gun," he said.

"What?" she said, seemingly confused. Letting go of his hand, she clutched the rifle possessively. Her hands tightened around the weapon. She pulled it in closer to her chest. "Tony, I don't understand."

"The gun, Ana. Just give me the gun." He smiled reassuringly at her and stretched out his hands, the palms turned upward beseechingly. Still, Ana hesitated, obviously reluctant to relinquish the weapon. For the first time, a horrible seed of doubt sprouted in Tony's thoughts. Could he really trust this woman? What if she had been brainwashed to betray him? It was certainly possible; she wouldn't be the first innocent prisoner to be "turned" by sophisticated mind-control techniques. For that matter, could he be sure she was really Anastasia Swift? What if this woman, materializing so conveniently in his cell, was some sort of imposter, maybe a Life Model Decoy or another form of android pretender? There was only one way to find out. "Let me have the gun, Ana," he said, carefully watching her reactions. "You can trust me. We're on the same side, right?"

If she refuses to surrender the rifle, he decided, *this is a setup.*

Ana stared at him blankly for an impossibly long moment. Then she shrugged and smiled sheepishly. "Of course. Here, take it." She passed the weapon over to him. The steel rifle felt heavy in his hands, but his spirits lightened considerably. "Sorry, Tony, I don't know what came over me. It's just that, well, after all that's happened, I hate feeling defenseless, even for a moment."

I can understand that, he thought. How many times in the last day or so had he wished for his Iron Man armor? He felt guilty for doubting her. "No problem," he told Ana. "This won't take long." Resting the butt of the rifle against his shoulder, he swiveled and aimed the rifle barrel at the computer that had dominated his life ever since he woke up in this cell. With a sense of tremendous satisfaction, he pulled the trigger. A single burst of gunfire echoed off the walls, as the computer screen exploded into sparks and flying splinters of plastic. Behind him, Ana flinched at the rifle's loud report. Smoke leaked from the gun's muzzle. *No silencer,* he noted. If there were any guards in the vicinity, this would surely bring them running. He quickly fired another bullet into the unit's hard drive, then handed the rifle back to Anastasia. "Thanks for the loan," he said. "Careful, the barrel's still hot."

Chances are, he realized, the armor schematics had already been transmitted to another location. Still, if there was even a chance he could keep that data out of Blank Screen's hands, he had to take it. Besides, he admitted to himself, shooting that blasted computer made him feel a whole lot better. "Let's go," he said, reclaiming Ana's free hand. She squeezed his own hand firmly.

"Follow me," she said. Without so much as a parting glance at his recent residence, he exited the cell with Ana. She led him down the gloomy hallway to another corridor, as white and sterile as the prison he had just escaped. Tony listened for the sound of oncoming guards, but the installation, wherever they were, appeared deserted. *That's odd,* he thought. If nothing else, shooting up the computer terminal should have alerted Blank Screen that his/her scheme had met with resistance. So where were the guards summoned to halt this escape-in-progress?

Hand in hand, they ran down the empty corridor for about fifty yards until they came to an intersection. *Which way now*, Tony wondered. *Left, right, or straight ahead?* Without a second's hesitation, Ana pulled him to the right. The corridor they found in that direction looked identical to the one Ana had diverted them from, as did the long white hall at the next intersection. This time she turned left, then right, then right again. Ana never paused or looked at all lost or uncertain; instead, she guided him through a bewildering labyrinth of indistinguishable white corridors as though she had the route committed to memory. No one pursued them, or appeared to block their headlong rush through the complex.

Tony quickly lost all sense of direction; he doubted that he could find his way back to his cell even if he wanted to, which he certainly didn't. None of the corridors seemed to lead anywhere except to more empty halls. He looked in vain for any sign of an office, a lab, or even another prison cell. Were the doors just as invisible from the hall as they were from the inside of his cell? *None of this makes any sense,* he thought as he ran. What sort of place was this anyway? Where were they going? He felt like a mouse running through an experimental maze that the Ana-mouse had already figured out. "Wait," he said. "What's going on, Ana? Where are we running to?"

"Please, Tony!" she said, pulling anxiously on his arm. "I'll explain as soon as I can. We're almost there!"

"Almost where?" he demanded. He wanted to trust Ana, but, blast it, he'd been in the dark for too long!

"Here," she said. They came to an abrupt halt in front of blank white wall. A dead end, he realized, amazed that any of these endless corridors ever came to an end. *Now what?* he wondered, half suspecting the answer. Sure enough, Ana pressed her palm against the smooth white surface of the wall, and a dark crack suddenly appeared a few inches away from her hand. After watching a door appear from nowhere in the wall of his cell, he was none too surprised when a similar division formed in the wall in front of him, expanding to reveal another doorway onto darkness. What he didn't understand was how and why Ana was able to activate the door. "Finally," Ana exclaimed. "We made it!"

"Made it where?" Tony asked again, driven almost to madness by the questions crowding his brain. Even more than he wanted his armor, he needed to know what exactly what was happening. Where were the guards? Why did Ana suddenly have the run of the place? *What became of her blasted tan?*

"To our only hope," Ana said. Her face was grim and deadly serious. "Come." She urged him over the threshold into the chamber beyond. The lights in the room came on automatically as they entered; it was the same unfocused illumination, emanating from no visible source, that had suffused his cell. Hearing another *whoosh,* he glanced over his shoulder and saw the door closing behind him—or, more accurately, vanishing back into the state of nonexistence whence it came. Tony experienced a stab of anxiety as the last sliver of a crack disappeared from the wall, sealing him in. He was trapped once more, but where?

"Look," Ana said, introducing him to their destination. Tearing his gaze away from the former site of the door, Tony took in the whole scene. Recognition hit him instantly, and Tony felt torn between excitement and horror.

They were in a combination laboratory/workshop,

easily three or four times larger than either his or Ana's cell. Gleaming, stainless steel machinery lined the walls, including computers, X-ray machines, motion detectors, holographic imaging systems, laser sensors for microscopic analysis, a solar generator, magnetic field projector, and numerous artificial arms—"waldoes"—individually designed to handle a variety of tasks, from sturdy arms intended for heavy lifting to intricate mechanical fingers fit for precision operations beyond the capacity of a normal human hand. Only a few feet away from Tony, a mounted display case held a selection of high-quality tools, from laser scalpels to micro-welding torches, neatly arranged and clearly identified with typeset labels printed in English. Tony was impressed, despite himself. Blank Screen had clearly spent millions outfitting this lab with the best possible equipment.

It was the centerpiece of the room, however, that really drew his eyes—and filled Tony's heart with profoundly mixed feelings. Supported by two massive waldoes that protruded from the high ceiling several yards above them, a partially assembled suit of Iron Man armor hung suspended in the air; the faceplate of the mask looked down on Tony expectantly, waiting to be brought to life. The final layer of gold and crimson plating had not yet been added to the armor; the suit was a uniform dull grey, much like the first suit he had built so many years ago in Southeast Asia. All over the armor, sections of circuitry remained exposed to the air, not yet covered by protective tiles.

Tony saw that the forward multispectral camera platform near the top of Iron Man's faceplate had not yet been integrated with the surrounding systems such as the headset's UHF/VHF antenna array. The lens over the tri-beam was missing, leaving a gaping hole in the center of the chest assembly. The main magnetic field timing circuit access, located over the right hip, jutted a few inches out of its proper location; apparently, someone intended to work on it further before sliding it all the way into its proper slot. And so on and so on, Tony noted. The suit was by no stretch of the imagination operational just yet, but the bulk of it was substantially, terrifyingly there.

Dumbstruck, he circled the armor, scanning every detail of its construction. He couldn't be sure without a closer look, of course, but a quick inspection suggested that the armor was fully two-thirds complete. Tony was impressed again, and appalled. The notes and schematics he had so reluctantly fed into Blank Screen's computer had become a physical reality without his knowledge.

"I never imagined they could get this far this fast," he said out loud. Turning away from the armor for a minute, he contemplated the display on a computer screen built into the wall. As he feared, there were his latest diagrams available for anyone to see. Shooting that other computer to bits had done no good at all. Everything he had entered into the machine in his cell had been transformed into iron and circuitry in this laboratory, either by Blank Screen or by his or her minions. "Blast it!" he blurted, feeling like a dupe. He pounded his fist down on a shining metal countertop.

And yet, he thought, it was still hard to believe that his enemies could have built so much of the suit already. He hadn't given them nearly enough information yet ... unless they had successfully extrapolated from the data he had provided them to figure out what was missing. It was not nearly as easy as simply connecting the dots, but it was possible, he supposed. If so, however, then he was dealing with scientific genius of even greater potential than he had feared. Tony looked more carefully at the diagram on the screen. On second glance, he saw that the blueprints were not exactly as he had last entered them. *Someone* had indeed modified his designs, extending the logic and direction of Tony's engineering techniques into areas that Tony had not yet revealed to Blank Screen. Like a technological mimic, aping Tony's distinctive methodology and reasoning, the inhabitant of this lab had raced ahead of him, designing armor systems in the "style" of Tony Stark.

But why the rush? Tony wondered. *Why not wait for the real thing, instead of a passable imitation based on admittedly inspired guesswork?* There were at least two possible explanations, he surmised. Either Blank Screen had realized that, when push came to shove, Tony was *never* going to share all of Iron Man's secrets, no matter what became of both him and Ana, or Blank Screen had a very specific plan in mind for this armor, a plan that ran on a definite time-table. Maybe he/she needed a suit of armor by a certain, firm deadline in order to carry out some diabolical objective, like assassinating a president or conquering the world. If that was the case, then a hasty escape became even more imperative. God only knew what atrocity was planned, but maybe there was still time to nip Blank Screen's evil ambition in the bud.

And the means to stop Blank Screen was hanging from the mechanical arms only a few feet away.

Ana was way ahead of him. She rested her rifle against the nearest wall, then waved her arms wildly towards the ominous grey figure dominating the center of the lab. "The armor!" she said excitedly. "Don't you see, Tony? This is our chance. You can wear the armor, just like the real Iron Man, and get us out of this terrible place!"

"Maybe," Tony agreed. Walking away from the screen, he peered at the armor. It waited, like Frankenstein's monster, for the spark of his genius to animate its mighty iron limbs. Ana was right. This suit was exactly the weapon he'd been praying for, so why did he feel so leery about this entire scenario? *Something's wrong.* His suspicions nagged him. *This is too easy, too convenient.* He glanced furtively at the automatic rifle propped up against the wall. *Suppose I just grab that gun and try to shoot my way out of here?* he thought, then shook his head. *That would be a much more practical notion if I had any idea at all where "here" is, or what sort of obstacles lay between us and freedom.*

"I don't know," he said, hedging his bets. "The suit's nowhere near complete."

"Then finish it!" Ana pleaded. She embraced him desperately, holding on to him as though her life depended on it. He felt her body press against him, and heard her voice crack as she sobbed on his shoulder, her lips next to his ear. "Please, Tony," she begged. "I can't go back to that . . . that torture chamber. You don't know what they did to me there! It was horrible. The pain, the helplessness . . . never knowing what was going to happen next, if I was going to live or die. I can't go back there. I'll kill myself first!"

"I know. I understand," he said soothingly, stroking her back. Her body racked with violent sobs, Ana trembled in his arms. All the strength and confidence she had demonstrated during their escape attempt (*if that's what it was,* the wary part of his mind amended) seemed to drain away suddenly, as though she had reached the very limits of her endurance and had no more emotional reserves to draw upon. He found himself largely supporting her weight, holding her up lest she collapse onto the laboratory floor. Tony couldn't blame her; after all she'd endured, it was a miracle she'd come this far. He remembered their sunny afternoon upon *Athena*, the taste of her lips and the sultry fire in her eyes, and his heart ached from the nightmare their brief idyll had become. *How can I tell her,* he thought despairingly, *that I witnessed much of her agony, agony she suffered largely because of me?*

"You have to complete the armor and put it on," she whispered plaintively. Her lips brushed his ear. Her quivering body sagged against his, as her voice rose, gaining passion and determination. "It's our only hope, Tony," she breathed urgently. "Become Iron Man . . . for me."

At that moment, as he held Anastasia's trembling frame protectively, while unforgettable images of her pale form writhing in a hell of unleashed lightning raced through his brain alongside sensuous memories of an incandescent bronzed figure lounging blissfully amidst sea and sunlight, Tony knew he would do anything, fight anyone, to keep this one, all-too-vulnerable woman safe from harm.

If only, he thought bitterly, *I could truly trust her as well.*

But he didn't.

FRIDAY. 11:34 PM. EASTERN STANDARD TIME.

The East Coast of the United States was a glittering tapestry of tiny lights speckling a rich, velvety cloak of midnight darkness. At least that was how it appeared to War Machine as he soared through the sky at an altitude of fifteen thousand feet. It was a clear, starry night with minimal cloud cover. *Go high enough,* he thought, *and I could probably see all the way from Miami to Maine.*

Well, maybe I'm exaggerating just a little. Still, it was a beautiful night to be flying. The world looked so peaceful from up here, like a miniature diorama in a museum exhibit. The reality on the streets and byways below was far different, he knew. All those tiny points of light represented homes and offices and vehicles filled with breathing, thinking individuals. Somewhere down there, in the Philadelphia neighborhood where he was born and raised, another small child might be faced with abuse or abandonment—or be tucked away in bed, dreaming of a life of adventure and accomplishment.

Hah, Jim thought, laughing at his own sober reflections. *I'm getting morose in my old age, not to mention alliterative. Better keep my mind on my job.* With several hours to spare before Madame Masque's deadline, he had decided to head for Avengers Mansion in New York City. His undersea battle with A.I.M. had left his armor in need of repairs and his arsenal badly needing replenishing, and his own California headquarters was several hours away. Until he got the suit checked out for any hairline fissures, he didn't want to risk another suborbital re-entry. Fortunately, Manhattan was only a short hop from Florida. Even though he had not been an active member of the Avengers for some time, Jim knew he could count on fresh supplies and a thorough once-over at the super team's headquarters. He did feel odd about dropping in so late in the evening, but one of "Earth's Mightiest Heroes" was bound to be on duty. Probably the Vision, Jim guessed. As an android, he didn't need sleep.

I wish I didn't, Jim thought. He yawned beneath his iron faceplate. Even though it was not even nine o'clock by California time, that brawl under the Atlantic had taken a lot out of him. Briefly, he considered dropping out of the sky for a cup of coffee somewhere, then decided he didn't have that much time to waste. *Too bad there are no truckstops at fifteen thousand feet,* he thought, yawning once more. *I feel like I could sleep for a week.*

He check his armor's chronometer. It was eleven-forty Atlantic. *It's about time for* Nightline, he thought, tuning in the audio portion of the show on his satellite link. Sure enough, they were covering Tony Stark's disappearance, but Jim discovered that the "coverage" was little more than half-baked rumors and spin control. *Maybe I should switch to Letterman. . . .*

Before he could pursue this half-serious thought,

an emergency message interrupted the transmission from ABC. The armor switched automatically to a priority channel, and War Machine heard Bethany Cabe's throaty voice come over his audio receivers.

"Jim," she began. "Bethany here. I got Sheva's message regarding the chip. Congratulations . . . and thanks. Do you still have the chip with you?"

"Affirmative," War Machine replied. If he hadn't been flying at Mach One, he would have patted the containment pouch on his belt. He had debriefed Sheva Joseph at WorldWatch on his successful raid on Advanced Idea Mechanics about a half an hour ago, shortly after his escape from the undersea lab. Good to know that Sheva had already brought Stark Enterprises into the loop. Now, he quickly updated Bethany on his immediate plans regarding Avengers HQ. "I figure either the Vision or Dr. Pym can look the suit over and, hopefully, give it a clean bill of health."

"Is that absolutely necessary, Jim?" Bethany's voice asked.

"Why?" he said. "Do you have a better idea?"

"Maybe," she replied. "I think I have a lead on Madame Masque. My sources at Interpol tell me that a major meeting of the world's top crime families is scheduled to be held in New York sometime this weekend. This meet is a very big deal in underworld circles. All the top people are supposed to attend, from the Yakuza, the Mob, *and* the Maggia. Including Madame Masque herself."

"Hmmm," he said thoughtfully. "You think maybe this summit meeting is why Masque wants the energy chip? She could be making a bid for more power, and if this gadget is half as powerful as it's supposed to be it would make one hell of a bargaining chip, no pun intended."

"Perhaps," Bethany agreed. "About the chip, did you learn anything more about it from A.I.M.? What did you find out about its real capabilities?"

"Only that the eggheads at A.I.M. thought it worth building a fortress around. That must count for something."

"I see what you mean," Bethany acknowledged. "Damn, I wish we had more time to analyze it. Maybe later—the important thing now is that I have an address in Manhattan where Madame Masque will supposedly be residing for the next six hours. Don't ask me where I got it; enough lives are at stake as is."

"Understood," War Machine said. He didn't care whose arms Bethany had twisted to uncover this info; it was the best lead they'd gotten since Tony had been snatched. "Give me the address."

Bethany recited the address, then had Jim repeat it back to her. "It's a penthouse on the Upper West Side," she elaborated, "near Central Park. Security is bound to be tight, but I'm fuzzy on the details. The sooner you strike, though, the better."

"Right," War Machine agreed. *So much for the tune-up,* he thought. The deadline was still over a day away. Madame Masque wouldn't be expecting a frontal assault now. This was his big opportunity to upset her meticulously planned operation and gain the advantage of surprise. His armor was not in the best of shape, perhaps, but it was still up and running, and that should be more than enough to take out a bunch of Maggia goons. Most importantly, he reminded himself, Tony was in potential jeopardy every minute he remained in the hands of the bad guys. *I'd never forgive myself,* Jim thought, *if Tony lost an arm or an eye or worse while Doc Pym tinkered with the suit.*

He checked his location finder. At top speed, Manhattan was less than forty-five minutes away. *Time to take a War Machine–sized bite out of the Big Apple,* he decided. "Anything else I need to know?" he asked Bethany.

"Plenty, I imagine," she said. "But that's all the inside dirt I've got for now. You're going to have to wing it, I'm afraid. Sorry." Bethany paused before continuing. "Good luck, Jim. Take care of that chip, okay?"

"Sure," he told her. It was probably too much to hope that Tony was actually being held at this particular address, but he felt more optimistic than he had for hours. He was getting closer to Tony. He could smell it. "Wait," he said before signing off. "I just thought of something. There's something I want you to send to me in New York, as fast as humanly possible."

"Anything you want, you've got it," she said.

Jim could hear the gratitude in her voice, as well as her eagerness to take action instead of simply waiting around for bad news. He explained to her exactly what he needed. "Of course," she said when he was finished. "I should have thought of that myself. I'll send it by suborbital transmodule immediately. Avengers Mansion okay with you?"

"Perfect," he said. "I'll pick it up after I've kicked some Maggia butt." *Assuming, that is,* he thought privately, *that I don't run into any unpleasant surprises at Masque's hideout.*

Bethany must have been entertaining similar concerns back in Los Angeles. "Be careful, Jim," she said. "I'm crossing my fingers for both you and Tony."

"Much appreciated, Beth," he told her sincerely. "War Machine, over and out."

Cutting off the transmission, he climbed to twenty thousand feet. The lights below dwindled to pinpricks as he revved up his jets to full speed. Rockets flared from his heels and Jim felt the surge of sudden acceleration.

Give my regards to Broadway, he thought. *New York, here I come!*

Only miles from Manhattan Island, his autonavigator beeped its proximity alarm and entered the necessary course corrections. Slowing his pace, War Machine descended towards the city proper. New York's magnificent skyline beckoned him like a gigantic crown of jewels, the lighted skyscrapers looming high above the city streets, dwarfing the Statue of Liberty where she raised her lamp above the harbor.

War Machine flew in from the south, passing far above Lady Liberty and Ellis Island. It was past one in the morning; traffic was minimal across the Brooklyn Bridge. Ahead of him, the twin towers of the World Trade Center dominated the horizon. War Machine dropped altitude until he was less than half a mile above the top of the towers. Soaring over them, deftly evading the huge antenna spike on the northeast tower, he headed uptown on Broadway, clocking his progress by the landmarks he passed: Wall Street, Trinity Church, the tangled labyrinth of shops and streets that was the West Village, the Flatiron Building, the Empire State Building, Madison Square Garden, the gaudy neon spectacle of Times Square. . . . Finally, Central Park stretched below him: an immense rectangle of greenery surrounded on all sides by concrete and skyscrapers. War Machine was always stunned by the sheer size of the park. Roughly fifty blocks long and four longer blocks across, the park was large enough to contain several bodies of water, as well as a playing field, tennis courts, a skating rink, gardens, monuments, and a small zoo. The last time he and his ladyfriend, Rae Lacoste, had spent a weekend in New York, they'd spent an enjoyable afternoon paddling a rowboat around the lake down there. Jim smiled at the memory. That had been a good day. Too bad this excursion to the Big Apple had a meaner agenda.

There were no couples, jubilant or otherwise, rowing upon the lake now, of course. At night, the park became a jungle inhabited by human predators more fearsome than anything found in the zoo. Masked by shadows, the park appeared deserted, its dense foliage hiding its nocturnal denizens from sight. War Machine was glad he didn't see any joggers here; he probably wouldn't have been able to resist the temptation to swoop down and carry them to safety whether they liked it or not. Instead, he veered left, following Central Park West.

According to Bethany, Madame Masque could be found on the top floor of one of the tall buildings bordering this side of the park. Switching on his location finder, he superimposed a Manhattan street map onto the city blocks below him. A quick mental command deleted the glowing green lines that indicated the presence of subway lines; he was looking for a penthouse, not an underground tunnel. Cybernetically, he entered the address Bethany had given him into the tracking computer. The location finder responded immediately, mapping the numerical address onto the scene before his eyes. Between the street lights and glowing windows of the City That Never Slept, he didn't need to announce his presence by using his chest searchlight; he flew by sight. A bright pink square flashed on his field of vision, identifying the correct building from the dozens of similar structures surrounding it. *That was easy enough,* he thought, switching back to normal vision.

The residence in question was stately edifice of marble and brick that practically dripped age and money. Stone gargoyles adorned the upper corners of the building. War Machine saw a kidney-shaped swimming pool, with accompanying putting green and helicopter pad, occupying the roof of the building while, ten stories below, a red carpet stretched from the sidewalk to the scarlet awning covering the front entrance. Golden tassels hung from the deep red fabric of the awning which showed no sign of fading or weathering. A long black limousine was parked in front of the building, which was guarded by at least three burly doormen whose scarlet, tasseled uniforms matched the awning. *Nice building, nice neighborhood,* War Machine observed. *Guess organized crime pays well.*

Hovering noiselessly above the building, out of sight of the almost certainly armed doormen, he recalled what he knew of the Maggia, both from research and from personal experience.

An international syndicate, the Maggia was the world's most powerful organization dedicated to conventional crime, as opposed to subversive activities. Unlike A.I.M. or Hydra, the Maggia was more interested in profit than political domination. Originating in southern Europe, the Maggia spread through non-Communist Europe and the Americas. Its baleful presence in the United States first came to public attention in the 1890s, and the Maggia's widespread bootlegging of illegal liquor during the Prohibition Era had become legendary. Even Al Capone was said to have feared the early Maggia, while Elliot Ness found its leaders truly untouchable. Today, War Machine knew, the Maggia controlled most of the illegal gambling, loan-sharking, and narcotics trade in the United States, as well as many legal gambling casinos in Atlantic City, New Jersey, Las Vegas, Nevada, and soon, most likely, New Orleans. Ruled by a loose coalition of so-called "families," it also had tremendous influence within various labor unions, and controlled politicians on every level of government. The Maggia also invested many of its illicit gains in legitimate businesses, even trying to buy into Stark Enterprises on occasion. Fortunately, Tony had always managed to keep his companies free from Maggia influence. *Was that why they chose Tony to snatch, aside from his well-publicized connection to Iron Man?* War Machine wondered. *For revenge, or to make an example of him to other business leaders?* It seemed as good an explanation as any. The Maggia specialized in extortion and intimidation.

In essence, the Maggia worked much like the plain old Mafia. The only difference between the two organizations, as nearly as he could tell, was that the Maggia had the technological edge. Where the mob tended to stick to its traditional forms of enforcement, guns and bombs and old-fashioned muscle, the Maggia, less bound to its infamous past, never hesitated to employ the most modern forms of terror: robot dreadnaughts, super-villains, death rays, and anything else they could get their greedy paws on. This whole energy chip caper sounded just like a typical Maggia power play. *No way,* War Machine vowed again, *am I giving these cutthroats another deadly toy to play with.* To date, WorldWatch had not devoted much effort to exposing the Maggia, preferring to ride herd on more political troublemakers. *That may have been my mistake,* Jim thought. The Maggia's corrupt reach tainted lives from street level to boardrooms, from neighborhoods to nations, making true social justice even harder to obtain. It was something he'd have to look into when he got back to California, after he rescued Tony.

Despite the lateness of the hour, the lights were still on in the penthouse. *Crime never sleeps,* War Machine thought angrily. *Good. I'd hate to disturb anyone's beauty rest, especially Madame Masque's.* He aimed his armored fists at a plate-glass window on the penthouse's south side and went into a power dive. The direct approach had worked fine with A.I.M., so why sneak around where the Maggia was concerned?

His fists hit the window like piledrivers. The glass was thicker than he expected, but no match for several hundred pounds of plummeting War Machine. Shards of broken glass flew like shrapnel, producing shouts of surprise and pain. Spinning in mid-air, War Machine landed smoothly on his feet. Glass crunched beneath his black metal boots. Bullets *pinged* off his chest and faceplate, but War Machine barely noticed them. He looked around quickly, searching for Madame Masque.

He was in a luxuriously appointed living room, decorated with expensive-looking antique furniture. A sparkling crystal chandelier hung from the ceiling. Wall-to-wall shag carpeting, indigo blue, covered the floor. A plush couch, upholstered with fine rose damask, was pushed against one wall, behind a low mahogany coffee table. A medieval tapestry reproduction hung on the wall opposite the plate-glass window War Machine had just crashed through, depicting a legendary encounter between a jousting knight in full armor and a mythical dragon that vaguely resembled Iron Man's old foe Fin Fang Foom. Two cozy, wingback chairs had been pulled around the coffee table. Judging from the playing cards and fifty-dollar bills scattered over the surface of the table, a high stakes poker game had been in progress when a black-and-white armored warrior came blasting into the room. War Machine glanced down at the discarded cards, noting that someone had tossed aside a royal flush when he attacked. *Tough luck,* Jim thought, shrugging.

There were five gunmen visible, all firing at him with automatic pistols. They looked like ordinary, if relatively prosperous hoods to War Machine: beefy looking men in tailor-made suits. All five had discarded their jackets and ties during the game. They wore shoulder holsters over pressed white shirts, their collars unbuttoned. Broken noses and scars marred their faces, testifying to the roughhouse nature of their lives and characters. Behind opaque lenses, Jim's eyes searched the room, but found no women in sight, masked or otherwise.

Maybe Bethany's unnamed source was mistaken, he thought, *or maybe the Boss Lady herself is lurking elsewhere in the penthouse.* War Machine spotted a heavy oak door across the room, partially covered by the hanging tapestries. The frantic gunmen stood between him and the door, emptying clip after clip of ammo at War Machine. Flames burst from the muzzles of their guns. Bullets ricocheted off his impenetrable armor plating, tearing holes in the living room's lavish furnishings. Stuffing burst from the back of a cushioned chair as a stray bullet pierced the front of the chair and came out the other side. A porcelain vase, ornamented with delicate streaks of gold filigree, exploded into shards, joining the fragments of broken window on the dark blue carpet. *What a mess,* War Machine thought, annoyed. The blare of the guns, as well as the constant ring of bullets bouncing off his armor, was getting on his nerves.

He leaned over and seized the coffee table with both gloves. Effortlessly, he lifted the heavy wooden object above his head and faced the gang of shooters. Hearts, spades, diamonds, and clubs, along with a handful of crumpled green bills, slid off the table, drifting downwards to the floor. ''Ante up, boys,'' War Machine said. The vocal changer in his mouthpiece made Jim's voice, ordinarily deep, sound like the roar of an enraged lion. He could see the blood draining out of his opponents' flushed faces as they realized his intention. War Machine hurled the mahogany table, cannonballing it into the knot of men with full force. Knocked off their feet, their shots pelted the ceiling, blowing holes in the plaster before the goons' pistols fell silent altogether.

War Machine doubted that any of the men would be getting up soon, but he didn't give them a chance to rise again. Casually kicking a bulky chair out of his way, he stomped across the room. Shoving the now-battered table aside with one hand, he grabbed the closest gunman by his shirt front and lifted him off his feet. The Maggia "soldier" was a big man, easily three hundred pounds of fat and muscles, with curly brown hair and a blackened eye. His feet, clad in polished black leather loafers, dangled two feet above the carpet. "I want Madame Masque," War Machine declared. "Where is she?"

"Huh?" Curlytop said. He acted dazed. War Machine couldn't tell if the man was faking or not. He channeled a very mild electrical sting to his right gauntlet, jolting the man back to his senses. "What the hell?" Curlytop shouted, suddenly more angry than confused. He fixed sunken, bloodshot eyes at the robotic creature staring up at him through a pair of cold, plastic lenses. "You're that Avenger, Iron Man, aren't you?"

"Close enough," War Machine answered. *I need*

to get a better publicist, he thought. The four other men stirred fitfully at War Machine's feet. He looked down at the tangle of mobsters, collapsed on top of each other. They groaned and twitched a bit, clutching their injuries, but didn't look like much of a threat. He'd knocked the fight out of them all right. He dismissed them with a glance, then returned his attention to Curlytop. "Madame Masque," he repeated. "I want her."

The disheveled gangster sneered at him defiantly. "I don't care what you want, Iron Jerk. All I know is you've just bought a whole mess of trouble." He spit a mouthful of blood at War Machine's face. The sticky red fluid slid down the reflective silver mask, making Jim very glad his eye and mouth slits were sealed. Several drops of blood pooled over his optic lenses, clouding his vision.

"The name's War Machine," he said angrily, shaking the man until his remaining teeth rattled. The electronic vocalizer added to the menace in his tone. "And you're in no position to make threats." He wiped at his bloodstained lenses with the back of his free hand, but the metal glove wasn't really suited to the task. *Invulnerable, yes,* Jim observed wryly. *Absorbent, no.*

"Wanna bet?" Curlytop gloated. As if on cue, the ornate tapestry behind the fallen mobsters was suddenly torn asunder by two enormous steel hands. Jagged spikes protruded from oversized knuckles, ripping through the fabric noisily. A huge metal foot emerged from behind the tapestry, trampling on the four recovering gunmen. War Machine heard bones shatter beneath the monster's heavy tread. *Oh hell,* he thought, guessing what was coming next. *I have a terrible feeling this fight's just beginning.* Dropping Curlytop like a sack of potatoes, he opened his eye-slits and closed them again, the motion clearing the gore from his lenses. The hefty gunman grunted angrily as he landed flat on his butt. He attempted to scramble to his feet, but War Machine rendered him unconscious with a single well-placed repulsor ray. He had more important things to worry about now.

The dreadnaught came through the tapestry, reducing it and the wall behind it to shreds. War Machine recognized the creature instantly. The robot fighting machines known as dreadnaughts were the most powerful and most feared weapons in the Maggia's capacious arsenal. They, along with the occasional super-powered mercenary, were what made the Maggia a match for the likes of Spider-Man, the Fantastic Four, and Iron Man. *Should have figured Masque would have at least one or two around with her,* he thought. He hoped this meant she really was nearby.

The dreadnaught was easily nine feet tall, more than two heads taller than War Machine, and its entire body was proportionally larger than any mere human being. Every inch of its exterior was protected by overlapping rings of solid steel. The dreadnaught's metallic hide reflected War Machine's own burnished exoskeleton. *Is this what I look like to ordinary people?* Jim thought briefly. It was a faintly disturbing revelation. Sharpened metal spikes lined the dreadnaught's knuckles, wrists, and outer thighs. Hollow tubes, capable of emitting gases or projectiles, coiled around the dreadnaught's head, two where a human's ears would have been and third mounted atop his skull. The back of the robot's head was protected by a raised steel collar that spread out behind the head like a bizarre metallic halo.

But it was the face of the dreadnaught that truly revealed its utter inhumanity. Although sculpted in chilling parody of humanoid features, with blank staring eyes and stylized representations of a nose and lips, not a trace of emotion or even consciousness could be seen in that lifeless visage. Jim had seen abstract sculptures that had more personality than the automation stalking towards him over the broken bodies of the Maggia hoodlums. The dreadnaught had a hinged jaw like a human's, even though he had never known a dreadnaught to utter a syllable or express a single thought. He assumed the thing's rudimentary mouth was an obscure, sick joke on the part of some Maggia weapons designer. *As War Machine,* Jim acknowledged, *my face is pretty goddamn artificial, but I like to think that my basic humanity comes through anyway.* The dreadnaught's empty gaze fell upon him. It raised its gigantic silver mitts ominously. *Maybe I'm deluding myself, but this thing isn't even trying.*

It has no spark to hide or expose. It's an "it" in every sense of the word.

The dreadnaught advanced across the room. War Machine heard the smooth hum of the robot's servo motors in action. Its metal feet left deep impressions in the glass-littered carpet. Taking a few steps backwards, War Machine raised his fists, ready to defend himself. *It's just another robot,* he thought hopefully. *How tough could it be?*

He waited for the dreadnaught to swing its large spiked fist at him. He was still waiting, with the dreadnaught about a foot out of reach, when a burst of red-hot energy struck War Machine in the chest. "What the . . . ?!" he exclaimed in shock. Beneath his armor, his bare chest stung as though burned. His gloved hand clutched his chestplate instinctively; the patch of armor above his injury felt hot and slightly molten to his touch. A heat-ray, not a force-beam then, he concluded. Not far away, the dreadnaught's right palm still glowed with a faint red radiance. *Damn,* War Machine thought. *I didn't know they were equipped with beam weapons.* He shook his head. His seared flesh throbbed painfully. *I can't take many more hits like that,* he realized.

The dreadnaught raised its other palm, but this time War Machine was ready. Jets flaring, he took flight mere seconds before the dreadnaught unleashed its second heat-ray. His head scraped the ceiling of the penthouse as he flew out of the path of danger. The brilliant red beam cut through the empty air beneath him. He could feel the intense heat of its passage; it was like standing too close to a blazing fire. The beam traversed the room until it hit a section of window that had somehow remained more or less intact. Cracks spread through the glass like spidery webs from the small circular hole left behind by one of the gunmen's deflected bullets, until the heat-ray hit the window. To War Machine's astonishment, the bullet-scarred glass simply vaporized at the beam's touch. It didn't break, it didn't melt, it turned to a pale white mist instantly. Jim remembered the correct term for what he had seen from his high school chemistry classes. *Sublimation.* The process by which matter went directly from a solid state to a gaseous state without passing through a liquid phase. The glass had *sublimed* before his very eyes. He marveled at the idea. What sort of temperature was required to pull off something like that? He didn't want to find out.

He caught a glimpse of red incandescence flashing at the periphery of his vision. Moving with lightning reflexes, he took evasive action, diving headfirst towards the floor. He barrelled into the antique couch like a bull in a china shop, toppling it over onto its side. He felt rather than saw the heat-ray miss his throat by inches. Wedged between the floor, the wall, and the remains of the couch, he found himself momentarily disoriented. Rolling over onto his back, he glimpsed a tall, silver figure striding mechanically across the room. Two silver palms pointed towards War Machine, two heat-ray projectors glowed in readiness, a heartbeat away from catching War Machine in a burning crossfire that threatened to cut him in half. Reacting automatically, War Machine reached up with both hands and grabbed the dreadnaught by the wrists. Metal spikes scratched against his gauntlets, scraping against the armor plating, but he refused to let go. Instead he twisted the dreadnaught's wrists so that the robot's palms turned towards each other even as twin heat-rays flared. Red-hot beams of energy met each other head-on, producing a blinding white light that made Jim blink and look away for an instant before the polarized lenses cleared his vision. He smelled metal melting and fusing together, then watched with satisfaction as the dreadnaught staggered backwards, jolted by the unexpected discharge of thermal energy. It tore its flailing limbs out of War Machine's grasp.

War Machine took heart from the robot's unexpected reversal of fortune. He leaped to his feet and confronted the towering metal monstrosity, hoping fervently that the dreadnaught's fearsome heat-rays had been taken out of the equation. Surely, he told himself convincingly, the ray projectors in the robot's hands couldn't have survived those powerful blasts from their respective counterparts. Too bad the lifeless robot couldn't actually feel the pain of its own searing beams, Jim thought vindictively; his chest still stung where the dreadnaught's surprise first attack had hit him.

The dreadnaught regained its footing. War Machine flinched involuntarily when the robot raised its right palm, but no crimson beam threatened him. To his relief, he saw the ray projector in the dreadnaught's hand was now nothing but molten slag. War Machine aimed his own gauntlets at the dreadnaught, eager to retaliate in kind. "Eat repulsor, Robbie!" he said, activating his weapons. He expected two purple rays to knock the dreadnaught clear across the room. Nothing happened, except that the dreadnaught charged at War Machine, swinging its massive spiked fist. *Damn,* he thought. Something was wrong with the repulsors in his gloves. He started to activate his chestbeam, then remembered that it had been damaged by one of A.I.M.'s underwater crab machines. He gulped within his armor. *I have a bad feeling about this. . . .*

A huge silver fist connected with his head. The impact penetrated the armor; even through multiple layers of padding, he still felt the concussive force of the dreadnaught's blow. The spikes on the monster's knuckles scraped across War Machine's faceplate, producing an ear-piercing, metallic shriek. War Machine fought back vigorously. He slammed both his fists into the dreadnaught's mid-section. The double punch left dents in the robot's abdomen and forced it back a couple of paces, but War Machine's counterattack didn't take it out. Another silver fist came at War Machine's face. He blocked it with his left arm, taking the blow on his forearm. His other arm delivered a roundhouse punch to the dreadnaught's chin.

Going for the knockout, he thought hopefully. *Talk about your heavyweight bouts!*

The dreadnaught's head snapped backward as War Machine's fist collided with its thankfully spikeless chin. Then, like a lethal jack-in-the-box, its head jerked back into position. Blank white eyes, devoid of pupils or irises, fixed on War Machine. Powerful, artificial hands grabbed War Machine's head and tried to break Jim's neck by twisting his helmet all the way around. War Machine's neck assembly, designed by Tony Stark to prevent spinal injuries, resisted the dreadnaught's efforts. The Maggia's metallic monster exerted more force. The magnetic fields holding War Machine's helmet onto the rest of his armor strained mightily beneath the dreadnaught's superhuman strength. Warning lights flashed before Jim's eyes. Jim could hear the neck assembly buckling. His head was turned far to the right; his chin clanked against his shoulder. His minigun was stowed upon his back, along with the empty missile launcher; if he deployed the minigun now, the barrel would smack into the side of his head at full speed.

He seized the dreadnaught's wrists once more. More spikes stabbed into his gauntlets, piercing the armor. The points of the spikes poked into the soft flesh of his palms, drawing blood. *Must be diamond-tipped*, he guessed, then remembered the same metal spikes gouging his gauntlets when he'd turned the dreadnaught's heat-rays against each other. *No won-*

der my repulsors don't work. The spikes probably tore the projectors up in a big way. He didn't let go of the monster's wrists, even though the spikes felt like daggers digging into his skin. He struggled to keep the dreadnaught from twisting his head off. He could feel his throat stretching, the muscles pulled to their limits. If he released the dreadnaught's arms, his spine would snap within seconds.

But was he completely unarmed? He tried to activate his laser. A tight red beam of light leaped from his left gauntlet, pointed towards one corner of the ceiling. He couldn't quite direct it at the dreadnaught, though, not without shifting his grip on the robot's arm. The angle was all wrong. *At least I know it works,* Jim consoled himself. *For now.* He shut down the saber once more; grappling with the dreadnaught at such close quarters, he was just as likely to slice himself accidentally as he was to connect the blade with the robot. Trying another tack, he prepped the minicannon in his other gauntlet. Its twin barrels extruded from the weapons pod on the back of the glove. Again, he couldn't aim the cannon at the dreadnaught in his current position, but the minute he got the chance, he'd shoot with extreme prejudice. *If* he got the chance.

He considered using his external heating systems to raise the temperature of his armor to unbearable degrees, then quickly discarded the notion. Any flesh-and-blood opponent would be forced to let go once the suit heated up enough, but a dreadnaught didn't feel pain or concern for its own self-preservation. He could easily imagine the machine continuing to exert pressure on Jim's head even as its melting silver casing slid off it in streams of liquid metal.

War Machine's head twisted further back over his shoulder. He couldn't see the dreadnaught at all now, only the cracked and battered ruins of the overturned couch behind him. War Machine was a one-man showcase of the latest in military technology, but none of Tony Stark's high-powered armaments could keep the relentless dreadnaught from removing Jim's skull like a twist-off cap on a bottle of Coke.

So Jim kneed it in the groin instead.

Naturally, a dreadnaught did not react the way an ordinary human would. Lacking reproductive organs, the silver simulcrum was not nearly so vulnerable in that area. Still, the unexpected impact staggered the dreadnaught. It wobbled upon its heels, and War Machine took advantage of the robot's lack of balance by throwing himself forward. He crashed against the dreadnaught's steel-ribbed chest, and, still clutching War Machine's helmet in its hands, it toppled over onto its back. War Machine landed heavily on top of the dreadnaught. *Thank God this thing doesn't have spikes along its front*, he thought. *Otherwise, I would have been impaled.*

The dreadnaught's grip on his helmet loosened. War Machine yanked his chin to the left and found himself staring into the dreadnaught's impassive visage. *Frankly,* he decided, *I prefer enemies who grim-*

ace when you knock them down. Squeezing hard on the robot's wrists, the spikes thrusting deeper into his palms, he pulled the giant silver fists away from his helmet. He shoved the dreadnaught's arms upwards, then released its wrists at last. The spikes hurt as much coming out as they did going in. *I'm going to need plenty of Bactine,* he thought angrily. Before the dreadnaught could react, War Machine rolled off the monster's metallic torso and onto the carpet. He sprang back onto his feet, only to find the dreadnaught already standing a few yards away. He glanced quickly at his gauntlets. As he feared, the repulsor units had been ravaged by the sharpened spikes on the dreadnaught's arms. Tiny white sparks flickered where his repulsor rays should have shot forth. Blood trickled from pinpoint punctures in the black iron gloves.

Its twisted steel collar almost touching the ceiling, the towering robot marched towards War Machine. He unsheathed his laser blade. The glowing red blade sprang from his gauntlet, then sputtered alarmingly. The laser light strobed on and off, the four-foot beam wavering like an unfurled ribbon in the wind. *Oh man,* Jim thought. *Now what?* The laser was probably waterlogged or something. Maybe the crushing pressure of the ocean depths had cracked some vital mechanism that had chosen right now as the perfect moment to break down. Hell, there were any number of possible explanations for the weapon's sudden malfunction; all he knew for sure was that his once lethal laser blade looked about as dangerous as a cheap flashlight. *I knew I should have gotten that tune-up,* he thought as the indefatigable dreadnaught advanced on him, still intent on War Machine's destruction.

Moving as quickly as a Wild West gunfighter, War Machine fired at the dreadnaught with the minicannon on his wrist. High-explosive ammo detonated upon contact with the dreadnaught's shining silver hide, but the firepower barely slowed the robot down. It shrugged off War Machine's hail of gunfire as easily as Jim had ignored the Maggia gunmen's bullets not too long ago.

"Okay," Jim said. "Let's do this the old-fashioned way. Hand to hand." He still hadn't tried the minigun stowed on his back, but he was afraid to really let loose with the armor-piercing shells, for fear of hitting the wrong target. For all he knew, either Madame Masque or Tony himself might be sequestered somewhere in this penthouse, maybe in the very next room. Turning the entire tenth floor into a smoking crater wasn't going to help matters, so he resisted the temptation to deploy the artillery on his back. *Besides,* Jim thought, his punctured hands feeling like hamburger, *right now I really want to hit somebody.*

The ringing sound of metal striking metal clanged harshly as War Machine slugged the dreadnaught with all his strength. The spike-covered colossus fought back mercilessly, hammering with its titanic steel arms. War Machine held his ground, and pummeled the dreadnaught with blow after blow. His armored fists left dents in its torso, but did nothing to discourage the robot's implacable attack. The dreadnaught's expressionless face never changed, no matter how hard War Machine pounded it. Impervious to pain or fear, it kept up its assault.

The formerly luxurious penthouse suite became a demolition site. Carved antique furniture that had survived intact for centuries was reduced to splinters by the furious combat of two futuristic warriors. Out of the corner of his eye, War Machine saw Curlytop and his fellow gunmen flee through the wooden door next to the shredded dragon tapestry. The door slammed shut behind them before War Machine could see what lay beyond. Not that he really had time to investigate further, what with the dreadnaught's nonstop onslaught keeping him a bit busy. Iron slammed into silver plating. Jagged spikes tore deep, uneven scratches into War Machine's protective armor. The dreadnaught never gave him a minute's respite. Jim felt like one of the Rock'Em-Sock'Em Robots he'd played with as a child, trapped in a sci-fi boxing match that was never going to end.

The dreadnaught threw another punch at War Machine, who bobbed and weaved to avoid the huge spiked fist. The metallic titan swung its fist like a mace, barely missing War Machine's helmet. *Used to be,* he thought wistfully, *Iron Man could take out a roomful of Maggia dreadnaughts without much trouble.* This was obviously the new-and-improved model. *Isn't this thing ever going to run out of steam?* he wondered. Exhaustion crept up on him, slowly sapping his strength. His breath was ragged. Beneath the armor, sweat coated his back. His arms felt heavier and heavier. His fist plowed into the dreadnaught's dense, unyielding frame and he felt the force of the collision vibrate all the way down his arm. Fatigue was his enemy now, as much as the dreadnaught, but his unliving foe showed no sign of tiring or of abandoning the fray. Surrender was not part of its programming.

Man and machine circled each other amidst the devastation. War Machine saw his unstoppable adversary silhouetted against the shattered picture window. Moonlight glinted off the creature's silvery casing, dark shadows pooling where War Machine's fist had left dents in the robot's armor. Beyond the dreadnaught, War Machine glimpsed the wooded expanse of Central Park, across the street and ten stories below.

War Machine suddenly realized there was one thing he could do that the Maggia's monster could not: *fly*. A plan occurred to him, and he backed away from the dreadnaught until his back touched the ruined tapestry. Strips of torn embroidery dangled over his shoulder. He ran a quick program through his navigation computer, then, taking a running start, launched himself into the air, hurling straight at the dreadnaught with his fists thrust out in front of him. The micro-turbines in his boots roared into action, accelerating War Machine at his foe. He hit the dreadnaught head-on, like a pool cue striking the eightball. The dreadnaught went flying backwards, its arms and legs flailing, out the shattered window and over the street below. Halting his own flight at the very edge of the window, War Machine watched the dreadnaught descend in an arc over the park like a silver meteor towards its shadowy recesses. *Silver dreadnaught in the corner pocket,* he thought triumphantly. Using the computer's guidance, he'd hit it at the right speed and angle so that the corner pocket was, in fact, Belvedere Lake. He grinned smugly behind his mask. Even if the dreadnaught survived the fall, it would take it a while to return to the scene of the fight. The thought of the killer robot, covered with seaweed and leaves, riding the elevator back up to the tenth floor made him chuckle.

Now then, he thought, *back to business.*

Cooling his jets, he landed heavily on the carpet. Deep footprints in the shag bore testament to the armored clash that had just taken place. Jim peered through his lenses and looked around. Broken furniture lay like casualties on a battlefield. The wing-back chairs were now heaps of kindling. Cotton stuffing piled in tufts on the carpet; he saw tiny white feathers floating in the air. The overturned couch had broken in two. The mahogany coffee table, still resting where he'd tossed it, looked like it had been run over by a bulldozer. The crystal chandelier had smashed into the floor; only broken wiring hung overhead. Bullet holes peppered the walls and ceiling.

His gaze fell upon the closed door at the other end of the living room. He wondered what lurked behind the door. A pack of frightened gangsters? More dreadnaughts? Madame Masque? Tony Stark bound and gagged?

There was only one way to find out. He stomped across the demolished living room, his faceplate locked in a permanent scowl.

The door swung open before he reached it. Jim tensed up instantly. Adrenalin surged into his weary muscles. He clenched his fists, ready for anything.

Madame Masque sauntered calmly out of adjoining room. Despite himself, she took Jim's breath away. A skintight black leather bodysuit showed off an impressive figure that spoke of strenuous hours in a gymnasium or health club. Whenever she moved, clinging shadows slid over her body like sinuous oil slicks. She wore long black gloves and high black boots with spiked heels. A gold-tinted gunbelt was slung low upon her hips; War Machine noted automatically that her gun was still in its holster. The bright, reflective hue of her belt matched the cold, metallic beauty of the golden mask that covered her face. Long, dark hair cascaded over her shoulders. Only her throat and part of an ear, slipping out from behind the rim of her mask, exposed her smooth pink skin. The lady was white, Jim observed, just as he'd expected. The Maggia was hardly an equal opportunity employer.

Arms akimbo, Madame Masque rested her hands defiantly upon her hips. Her gaze swept the living room, taking in the desolation. Behind the sculpted golden metal mask, her eyes lingered on the ravaged tapestry. Reaching up, she ran a ragged ribbon of the torn tapestry between her fingers, then dropped it disdainfully. She stared coolly at War Machine, her eyes meeting his.

"Shall I bill the damages to WorldWatch or Stark Enterprises?" she asked. Jim didn't recognize her voice, nor could he place her background from its sound. She had the formal, unaccented tones of a TV newsreader. To his annoyance, she seemed neither angered nor intimidated by his defeat of the dreadnaught. No emotion escaped her metal mask.

"Forget the household repairs," he barked at her. "I want Tony Stark and I want him now." He stepped closer to her, grinding shards of crystal into the indigo carpet. With her spiked heels, Madame Masque was nearly six feet tall; still, War Machine towered over her. "You have a choice," he said. "We do this easy or we can do it the hard way. You decide."

Madame Masque didn't even flinch at his approach. Her arm swept languidly through the air, gesturing towards the wreckage surrounding them. "Tell me," she asked sarcastically, "is this what you consider the easy way? One shudders to contemplate your idea of the forceful approach."

"Cut the crap," War Machine said. "You brought this on yourself the minute you snatched

Tony Stark. The man's got friends, lady. When you messed with him, you bought a whole pile of trouble." *And siccing your pet robot on me didn't improve my disposition any,* he added silently.

Madame Masque looked up, apparently unconcerned. Her golden lips didn't move when she spoke. "You might have a point," she conceded, "if I was indeed responsible for Tony Stark's recent abduction. But I'm not."

What the hell? Jim thought, momentarily rendered speechless. If Madame Masque was telling the truth, then that changed everything. This whole New York excursion might be one big goose chase, and his grueling battle with the dreadnaught a total waste of time. He prayed Masque was lying.

"Before her unfortunate demise," she continued, "my predecessor was quite fond of Mr. Stark. I have no strong feelings regarding him one way or another, and certainly no reason to remove him from his yacht." Jim wished he had a lie-detector built into his armor; he couldn't tell if the masked woman was being honest with him or not. *Did she know about the energy chip in his belt?* he wondered. That was certainly motive enough. It didn't seem wise to mention that right now. There could very well be more dreadnaughts lurking in the next room, and the energy chip might entice Madame Masque into unleashing them upon him.

"If you had nothing to do with this," he challenged, "how do you know so much about the kidnapping? Stark's people have been keeping a tight lid on the details.''

Madame Masque sighed wearily, as if growing bored with the conversation. ''I have sources of my own, Mr. War Machine.'' She tilted her head towards him. ''By the way, what *do* your friends call you? War or Machine?'' She shrugged dismissively. ''You may inform Ms. Cabe, incidentally, that her informant will not be talking to her again. Or anyone else for that matter.'' An icy edge crept into her voice, leaving no doubt that Bethany's inside connection was no longer among the living. *Probably supporting a highway overpass somewhere,* he thought, *a few miles down from Jimmy Hoffa.*

War Machine clenched his teeth. Glamorous or not, Madame Masque's cold-blooded *hauteur* was getting on his nerves. He didn't care how smart or sexy she was. He fought the temptation to shove his minicannon in her face.

''What about that video Bethany received?'' he asked ''She said you personally took credit for grabbing Tony.''

''As far as I can tell, that was a computer-generated simulation of myself.'' Madame Masque glided past War Machine, ducking under his arm. Bending over, she picked up a fragment of the shattered vase. The gold leaf flaked off onto her fingers. ''Didn't you see *Forrest Gump*?'' she asked snidely.

Turning around, he grabbed her roughly by the shoulder. ''Not so fast,'' he snarled. His fingers dug, none too gently, into the glossy black leather covering her flesh. He half-hoped she'd go for the pistol on her hip, but no such luck. She just dropped the piece of broken porcelain from her fingers. The tip of her boot calmly kicked it across the room. "Maybe you're telling the truth," War Machine said, "and maybe you're not. But you're still a wanted criminal and a killer. Give me one good reason why I shouldn't take you in."

"Because I know where the transmission really came from," she said softly.

War Machine released her shoulder. Madame Masque stepped away, then spun on her heels to face him. Her golden face, like a classical statue of some heartless pagan goddess, looked up at his. "I thought that would intrigue you," she said.

"Talk fast," he said.

She shook her head. "First, I want your promise that you will leave these premises without any further unpleasantness." She glanced around the demolished penthouse. "I think you've inflicted quite enough havoc on my operations this evening."

Not nearly enough, Jim thought bitterly. He didn't trust Madame Masque nearly as far as he could throw her, which was probably all the way across the park if he tried. Still, rescuing Tony was the important thing. Time was running out, and Masque's offer was the only lead he had. Trashing the Maggia, and putting Madame Masque's shapely butt behind bars, could wait. *If nothing else,* he thought, *it will give me something to look forward to.*

"It's a deal," War Machine said. He didn't offer to shake her hand. "But if you're feeding me a line of bull, you're going to regret it. I don't care how far you run or how deep you hide, lady. Play dirty with me and I'll be in your face in a big way."

Madame Masque's dark eyes flashed behind her mask. "That might be interesting, metal man," she said provocatively. "But my information is very reliable. Few people are brave enough, or foolish enough, to lie to me. Stark's kidnappers transmitted their message from New Orleans."

Louisiana, Jim thought. *Jesus, this is turning into a cross-country road trip.* "Where in New Orleans?" he demanded.

"I don't know," she said, "and that, I promise you, is the truth. I can't even guarantee you that Mr. Stark is being held there, only that New Orleans is where the ransom demand originated." She paused momentarily, then eyed him quizzically. "Curiosity compels me to ask: do you have the energy chip?"

Playing all the angles, were you? War Machine thought suspiciously. "Maybe," he said.

Madame Masque sighed loudly. She glanced briefly at the window he had destroyed. A faint breeze blew through the penthouse, stirring up the bits and pieces of torn upholstery scattered around the room. "One of these days," she said, "we'll build a better dreadnaught. Then we'll see who holds on to what, War Machine."

"Sorry to disappoint you," he said gruffly.

"*C'est la vie.*" Madame Masque looked away from the window. Jim wondered if she was planning to retrieve her robot bodyguard after he flew away. "If I were you," she said, "I would head for New Orleans immediately." She turned her back on him and walked back towards the ripped tapestry and the adjacent rooms. She laid a black-gloved hand upon the doorknob.

War Machine was not so easily dismissed. "This isn't over," he called out, meaning it. The Maggia had just moved closer to the top of WorldWatch's hit list. One way or another, he was bringing her down. Maybe not today, maybe not tomorrow, but someday soon, Jim vowed, he'd show Madame Masque and her whole rotten organization what a War Machine was really capable of. And not all the dreadnaughts in the world could stand between them and the kind of justice they deserved. "Watch your back, babe," he said.

Wrapped in skintight darkness, striding proudly through wrack and ruin, Madame Masque stiffened almost imperceptibly. But she did not look back.

"I can't really explain it, Tony," Anastasia said. "I was pounding on the walls of my cell like a madwoman, when I heard something click within the wall. Then the door appeared out of nowhere. Maybe I just happened to hit the correct rhythm, the right sequence of taps, or perhaps those awful lightning bolts had damaged a hidden lock somewhere. I don't know. All I saw was a way out and I took it."

Anastasia leaned against a gleaming steel workbench. Her rifle, fully loaded, rested less than two feet away, within easy reach of the blonde model. On the other side of the lab, Tony Stark closed the swinging glass door that protected the mounted tool display. He held a pen-sized laser soldering iron in his right hand. Partially assembled, the new Iron Man armor hung between him and Ana.

"What about the gun?" he asked, gesturing towards the forbidding automatic weapon with his free hand.

Ana brushed her golden bangs away from her eyes. "I found it here in the workshop, the first time I stumbled onto this place. Whoever was working here must have left it behind. I don't why." She glanced nervously towards the location of the lab's hidden door. "Tony, they could be back any minute. You must hurry!"

"Who, Ana? Who could come back?" he asked. He hated grilling her like this, but none of her story rang true. It was too pat, too convenient. "How did you find me?"

"These computers. They told me where you were and how to get there." She pointed towards a monitor still showing his recent armor designs, as well as another screen featuring a black-and-white image of his now-empty cell. It reminded Tony of the security cameras that were in most shops and businesses, not to mention every modern-day prison. Judging from the angle, the camera must have been concealed in the northwest corner of the ceiling. *I searched every inch of that cell,* Tony thought. *How did I miss it?*

"I may pose in bathing suits for a living," Ana continued, "but I'm not a stupid woman. I know how to use computers. I can even program my VCR." A note of exasperation snuck into her voice. "What is this, Tony? An interrogation?" She glared at him, obviously hurt and angry. "Don't you trust me?"

No, Tony admitted reluctantly. Every instinct he had was screaming at him that there was something very wrong about this entire scenario. The pen-laser felt like a coiled viper in his hand, eager to betray him the minute he put it to use. He contemplated the empty iron shell suspended before him, needing only his expertise and technical know-how to transform this rough assemblage of steel and circuitry into one of the most powerful weapons on the face of the earth. *Someone* wanted him to complete the suit, but he doubted it was Ana.

Unless. . . . A horrible thought occurred to him. What if Ana was Blank Screen? How well did he truly know her anyway? They'd shared a couple of dates, a few brief moments of passion, but beyond that she was still a stranger to him. It was hard to imagine that a celebrity supermodel out of the pages of *People* magazine could also be a ruthless criminal mastermind, but how many people guessed that millionaire playboy Tony Stark was also the invincible Iron Man? Appearances could be deceptive.

If she was really Blank Screen, then Meryl Streep had nothing on her. Ana deserved an Academy Award for her performance as both a carefree, seductive sunbather and a hysterical victim of inhuman cruelty. Tony stared at the woman urging him to finish the armor. Her clean white prison uniform matched her smooth, pale skin.

"What happened to your tan?" he asked.

"Huh?" she replied, apparently caught off-guard by the question. "Come again?"

"Your tan," he repeated. "You'd developed quite an impressive tan the other day on the yacht. I don't see any sign of it now."

Ana's jaw dropped. She lifted her hands above her head and shook them in frustration. "This is absurd," she protested. "I mean, I'm glad you noticed the tan, Tony, but this is hardly the time to discuss my complexion. Have you completely lost your mind?"

"No," Tony said quietly, now convinced he was onto something. He wasn't imagining things; it was this entire situation that was insane. Ana as Blank Screen? He shook his head. He was getting closer, but that wasn't quite it. There was more wrong here than just Ana's now-you-see-it, now-you-don't tan and her flimsy escape story. Melanin did not evaporate overnight, but neither could meals come and go through walls that might or might not be solid, depending on the moment. Why build a prison complex that consisted of nothing but endless, unguarded white halls? Tony rubbed his chin thoughtfully, noting once more the conspicuous absence of even so much as a five o'clock shadow. He sniffed the air. Despite his hours of labor at the computer terminal, his body still smelled fresh and unsoiled. "Listen to your body," Ana had counseled him on the yacht several eternities ago. Tony listened now, and what he heard was deception. *This is not reality as I know it,* he thought. *This is not my body.*

All at once, everything clicked into place. Tony recalled, almost nostalgically, controlling his telepresence unit from the lower deck of *Athena.* He had never really left his cabin on the yacht, but it felt like he had actually been there in San Francisco, rescuing that poor woman from her perilous situation atop the Golden Gate Bridge. He had experienced every sight, sound, and sensation of his encounter with the Hydra wannabe, thanks to the modern miracle of virtual reality.

Tony glanced around the lab. As in his cell, the light illuminating the scene seemed to come from everywhere and nowhere. There were no shadows in the room, no scuff marks on the polished floor. None of the equipment showed *any* signs of wear and tear. He looked more closely at his surroundings, squinting his eyes. No dust motes floated in the air. The room temperature was so comfortable as to be completely unnoticeable. Everything about the setup was pure, pristine . . . and artificial. "This isn't real," Tony declared.

"What was that?" Anastasia asked, as if she thought she'd heard him incorrectly. Her brows wrinkled beneath the bruise on her forehead. Her lovely face looked puzzled.

"It's not real," Tony said. "None of it is. Not the lab, not my cell, not this armor. Not you." He looked at her sadly, wondering what had happened to the real Anastasia Swift. Perhaps she was already dead, or maybe she had never been taken prisoner in the first place. He hoped fervently that she was alive and well and free, someplace far from here.

He strolled over and tapped the armor's iron chestplate with his knuckles. It made a convincingly solid ring. "Impressive," he mused out loud. "I'm not surprised I was taken in for so long. The minimalist design of the prison must have made the illusion easier to maintain, but that's all this was: an illusion. Everything I've experienced since being captured, including the cell and your sudden reappearance, has been one elaborate virtual reality simulation. And a good one, too, despite a few minor slip-ups like the missing tan." He eyed the striking blonde woman appreciatively. "They must have assembled your image from some earlier film footage, taken when your skin was paler than it was after our vacation in the Gulf of Mexico. Sloppy." Tony ran his free hand along the blank white wall they had appeared to enter through. It felt like genuine concrete. From a technical standpoint, he couldn't help being intrigued by the sheer verisimilitude of the artificial reality that had been constructed to deceive him into thinking he was actually standing in a working laboratory. His respect for Blank Screen rose a notch.

"Your bruises and other injuries were a nice touch," he commented off-handedly. "They almost convinced me." In a sense, he realized, he was talking to himself. This "Ana" was just a construct, part of an interactive V.R. simulation. He observed the stunned, disbelieving expression on her face, and wondered if she'd been programmed to respond to this turn of events.

For a minute, she looked uncertain as to what to do next. Then she grabbed for her gun. Startled, Tony leaped to intercept her, then realized there was no time and no point. He watched motionlessly as Ana (or rather, he corrected himself, a computer-generated image of Ana) directed the muzzle of the rifle at his head. He heard her release the safety on the gun. Her blue eyes narrowed, her mouth formed a grim straight line. Her finger rested on the rifle's trigger. A moment's twitch would cause the gun to fire.

"Sorry, Tony darling," she said. "I hate to do

this, but you've obviously gone insane, and I don't have time to deal with your craziness. Fix the armor. Now.''

He stared down the barrel of the gun. It looked more real than virtual. His mouth went dry. He gulped involuntarily. *What if I'm wrong?* he thought. Death by automatic weapon fire stared him in the face. Once Ana pulled that trigger, there wouldn't be time to revise his theory. If, in fact, this was his actual body, it would be riddled with holes within seconds. He squeezed the pen-laser in his right hand. It wasn't much of a weapon, but it was all he had. He estimated the distance between himself and the gun-toting young woman, and tried to calculate the odds that he could disarm her before the high-powered rifle reduced him to a bloody carcass on the floor. She was over two yards away; the odds weren't good. Tony felt his heart pounding in his chest.

No, he thought firmly. He mustn't panic. He was right. He knew he was. None of this was real. There was no gun. He closed his eyes, blinding himself to the deadly illusion. The miniature laser dropped from his fingers, clattering onto the floor.

''Open your eyes,'' said Ana's voice. It sounded just like her. He heard footsteps coming nearer. The muzzle of the rifle suddenly pressed against his forehead; it felt hard and cold and very real. ''Damn you, Tony. Open your eyes this minute. Look at me!''

Tony kept his eyes screwed shut. His heartbeat slowed. Mentally, he retreated from Ana, the threat of her gun, and the supposed laboratory itself. *Blank Screen has underestimated me,* Tony realized. His artificial nervous system, developed as a last-ditch defense against the techno-neurological virus that had literally killed him for a time, had capabilities beyond the flesh-and-blood wiring of an ordinary man, capabilities Blank Screen could not possibly have anticipated. Tony Stark's new nervous system could do more than simply transmit sensory data about his environment; Tony had programmed his nervous system himself, and he could reprogram it at will. It wasn't easy, but he could do it.

Eyes shut, Tony concentrated on accessing his built-in cybernetics. At first all he could see was darkness, punctuated by the random streaks of color a person usually saw when focussing on the interior of their eyelids. Slowly, however, those sparks and streaks came together, coalescing into coherent patterns resembling circuit diagrams. Command codes appeared upon his retinas. By shifting his attention from one code to another, he could move the sparks about like cursors on a computer screen.

Booting up, he thought. *Autonomic system override.* The internal functions of his body appeared as streams of data flashing past his consciousness. He rifled through subroutines relating to his digestion, his respiration, blood circulation, and all his other biological functions until he isolated the flow of information he was looking for, the ongoing programs that regulated and monitored all his sensory input.

"Look at me, Tony, or I'll shoot you now," Ana said. Her voice seemed to be coming from miles away and was growing fainter every instant. "I'm not joking, Tony. I swear I'll blow your stupid head off if you don't open your eyes and get to work on that armor. I'm counting to three. One . . . two . . ."

Tony ignored her threats. He existed in a different world now, a reality made up of data and preprogrammed commands, visualized as glowing icons of pure mental energy. *Welcome to cyberspace*, he thought, with apologies to William Gibson. In its own way, it was just as unreal as the illusory prison he had escaped from. Curiously, however, he felt much more at home among the blatantly symbolic landscape of cyberspace. At least this simulation wasn't pretending to be the physical world.

No wonder I couldn't break that damn computer in my cell, he realized. *It wasn't made out of plastic and silicon at all, just digitized information.*

His mind, adjusting to its new environment, moved in time with the electrons coursing through his nervous system. He heard, as if from a distant continent, the virtual Ana count to three, followed by the muffled boom of her rifle firing at point blank range. Reacting at high speed, he monitored his external inputs and located the incoming data that simulated the report and impact of a fatal gunshot. From his altered perspective, the lethal illusion resembled a blood-red pellet forcing its way towards his brain like a poisoned ostrich egg sliding down the gullet of an elongated python. Left to its own devices, would the false data actually convince his body it had been shot through the head? Tony wondered if his brain would spontaneously hemorrhage in response. Curious, and feeling quite removed from the physical world, he was tempted to watch and find out. Instead, quite casually, he plucked that particular piece of data from his nervous system with a pair of psychic tongs. *Delete,* he commanded and the poison pill blinked out of existence.

So much for that, he thought. *Ana's bang was worse than her byte.* The rest of the illusion—Ana, the lab, and so on—continued to flow directly into his brain. Tracing the transmission to its origin, he discovered that all of his external sensory data— sights, sounds, smells, tastes, and textures—were being fed into his nervous system through a single discrete location. *The neural port behind my ear,* Tony realized. *I'm plugged into a computer that's creating everything I sense.*

A surge of exhilaration suffused Tony with new energy and excitement. From his current vantage point within his own nervous system, he watched as autonomic systems flooded his body with adrenaline. Serotonin levels in his brain rose with his spirits. Blood vessels expanded, carrying nutrients and oxygen through his body at an accelerated pace. Tony Stark had a front-row view of his own renewed hope.

No doubt his built-in neural port had made life

easier for Blank Screen when implementing this duplicitous operation, but it was more than convenient for Tony as well. Now that he fully understood the true nature of his captivity, had scoped out the lay of the cyber-landscape, as it were, he could take advantage of his connection to the computer programs maintaining this artificial reality. Every access point could be an exit, too, and each interface was a two-way street. Tony grinned triumphantly; he watched the neurons travel from his frontal lobes to the tiny ligaments controlling his lips. At last, after all his fruitless searching, he had finally found his escape. He felt like the Count of Monte Cristo once more, staring out at the sunlight at the end of a tunnel he dug with his own hands. *My body may be trapped,* he reminded himself, *but my mind can go anywhere.*

The consciousness of Anthony Stark, the unique bioelectrical patterns that comprised his memories and personality, flowed towards the neural port connecting him with the outside world. He hovered apprehensively at the point of interface, warily contemplating the all-too-permeable barrier between his own distinct nervous system and the unknown cybernetic realm beyond. *The last time I tried this stunt,* he recalled, *I almost didn't make it back to my body.* VOR/TEX, a malevolent artificial intelligence, had lured him into cyberspace, then had taken up residence in Tony's nervous system, stealing his body and stranding Tony in the surreal universe of electronic frontier. Only VOR/TEX's own unfamiliarity with the pains and pleasure of biological existence (including, Tony remembered with disgust, his flesh's weakness for alcohol) had given Tony the edge he needed to regain his rightful place within his own brain. *That was bad,* Tony thought. *I never want to go through that again.*

VOR/TEX had been deleted forever, though, and he had nowhere else to go except back to a phony, imaginary Ana intent on killing him. Blank Screen's insidious deception continued to flow into his nervous system via this very port, filling his mind with a false reality. *Now or never,* Tony thought. Swimming upstream against the flood of artificial stimuli, he exited his body.

It was like stepping out of a cramped closet into a vast and spacious plain, expanding infinitely in all directions. Data trails, resembling multicolored bands of shimmering energy stretched to the horizon and beyond. Bytes of information coursed over the bands, sparkling like fireflies. Gravity was binary; up was 1 and down was 0 and he could move freely either way. The trails shifted constantly, intersecting each other and breaking apart, while the glowing bytes navigated from trail to trail at blinding speed. The entire vista was in a constant state of motion, reshaping itself every instant, with Tony floating, awestruck, at the eye of the most magnificent lightshow he had ever beheld.

In a way, this realm reminded him of some of the mystical dimensions he had reluctantly entered alongside his occasional ally, Doctor Strange, sorcerer supreme and master of the mystic arts. Like the dark dimension of the dread Dormammu, this strange new world bore little resemblance to conventional, Newtonian reality. Geometric shapes floated in midair, defying earthly gravity, while data streams looped back on each other like Escher paintings. A committed scientist at heart, Tony Stark had never enjoyed the irrational fantasy worlds his sorcerous colleagues seemed to take for granted. Cyberspace was another matter, though. Despite a superficial similarity to the hells and heavens of the unseen world, it was a reality created by technology. Its rules obeyed the inexorable laws of logic and mathematics. As far as he was concerned, that made all the difference.

Intellectually, of course, he knew that the wondrous world he had entered was really no more than a system of electronic impulses transmitted via a variety of physical media including copper wiring, silicon chips, and magnetic memory systems. No matter. The human mind had no choice but to translate cyberspace into visual images that made some sort of sense to creatures that had evolved using their eyes, ears, and other senses to perceive the world around them. Hence, the fluorescent ribbons to indicate routes of transmission and brightly-colored objects to represent discrete packets of information. He wondered what cyberspace would look like to someone blind from birth. A universe of sounds, each byte a musical note, each program a symphony, or an endless parade of elevated braille characters? Tony knew that even his own consciousness was now just a series of interactive commands, uploaded into whatever machinery had been linked to the nervous system he'd been forced to leave behind, but that was even harder for a human intelligence to conceive. He visualized himself standing on two ordinary legs on a shimmering plateau of solid light. He looked down at his hands and body. His imagination had maintained the self-image fed into his brain by Blank Screen's virtual reality software. He found himself wearing the same dull white uniform. His bare toes wiggled over the edge of the plateau.

To blazes with this, he thought emphatically. He was running the show now. It was time to take control of the steering wheel. For what felt like days now, he had wished for his armor. If he couldn't have the genuine article in the material world, he'd have to settle for the next best thing. Concentrating carefully, he visualized himself wearing a complete, state-of-the-art suit of Iron Man armor. Having just spent countless hours re-creating the designs in his cell, it was incredibly easy to call every last detail of the suit to mind. Layer by layer, the armor began to form over his body until he was completely encased. Red and gold metal, the colors even more vibrant here than in the real world, reflected the scintillating pulses of light and energy flowing all around him. He lifted his hands before his eyes. Through two narrow slits he saw a pair of bright red gauntlets flexing fingers wrapped in overlapping rings of iron and enamel. He smiled beneath a gleaming golden mask. The transformation was complete. Tony Stark had vanished from sight. In his place stood the imposing figure of Iron Man.

An eerie calm fell over him. He recognized the feeling, or rather the lack of feeling. Despite all appearances and visualization exercises, he no longer possessed a body of flesh and blood. All the glands and hormones and neurotransmitters that fueled his emotions had been left behind on the other side of the interface. Iron Man glanced over his shoulder. The access port leading back to his body pulsed like a living thing. Red and engorged, it dripped stray electrical impulses that flickered briefly and died once they passed beyond the port onto the plateau. *Interesting*, Iron Man thought with a growing sense of detachment. Symbolically at least, the access port represented the only door back to the wet, messy, tempestuous world of biological existence. He experienced only the mildest twinge of loss. After all the stress and trauma of the last few days, the heights of anger, guilt, and despair, it felt good to take a break from emotion for awhile.

This could get addictive, he thought, *especially for a recovering alcoholic like Tony Stark.* Out-of-body jaunts into cyberspace could become a new way to deaden his feelings, the same way bourbon used to. The sooner he got back to his body, the better, before he forgot what being human was all about.

Enough sightseeing, Iron Man thought. *Time to*

get to work. Igniting his imaginary boot jets, the Golden Avenger lifted off the plateau. He flew head-first into the ever-changing cyberscape. The armor's internal sensors represented the efforts of his own free-floating consciousness as it explored and manipulated the luminescent shapes and paths ahead of him. *First things first,* he decided. He had to delete every last bit of his armor designs from Blank Screen's general database. He constructed a search-and-destroy program designed to find and delete any reference to armored exoskeletons and released it into the nearest data trail; the program manifested itself as incandescent, chartreuse pulse bolts that shot from Iron Man's gauntlets and zoomed along the interconnected strands of light. The bolts spread throughout the web, seeking out Iron Man's stolen secrets. Blinding flashes of white light detonated whenever a pulse bolt caught up with its target. The light incinerated both the lime-green pulse bolt and the roaming clusters of glowing bytes that contained part of the technological data Tony had fed into the virtual computer in his cell. Iron Man watched the first few explosions cascade into a flurry of simultaneous flashes going off like strings of firecrackers. The whole process took only nanoseconds. The explosions died down quickly, except for a few stragglers that burst sporadically thereafter, like the last few kernels in a bag of popcorn. Soaring above the cleansing fire, Iron Man felt confident that his designs had been thoroughly expunged from his surroundings. Lacking the hormonal ingredients to truly celebrate his victory, he merely nodded, savoring the calm satisfaction of a job well done.

Reconnaissance was the next item on his agenda. Where was he, exactly? What kind of setup was his disembodied consciousness now exploring? And, perhaps most importantly, where had his physical body actually ended up, if indeed it wasn't really sharing a laboratory with the false Ana and her automatic rifle?

Iron Man cruised methodically along the bands of neon. He extended his sensors in all directions, including 1 and 0, sampling the individual packets of information traversing the bands, and electronically eavesdropping on the never-ending interchange of commands and responses. Very quickly, according to his accelerated frame of reference, a picture formed in his mind of the basic parameters of the situation.

The body of Tony Stark was confined in a coffin-like apparatus, fed by intravenous tubing. A neural block kept him paralyzed from the neck down, while all the sensory details of the ''prisoner in a white cell'' experience were transmitted directly into his brain via the access port behind his ear. A variety of systems were in place to monitor his genuine biological functions and maintain his life. Biofeedback mechanisms supplied him with oxygen as needed, as well as disposing of his bodily wastes.

Amazing, Iron Man marvelled, impressed despite his lack of glandular responses. All this time, while his mind roamed from his cell to the laboratory to the sprawling expanse of cyberspace, his actual body had been locked in a box somewhere. Iron Man lifted his head to behold the glowing expanse of the electronic realm stretched out before him like an uncharted wilderness.

I could be bounded in a nutshell, and count myself a king of infinite space, he recited, quoting Shakespeare's *Hamlet.* Shaking his head to clear it of the staggering implications of the virtual world, Iron Man forced himself to concentrate on the matter at hand.

The entire operation was automatic and self-contained; no human technicians had access to the system once it was up and running. Iron Man searched in vain for any trace of Blank Screen; as far as he could tell, he had never actually had a dialogue with the instigator of this perfidious scheme. All of Blank Screen's threats and demands had been programmed into the virtual reality scenario before Tony was ever hooked up to it. The only clue Iron Man ran across was a single inactive file, tucked away in a virtual dead end on the outskirts of the data trails, containing several years' worth of financial records. The file recorded hundreds of transactions, involving millions of dollars, pounds, francs, lira, yen, and marks, all revolving through a single account in a German bank in the name of ''The Second Labor Party.''

Hmmm, Iron Man murmured. *Germany. Second Labor. . . .* His mind made the connection in-

stantly. For the first time since God knew when, he
felt much less in the dark. He had a theory now, and
a suspect, but he could pursue his suspicions later.
Blank Screen could wait. First, he had to free his body
as well as his mind. He was relieved, however, to find
no specific software designed to hold Ana captive as
well. It now appeared likely that every glimpse he'd
had of Ana since waking up in his barren white cell,
including those grueling scenes of the captured
woman screaming in agony and fear, had been computer-generated simulations like everything else. Her
torture had been a hoax, specifically manufactured to
make him comply with Blank Screen's demands.
Thank God, he thought. Even with his emotions flattened by his current state of being, he still felt a great
weight lift from him. He looked forward to finding,
and embracing, the real Anastasia Swift once more.
She'd never realize how glad he was to see her.

Their reunion would be more satisfying, of
course, if he could manage to liberate his body first.
He was already starting to forget what it was like to
be flesh and blood. He recalled the experience of being human, but only as a vague abstraction. Time
passes more quickly in cyberspace, he recalled. It felt
like hours since he'd uploaded his awareness into this
new world, even though mere minutes had probably
passed in real life.

Time to find a way out, Iron Man resolved.

The cybernetic web around him, although seemingly big as all outdoors, consisted entirely of the var-

ious programs and subroutines supporting Blank Screen's virtual reality prison. Iron Man had yet to connect with the larger world beyond this operation. From inside, this maze of fiery data trails, branching out and doubling back on each other in ever more complicated configurations, looked like the world's biggest and most byzantine highway system, but in terms of the global Internet, he was just wasting time following the tracks of an elaborate toy train set. There had to be way to link up with the outside world, he knew. He just had to find it.

Back in his cell, seated on the stool in front of Blank Screen, he had tried to hack his way out and failed. But that was different. The computer, the keyboard, and everything else had been an illusion. He hadn't realized then that he was already hooked up to Blank Screen's real computer system, in a way far more intimate than he could have possibly imagined—or than Blank Screen could ever have anticipated.

Iron Man activated his searchlight. The beam shot from his chestplate, sweeping over the spiraling streams of data. He concentrated on locating a system that did not feed back into the homeostatic processes keeping Tony Stark alive, inactive, and enmeshed in an imaginary world of blank white walls and disappearing doors. At first, he found nothing. Iron Man flew above and below the twisting energy bands, diving through the narrow interstices of the web and weaving among flowering, polychromatic structures of programming. His searchbeam preceded him, casting a constant emerald radiance on all that fell in its path. An old comic book character had used a beam like this to uncover the truth, Iron Man dimly recalled. He couldn't remember the hero's name, but the green light had always served him well. Iron Man hoped he'd be just as successful.

Metaphor could be reality, according to a mortal's perceptions of cyberspace. Iron Man was almost ready to give up when the beam passed over a single slender thread heading off towards the horizon. Iron Man came to an abrupt halt. Unlike the constant, coruscating traffic running along most of the data trails he had swooped past, this conduit was literally abandoned. Not a single glowing byte traversed the skinny little pathway. Its hue was dull and muted, a muddy grey the color of grave dust, and portions of its substance had faded away, leaving gaps and fractures along the way. Upon closer inspection, Iron Man realized it was not really an active stream at all, just the trace remains left behind by the long-ago passage of bygone data. He focused his beam on the pathetic remnant. The minute the emerald ray touched it, the entire path lit up. A spectral green flame raced down the line, leaping over the cracks and fissures in the path, blazing a trail that stretched away from the more heavily frequented regions of cyberspace towards a distant point too far away for his sensors to reach.

This is it, Iron Man felt convinced. If he had still been connected to his heart, it would have leaped.

Iron Man followed the flickering green fire with determination. He was leaving the access port back to his body even further behind, but that didn't matter. This was the way out. He could feel it in his bones . . . sort of.

The blazing path grew wider and more substantial as he followed it. Bits of old, discarded data strewn along its path, like litter tossed from the window of a speeding car, gave him a better idea of the path's former function. It was a communication channel of some sort, long unused but still recognizable, calling to mind the ancient Roman roads that still ran across portions of Europe. *This isn't hacking*, he thought, *it's archaeology.* Yet even old roads, he recalled, eventually connected with a modern thoroughfare. You just had to follow them long enough. He increased the power to his jets and upped his speed. *What the hell,* he thought, *it's not like I'm burning real fuel. . . .*

Minutes later, the path came to end. The green flame sputtered and died, leaving him in virtual darkness. He cast his searchbeam about, seeking some clue to his new surroundings. Bits and pieces of dormant command codes hinted at past usage. They coiled around him like copper tubing, unmoving and unilluminated by the Day-Glow colors that the active systems had radiated. What was this place? The commands looked familiar. . . .

Suddenly, the pieces came together in his mind, and a bright light literally sprang to life somewhere overhead as Iron Man identified his location. It was a satellite link. The software around him was designed to support a defunct communications node. At one time, Blank Screen had received and transmitted broadcast messages using this programming. Probably while the virtual reality coffin was being installed, he guessed. It dawned on Iron Man that none of the data he had examined since leaving his body had given him an indication of where, geographically, he was being held. The aquatic commando team had thrown him off *Athena* somewhere in the Gulf of Mexico, but he could be anywhere now. *Wouldn't it be ironic,* he thought, *if it turns out I've been buried alive in my own backyard?*

There was no time like the present to find out. All he had to do was get the satellite link up and running again. He scanned the dormant pathways until he found the one he needed. It looked like a long cylindrical cable running up to the sky. He reached out and wrapped his fingers around the diameter of the cable. Establishing a link, he channeled power through his gauntlets into the cable. Energy crackled loudly as the cable jerked violently. It bucked strenuously in his hand, flailing and thrashing about like a wild animal. *Good,* Iron Man thought. There was life in the old software yet. Lightning sparked along the length of the cable, coursing up the line to a satellite orbiting overhead. He activated the antenna and loudspeaker in his helmet. Back in the real world, he assumed, a genuine antenna was now broadcasting for the first time in weeks.

He tried to contact Stark Enterprises in California, but that proved trickier than he'd hoped. Blank Screen had transmitted on an unusual frequency, one that didn't immediately correspond to any receiver he knew. Manipulating the programming cable through his gauntlet, he struggled to switch the transmission to another frequency, any frequency. He didn't *need* to communicate directly with Stark Enterprises. At this point, he'd be delighted to reach a ham radio operator in Peoria, just as long as that person would be willing to take a message.

Unfortunately, the communications programming seemed to be explicitly designed to prevent any transmissions except on the approved frequency. *Figures,* Iron Man conceded. Blank Screen had reason to be paranoid about keeping his messages private. Kidnapping, extortion, and industrial espionage required a certain degree of secrecy, after all.

With no better alternative, Iron Machine sent out an SOS on Blank Screen's personal frequency. He had no idea where he was transmitting from or who might be listening, but it was his only hope. "This is Tony Stark. I am being held captive at the source of this transmission. I believe I am in danger. If anyone is receiving this, please contact the authorities. Repeat: This is Tony Stark . . ."

Iron Man recorded his plea into the system, then set it to repeat continuously at five-minute intervals.

There was a good possibility, he realized, that Blank Screen or one of his minions would hear his SOS before anyone else. They'd realize something had gone wrong with their scheme the minute they tuned into his broadcast, even if they couldn't figure out how he'd escaped the virtual reality simulation. Quite possibly, they were on their way this very minute, keen to shut him down permanently. But there was always a chance that someone else might intercept his message first.

Surprisingly, someone did.

"Tony? Is that you, man?" Iron Man recognized the deep, gruff voice immediately, but he couldn't bring himself to believe until he heard it again. "Talk to me, Tony."

Iron Man switched off the automatic recording. "Jim. My God. Jim Rhodes." His iron glove held on to the communications program as though his life depended on it. "Can you hear me?"

"Clear as mud," Jim's voice responded. A burst of static crackled in Iron Man's ears. "Let me adjust my receiver. There, that's better. Are you okay, Tony? You sound kind of zoned out."

He's picking up on my flattened affect, Iron Man thought, *not to mention the fact that I'm not actually speaking, but rather transmitting electrical impulses into Blank Screen's antenna that cause the hardware to duplicate the sound of my voice.* For a man with no body and no emotions, he was lucky he sounded human at all.

That was too much to explain to Jim right now. "Don't worry," he broadcast. "I'm fine. Where are you? For that matter, where am I?"

"I'm about fifty miles northeast of New Orleans, flying at about ten thousand feet." Jim Rhodes's background as a pilot revealed itself as he spoke. "E.T.A. in less than fifteen minutes. I have a lock on your location now. I'm reading an address somewhere in the French Quarter."

New Orleans? Iron Man was briefly taken aback. How had Blank Screen managed to smuggle him from the Gulf of Mexico to the Big Easy? *And how come,* he thought humorously, *in a city famous for its fine cuisine I get fed through an IV drip?* It was one more thing to hold against Blank Screen, when they finally met face to face.

"Don't stop for beignets," he told Jim. "I'm anxious to get out of here. You'll understand why when you see me. Be prepared for a shock."

"I'm on my way," Jim replied. "And, Tony, I'm bringing you a present."

SATURDAY. 4:18 AM. CENTRAL STANDARD TIME.

This place is a swamp, War Machine thought, descending towards the city of New Orleans. Below him, the bayous dripped with spanish moss. Stagnant pools of muddy brown water, clotted with algae, peeked out from behind the lush overhanging greenery, reflecting the moonlight. The sun was hours away from rising, but Jim imagined he could hear alligators snapping their jaws in the night-shrouded swamps. He could feel the humidity even through his armor; the night air was hot and sticky, reminding him of a Brazilian rain forest. The scent of the swamp, redolent with growth and decay, tantalized his nostrils. The rich, organic odors almost made the discomfort of the humidity worthwhile. *Almost.* Reluctantly, he sealed his armor and turned on the air conditioning.

War Machine zoomed over the bayous at top speed. Hearing Tony's voice over the receiver in his helmet had been like a jolt of pure energy, lifting his spirits and renewing his faith after Jim's frustrating tête-à-tête with Madame Masque. *She may be a world-class snob*, Jim thought, *but at least she'd delivered the goods.* Tony was definitely in New Orleans, and, from the sound of him, ready to be rescued. *Good thing,* he thought, *that I started scanning the airwaves on all frequencies as soon as I got within range of New Orleans.*

He yawned loudly in his helmet. Despite his improved mood, it had been a long day. It was only a little after two AM California time, but it felt like he'd been up all night. Fighting killer subs and dreadnaughts would do that to you. He was hungry, too. He'd barely eaten since breakfast, over seventeen hours ago, except for the small roast beef sandwich he'd wolfed down at Avengers Mansion before flying off for New Orleans. Jarvis, the Avengers' faithful butler, had fixed him the sandwich, along with a much-needed cup of coffee, when he arrived at the mansion minutes after leaving Madame Masque's devastated penthouse. The android Vision had not been present—Jarvis had mentioned something about a renegade Skrull warrior running wild through New York's subway system—but Doctor Henry Pym had readily agreed to give his battered armor a quick once-over. Pym, the Avengers's resident mad scientist, was a super hero himself, known at various points in his career as Ant-Man, Giant-Man, Goliath, Yellowjacket, and, more prosaically, Dr. Pym; *the man went through costumed identities like they were going out of style*, thought Jim, who had fought evil with merely two identities, War Machine and Iron Man. There was only so much Pym could do in the limited time War Machine was willing to spend at the mansion, but at least his mask was clean now, his laser blade had come back online after only a little tinkering, and most of the cracks in the chestplate and gloves were sealed.

And, most importantly, the package from Bethany had arrived as promised. Jarvis handed it over to

him the minute he landed on the Avengers' doorstep.
"I believe you are expecting this, sir," the butler said
in the formal tones of a proper English gentleman's
gentleman. Among the contents were a fresh supply
of missles and ammo for his artillery, which he hap-
pily reloaded. Then he stowed the package with its
remaining contents away in a storage compartment on
his back, between the positioning rails for his missile
launcher and Gatling gun.

Now, as he followed the Mississippi towards
New Orleans, War Machine was anxious to turn the
package over to Tony. He wished his friend hadn't
mentioned beignets, though; the sweet French pastry,
doused in powdered sugar, were a specialty of the
city. His stomach growled, anticipating a heavy
breakfast in one of many sidewalk cafés around Jack-
son Square. *Later,* he promised himself. Tony was
waiting.

The Mississippi wound lazily towards the city.
Moonlight shimmered on the wide, rippling surface
of the river. War Machine flew ahead of the slow-
moving current, coming in low over the rooftops of
the city. Jim Rhodes had visited New Orleans before
on both business and pleasure, and his eyes took in
the familiar sights and sounds as he quickly zeroed
in on the French Quarter, a six-by-twelve block section of the city along the Mississippi.

The Quarter, also known as the Vieux Carré,
was the pulsating heart of New Orleans, packed to
overflowing with fine restaurants, smoky jazz clubs,

souvenir shops, and live sex shows. Despite the Louisiana Purchase in 1803, when a growing youngster called the United States of America acquired New Orleans from the French, the Quarter had never truly succumbed to Anglo-Saxon notions of propriety; it remained a bastion of old-fashioned Creole hedonism, sleeping till noon every day and partying all night. Even now, despite the lateness of the hour, he could hear the sound of music and laughter coming from Bourbon Street, where crowded bars thrived side-by-side with "Nude Amateur Wrestling" and voodoo supply stores. Friday night celebrations, apparently, had not yet given way to Saturday morning regrets. Bourbon Street was the only place he knew where they *encouraged* you to drink in public; hell, you were practically fined if you weren't sipping a mint julep or hurricane as you strolled down the middle of the street, under the ornate iron balconies that overlooked every block.

Such balconies, usually overflowing with jungles of vines and potted plants, were everywhere in the French Quarter, jutting out like garden patios from the second floor of nearly every household and business. Few structures in the quarter were more than two stories tall. The Quarter was built on swampland after all, and any building too big and heavy would quickly sink into the watery soil. War Machine glanced down at the old, 17th-century homes built by the city's original French settlers. Hand-wrought iron gates concealed intimate private courtyards tucked away from the bustle of the streets.

War Machine passed over one of the many ancient cemeteries bordering the Quarter; even the tombs were built above the ground, in crumbling brick mausoleums that often held several generations of the same family, because the water table was so high. The cemetery gates were locked, but his radar detected furtive movement down among the night-cloaked monuments. Probably grave robbers, he guessed, ransacking the tombs for skulls and bones and grave dust to use in their voodoo ceremonies, or else someone making a nocturnal pilgrimage to the final resting place of Marie Laveau or another long dead voodoo priestess, seeking her supernatural intervention by leaving a sacrifice or offering behind. Jim had toured this cemetery in the past; you could spot the graves of deceased voodoo practitioners by the chalk markings on the monuments and the gifts of food and liquor at the foot of the tombs. New Orleans was more than just the birthplace of jazz; it also had the largest, most active community of voodoo worshippers this side of Haiti.

But War Machine wasn't looking for snakes, zombies, grave robbers, or even good jazz tonight. With Tony still a prisoner, he had no time to play bodyguard to a bunch of old bones. He zipped over the cemetery, leaving its mysterious intruders behind, while he homed in on the signal Tony had broadcast.

The source of the transmission turned out to be

an unassuming, two-story house on Dumaine Street, less than a block away from Louis Armstrong Park. Untended vines had completely covered the iron balcony in lush, green foliage. The house was painted blue with white trimming; blue and white, he knew, were the colors of protection according to voodoo tradition. He wondered if the paint job was intended to discourage burglars and whether or not it did any good. He spotted a satellite dish giving off a familiar signal mounted to the roof of the house, next to a small stone chimney, and he knew he'd found the right place.

At nearly five in the morning, and several blocks from the nonstop carousing on Bourbon Street, Dumaine was largely deserted. The streets and sidewalks were empty. All the lights were out in the blue-and-white house, as well as in the neighboring residences. War Machine couldn't tell if anyone was at home or not.

Tony hadn't mentioned any guards, but War Machine thought it best to be prepared for any resistance he might encounter. He scanned the house with both ultrasound and infrared sensors, but his signals bounced back to him. Despite its quaint, antique appearance, the entire house had been shielded from electronic surveillance. Tony's kidnappers seemed to have thought of everything. There *have* to be guards posted inside; he thought. Otherwise, why couldn't Tony simply walk out under his own power? Madame Masque had denied any responsibility for Tony's abduction, but War Machine had no illusions about her honesty. He half-expected to find half a dozen Maggia dreadnaughts inside the house. He considered trying to contact Tony again, but decided against it. It was possible that their communications were being monitored by someone within the house and that Tony, whether he knew it or not, was being used as bait to lure War Machine into a trap. Now that he had irrefutably located the site of Tony's prison, War Machine didn't feel like sacrificing the element of surprise, not if he had to fight his way through to Tony as he expected.

Anticipating trouble, War Machine aimed himself straight for the balcony. Painted wooden shutters covered a trio of tall picture windows at the back of the balcony. An awning, decorated with intricate iron grillework, hung over the vine-choked terrace. War Machine hit the shutters with both iron fists extended in front of him. Wood splintered and glass shattered as he smashed into the house like a runaway cannonball. "*Laissez les bon temps rouler*," he muttered under his breath as he invaded, ready to take on anything that A.I.M. or the Maggia threw at him.

Darkness greeted him, and silence. Except for the delicate tinkling of falling glass from the broken window, the second floor was as quiet and lifeless as a museum after hours. Switching to night-vision, War Machine scoped out his surroundings. He found himself in a dusty, abandoned parlor that looked as though no one had lived there for months. White sheets were draped over the furniture. A crack ran down the center of a large, gilt-framed mirror over an empty fireplace. The painted roses on the peeling wallpaper were dull and faded. The carpeting had been rolled up and stacked against one wall; walking across the abandoned parlor, War Machine's boots left footprints in the thick layer of dust covering the floor. If he didn't know better, he would have assumed the house had been deserted since the Reagan years at least.

"Tony!" he shouted loudly. "Tony, can you hear me?" The loudspeaker in his helmet amplified his voice until he figured they could hear him on Bourbon Street. After his spectacular entrance into the house, amidst much flying timber and glass, stealth was no longer a concern. Already, he could hear noise and confusion from the street outside, as lights came on all over Dumaine and curious heads poked out of suddenly opened windows. *Probably woke up the whole neighborhood,* War Machine thought, *let alone whomever may be hiding in this old firetrap.* The Louisiana police would be here soon. War Machine decided to find Tony before he was booked for breaking and entering.

"Tony?" he called again, but no one answered. For the first time, War Machine entertained the awful notion that maybe Tony was not on Dumaine at all. Or, worse yet, that his friend had been seriously hurt or killed shortly after broadcasting his SOS. War Machine stomped across the empty parlor, hoping that he wouldn't end up stumbling over Tony Stark's lifeless body somewhere in this far too quiet house.

Beyond a pair of double doors, a narrow hallway stretched away from the parlor. Ancient oil paintings of smiling riverboat gamblers and flirtatious Southern belles lined the corridor. From the frivolous and mildly scandalous nature of the portraits, Jim suspected this building might once have housed one of old New Orleans' many notorious houses of ill repute. He tore his eyes away from a revealing painting of a dusky quadroon beauty in a low-cut saffron gown and looked in the opposite direction. To his right, a circular staircase descended to the first floor. The hall was as dark and desolate as the parlor, but War Machine thought he heard a humming sound coming from downstairs, a low, steady vibration that might indicate machinery running. Grabbing hold of the wooden railing for balance, War Machine trotted hastily down the stairs. He was careful not to squeeze the rail too hard, for fear of crushing it to splinters beneath his powerful grip. In full armor, War Machine weighed four hundred and fifty pounds, but, to his considerable relief, the old staircase supported his weight. He rounded the final set of spiraling steps and came upon a surprising sight. Beneath his mask, Jim's eyes widened in amazement.

The difference between the second floor and the first floor was the difference between *Interview with the Vampire* and *Star Trek*. Unlike the dust-covered antiques one story above, the entire ground floor of the building had been completely refurbished, and transformed into an advanced scientific wonderland that rivaled anything Jim had seen at the laboratories of Stark Enterprises. Fluorescent overhead lights came on the minute he marched off the bottom step, exposing a large, spacious room to view; War Machine switched off his night-vision and, for a moment, stood gaping at the unexpected contents of the chamber. Row after row of sophisticated computer technology lined the polished steel walls; a constant buzz indicated that the computers were perpetually in operation. Electricity hummed beneath the floor, coming up through scuffless, white ceramic tiles to rattle the soles of his boots. A steel door, the size of a bank vault's, sealed the room off from the outside world. War Machine glanced around quickly; from the dimensions of the room, he guessed that it took the whole ground floor. *They must have knocked down most of the original walls to build this place,* he guessed. *Wonder how they're holding up the top floor?*

His gaze was instantly captured, however, by something—and someone—resting in the southwest corner of the room. "Tony!" he gasped out loud, both relieved and horrified by the sight before him:

Tony Stark floated, seemingly unconscious, in a vertical, high-tech sarcophagus mounted between two adjacent banks of computers and what looked to War Machine like life-support equipment. A tall transparent tube, made of reinforced plastic, held Tony's body in place. The cylindrical tube was supported by a gleaming steel pedestal, and capped by a piece of bulky metal apparatus linked by thick, insulated cables to the adjacent machinery. A skintight, nylon bodysuit, wired to numerous tiny electrodes, covered Tony's body from the neck down. Automated monitors reported continuously on Tony's heartbeat, EKG, and metabolism, reassuring Jim that, despite Tony's immobile appearance, his friend was indeed alive inside his plastic coffin. Jim walked over and, hesitantly, laid a gloved hand upon the tube; it felt warm, almost normal body temperature. He peered through the thick plastic. Upon closer inspection, he saw that the tube was filled with a clear, viscous liquid. A tiny stream of bubbles escaped from Tony's lips. Jim guessed that the fluid, whatever it was, was super-oxygenated to allow Tony to breathe without the aid of a respirator. Intravenous tubing ran from Tony's uncovered wrists and ankles. A capillary-width piece of electrical wiring ran from a location near the back of Tony's head to the complicated-looking mechanism topping the tube. A steady whirring noise came the lid of the sarcophagus. Tony's eyelids flickered and twitched sporadically, as though he was trapped in a dream he could not wake up from. War Machine experienced an unwanted flash of *déjà vu* as he recalled the above-ground tombs in the New Orleans cemetery. This concealed, stainless steel chamber of horrors was like one big, futuristic mausoleum, imprisoning Tony Stark between life and death.

Oh Jesus, Tony, War Machine thought sympathetically. *What the hell have these bastards done to you?* He glanced around once more, looking for someone he could vent his rage on, but the chamber was just as deserted, if better maintained, than the floor above. Only the all-surrounding machines kept guard over Tony Stark, noting his every bodily function with greater care and precision than any human jailer. The perfect prison, War Machine realized, with no wardens or turnkeys to bribe, subvert, overpower, or outwit. No fallible mortal guards. No possibility of human error. He could almost admire the cold, ruthless efficiency of it all.

Except, War Machine recalled, that Tony had somehow succeeding in calling for help anyway. Watching his friend float helpless and unaware in the sealed plastic sarcophagus, Jim had to wonder how Tony had managed it.

''Tony?'' he asked speculatively, lowering his voice to ordinary human volume. The man in the tube did not respond; he looked comatose. Another stream of bubbles rose from his lips. *I have to get him out of there,* War Machine thought, *but how?* He contemplated the sophisticated machinery surrounding the coffin. Given time, he could possibly figure out how to operate this equipment and release Tony without harming him, but how much time did he have? If the kidnappers picked up Tony's SOS, they could be here any second. He looked for an access port where he could jack his suit's computer into the one controlling

Tony's prison. Maybe he could override the inevitable security systems and initiate some sort of automatic shutdown. He hoped that waking Tony now wouldn't pose too much of a shock to his system.

Spotting a promising-looking outlet, War Machine extended a single armored finger towards what appeared to be a control panel in the primary apparatus atop the man-sized plastic tube. A black ceramic tile flipped open at the end of his fingertip and a two-pronged electrical plug protruded from his gauntlet. His finger hovered over the socket. *Here goes nothing,* he thought.

Then, an instant before the plug came into contact with the socket, Tony Stark's eyes suddenly snapped open. War Machine jerked in surprise. His heart pounded. For a second, he was convinced he'd done something wrong, but, no, he hadn't touched a thing yet. *Tony,* he thought instantly. Instinctively, he knew that was the answer. This was Tony's doing. Somehow, someway, Tony was freeing himself, the same way he had impossibly managed to call Jim to this address. Jim's soul surged with pride and relief. At last, everything was working out. Together, they'd get Tony out of here.

Within the vertical sarcophagus, Tony's eyes shifted from right to left before focusing on War Machine. Jim saw a reassuring smile appear on Tony's lips. Tony flexed his fingers experimentally and nodded his head. He closed his eyes again, but War Machine could tell he had not lapsed back into unconsciousness. Tony Stark's brow furrowed in concentration, and the machines around began to respond. War Machine watched with growing excitement as, one by one, the systems supporting Tony's prison blinked and shut down. The clear, oxygenated fluid drained out of the tube, flushed down concealed pipes underneath the floor. The IV needles retracted from Tony's hands and feet, dripping such minute quantities of blood that War Machine assumed a clotting agent had been applied at the same time that the needles exited Tony's veins. Only the cord running from Tony's skull to the computer on top of the tube remained in place, as the last of the fluid disappeared into the floor. Tony coughed violently, his lungs discharging what looked like gallons of the clear liquid, vomiting it onto the base of his plastic coffin.

Afraid that Tony would suffocate in the now-empty tube, War Machine drew back his fist, prepared to smash the tube and pull Tony to safety. His coughing fit subsiding, Tony Stark shook his head. Seconds later, the plastic covering retracted into the wall behind the sarcophagus, leaving Tony standing, shivering, on the metal pedestal. Visibly struggling to stay on his feet, he reached up behind his head and carefully detached the cable connecting his head to the surrounding equipment. The moment it came loose, his strength seemed to evaporate. Knees buckling, he collapsed forward, falling off the pedestal towards War Machine. Jim rushed closer, catching Tony in his arms before the other man hit the floor. He propped Tony up against his armor, supporting his weight. The clear liquid had left a slick, viscous coating over his flesh and clothing. The wetness made him slippery and difficult to hold onto, but War Machine maintained a tight grip on his friend, keeping him standing.

Tony's breaths were harsh and ragged. He clung, gasping, to War Machine's armored shoulders. "You okay, pal?" War Machine asked, concerned for the other man's safety. There was a teaching hospital on Canal Street, he recalled, across the street from the Clarion Hotel. If necessary, he could fly Tony to the emergency room in minutes flat. "How're you doing?"

"I'm fine, I think," Tony said. His voice was hoarse and raspy. "My legs feel like rubber, though, like I haven't walked in days." He jerked his head towards the empty coffin. "How long was I in there?"

"Since Friday afternoon, probably," War Machine said. He did some quick calculations in his head, trying to compensate for all the different time zones he crossed since learning about the kidnapping. "Twelve, fifteen hours maybe."

"Is that all?" Tony said, seemingly shocked. "I could have sworn it's been days." His eyes narrowed. His voice took on a detached, analytical tone. "Unless, subjective time is accelerated in the virtual environment, to the extent that muscular atrophy takes place psychosomatically. . . . Fascinating!''

War Machine had no idea what Tony was talking about, although he recognized the look in his friend's eyes. He'd often seen Tony get caught up in the scientific and engineering possibilities of a brand-new idea, sometimes at the worst possible moment. ''Uh-uh,'' he said. ''Not sure what you're going on about, buddy, but now is not the time.'' He could hear sirens approaching on the street outside, the sound coming down the stairs from the shattered window up in the parlor. He could explain everything to the police, of course, but that would probably take a while. He needed to debrief Tony himself, while there was still a good chance of catching the bad guys responsible.

Tony lifted his hand to his chin. War Machine noted that Tony needed a shave. Tony chuckled; coming from his rusty throat, the laugh sounded painful. ''Finally,'' he said. ''I never thought I'd be so glad to feel stubble in my whole life, but now the universe makes sense again.'' He looked around the room, blinking against the bright fluorescent lights. ''So this is reality?'' he said wonderingly. ''It's good to be back.''

War Machine remembered Tony's eyelids twitching in his liquid-filled coffin, and he wondered what strange dreams Tony had awoke from. ''Think you can sit down?'' he asked. Tony nodded affirmatively, so War Machine lowered Tony onto the pedestal. Slowly letting go of Tony, he watched the other man carefully, ready to catch him again if he started to topple over. But Tony stayed sitting upright. He rested his head in his hands for a minute, until pounding noises came from the dense titanium door. He looked towards the door apprehensively.

"Just the local constabulary," War Machine explained. "I created a bit of a disturbance busting into this place. Figure we can talk to them later." He glanced towards the door, designed, from the looks of it, to fend off the likes of Iron Man or the Hulk. "They're not getting through that anytime soon."

"I see what you mean," Tony said. He gave War Machine a searching look. "You mentioned bringing me a present before. Could it be what I hope it is?"

"What else?" War Machine replied. He reached over his shoulder and opened the storage compartment on his back. The item Bethany had expressed to New York, the same delivery he'd claimed at Avengers Mansion, was still there, safely tucked between his missile launcher and minigun. With one smooth movement, he pulled the package from its compartment and handed it over to Tony Stark. "Santa's come to town," he said.

Tony grabbed onto the brown leather attaché case the way a man dying of thirst seizes a canteen full of fresh water. His ordeal in the tube had left him weak, and his hands were shaky, but he quickly keyed the correct combination into computerized lock. The latch clicked open and the lid of the case sprang upwards. War Machine caught a glimpse of red and golden armor, gleaming beneath the fluorescent lights. Inspecting the contents of the case, Tony Stark's eyes looked more alive than they had since they first opened in the cramped confines of his transparent coffin. "Thank you, Jim," he said hoarsely. "For everything."

"No problem," War Machine said. "What now? Search the place from top to bottom?"

"No," Tony said. "If those computers are to be believed, this facility is entirely automated. There's no one here but you, me, and those cops outside." He staggered to his feet and started pulling on his armor. Flattened sheets of flexmetal took on three dimensions as he removed them from the briefcase. Modular components, linked by magnetic fields, snapped together as soon as they slid over his limbs. War Machine noticed that Tony's face grew flushed with exertion. Dark, weary shadows hung beneath his eyes.

"You need any help with that?" War Machine asked. He reached out to steady Tony while the other man pulled an iron boot over his bare foot.

Tony shook his head. He gently pushed War Machine's helpful hand away. "I need a shave and a shower and several hours of real, as opposed to virtual, sleep, but the day I can't put on this tin suit under my own power is the day I just lay down and die." Grunting, he pulled on the other boot. He almost lost his balance and fell, and War Machine had to fight the temptation to catch him once more, but, at the last minute, Tony planted both boots firmly upon the white ceramic floor. Breathing hard, he stood tall less than a foot away from his former prison.

War Machine groaned heavily inside his own armor. Tony's stubborn pride could be infuriating sometimes. But, he had to admit, it was that same sheer cussedness that had allowed Anthony Stark—and Iron Man—to overcome all the obstacles, physical and otherwise, that an unusually difficult life had thrown up against him. He watched with admiration as Tony dragged his heavy helmet over his head until its neck joints automatically connected the headpiece to the rest of the armor. Tony Stark's wan, exhausted face was supplanted by the resolute, implacable mask of Iron Man.

Footsteps sounded on the stairs. The two heroes turned their respective eye slits towards the noise. A flashlight beam came down the steps, followed momentarily by a huffing New Orleans city policeman, his face damp with sweet and humidity. *Must have climbed over the balcony,* War Machine deduced, *and through the broken window.* "You freeze now," he called out, his voice tinged with a Cajun accent. He raised his pistol, then lowered it slowly, along with his jaw, as his flashlight, its beam almost invisible beneath the overhead lights, fell upon two imposing armored figures: one black and white and bristling with artillery, the other crimson and gold and streamlined like a bullet. "Lord almighty," he whispered.

"There's no cause for alarm, officer," Iron Man said. Electronically amplified and distorted, his voice no longer sounded tired or hoarse. Raising his right gauntlet slowly, he projected a holographic image of his Avengers Security Clearance. War Machine did likewise with his own Clearance. Though neither were active Avengers at present, it seemed sufficient based on the wide-eyed look of the policeman, who stared at the images hovering in the air in front of his nose. "My colleague and I are investigating the recent abduction of Tony Stark. Perhaps you're familiar with the case?"

"Saw something about it on the news," the man admitted. He was a beefy white man with a sunburned face and a blonde crewcut. Blinking, he stared for a second or two at Iron Man's holographic I.D. card, then looked away. Iron Man closed his palm and the image vanished. War Machine did the same. The dumbfounded cop thrust his pistol back into its holster.

"I would appreciate it, officer," Iron Man said. "If you'd secure this site for us. I'm sure the FBI and S.H.I.E.L.D. will want to go over it at their leisure."

"The F-B-I," the man repeated slowly, drawing out each syllable. The Federal Bureau of Investigation seemed to impress him even more than two armored super heroes, possibly, War Machine guessed, because the FBI actually had some relevance to his life. For whatever reason, the man suddenly became very cooperative. "Whatever you say, sir," he said, almost snapping to attention. "I'll string up some yellow tape immediately, and notify my sergeant that this site is off-limits to all but authorized personnel. *Sir.*'' He started to head back up the stairs, then glanced over at the massive steel door blocking the first floor exit. ''Er, do you think we could get that big door open?'' he asked sheepishly. ''It would be more, well, convenient.''

He doesn't want to climb down the balcony again, War Machine realized. He could certainly sympathize with the man's position. Not everybody could fly out of here. ''Hang on,'' he said.

War Machine strode over to the door. A digital, pushbutton lock was affixed to a heavy steel wheel, similar to those found on an airlock door. He didn't know the combination, so he didn't bother with the keypad. Instead, he grabbed the metal wheel with both hands and gave it a firm turn. Titanium shrieked in protest, but War Machine spun the wheel a full 360 degrees and heard something snap satisfactorily inside the door itself. He tugged on the wheel and the entire door swung inward, opening up onto a nondescript wooden porch. A gust of hot, humid air rushed into the computerized prison.

The policeman's eyes looked like they were going to pop out of his head. ''Good God,'' he said, eyeing War Machine with new respect. ''That is, thank you very much for your assistance, sir. That was very obliging of you, sir.'' He walked stiffly past War Machine towards the porch. War Machine half-expected the police officer to salute him on his way out the door.

I wonder if he'd be half so deferential, Jim wondered, *if he knew I was black under all this armor?* It was a stereotype, he knew, but he couldn't help having his suspicions about white Southern cops. Or white Los Angeles cops, for that matter. He tried not to think in those terms, but history could be hard to forget.

"Ready to go?" Iron Man asked him, interrupting his depressing ruminations.

War Machine looked around the room. "Any chance the bad guys will be coming by to investigate?" he asked Iron Man. "I'd hate to put our nervous friend out there in the line of fire."

"I don't think so," Iron Man said. "Before I downloaded myself back into my body, I programmed the V.R. generator to proceed as though I were still confined to the life-support module. If anyone checks in, it should appear as though I'm still a captive here."

"Unless," War Machine pointed out, "they also intercepted that SOS you sent out."

"Unless indeed," Iron Man agreed. "Fortunately, you were already in the vicinity, so perhaps you intercepted the message right away, before Blank Screen detected it." He shrugged burnished crimson shoulders. "In any event, he's not likely to send anyone here, not if he thinks his cover's blown and the place is crawling with authorities. Which it will be in no time at all.''

Iron Man marched out the large steel porch. The blue wooden porch sagged under the weight of his armor. He lifted his chin, looking upwards at the sky. Following him, War Machine saw the darkness lightening to the east. The sun was coming up.

''Wait a sec,'' War Machine said. Beneath his grim, grey mask, his face held a puzzled expression. ''Blank Screen? Who's that?'' He stared at Iron Man. ''And what was that about downloading yourself into yourself?''

''It's a long story,'' the Golden Avenger informed him. ''I'll tell you about it on the way.'' His boots ignited, leaving scorch marks on the porch and flinging him towards the dawn, far away from the house on Dumaine Street. War Machine ascended as well, joining his friend as they headed for the sunrise.

I guess breakfast can wait, he thought, *as long as we can have this Blank Screen character for lunch.*

''Weird,'' War Machine commented after they had filled each other in on their recent experiences. Side by side, they flew over the Louisiana swamps. Now that the sun was coming up, War Machine was impressed by just how green the bayous were. Mist rose like steam off the brackish waters, the ancient cypresses with their drooping shawls of Spanish moss reflected in the slow-moving currents of the meandering tributaries and shadowy sloughs of the swamp so that it was often hard to tell where the foliage ended and the water began. Several hundred feet below them, a white egret lazily flapped its wings over the bayou, staying safely above the lurking gators.

Still, nothing in the mysterious swamps matched the mind-boggling strangeness of Tony's imprisonment in virtual reality. *When you can't trust your own senses,* Jim wondered, *what else can you rely on? How do I know that I'm not being fed a cybernetic hallucination this very moment?* Despite the rising heat and humidity, Jim felt a chill run through his bones.

"So Anastasia is definitely okay?" Iron Man asked him for probably the third time since they'd flown out of New Orleans. Jim had never met the lady but, like everyone else in the country, he'd seen her posters and calendars. He wasn't surprised she'd gotten under Tony's skin.

"As far as I know, yeah," War Machine answered. They communicated by short-range radio; it was easier than shouting over their own jetstreams. "Bethany's people picked her up and checked her out after the attack on the yacht. Last I heard, she was resting safely at home, at least until *The National Enquirer* gets hold of her."

"Great," Tony said. "You have no idea how glad I am to hear that."

Oh, I think I have an inkling, Jim thought. He tried to imagine what he would do if Rae Lacoste was apparently tortured in front of his eyes. His blood boiled just thinking about it. Fortunately, none of his enemies had come after Rae just yet, although that was probably only a matter of time. *The only thing more dangerous than being a super hero,* he thought grimly, *is being a super hero's significant other.* He needed to have a serious talk about that with Rae sometime soon, make sure she knew what she was getting into. . . .

As if on cue, a female voice suddenly resounded inside his helmet. Only it wasn't Rae Lacoste, it was Bethany Cabe. "Jim," she said. "Bethany here. Hope this isn't a bad time, but I have important new information about Tony. . . ."

"Before you say anything else," he said, interrupting her, "I have a pleasant surprise for you." He grinned behind his faceplate. "Hold on, I have to transfer this call." Without further ado, he patched Tony into the conversation and listened joyfully as Bethany whooped with delight at the sound of Tony's voice. Together, they updated Bethany on Tony's rescue. She listened carefully, occasionally asking succinct and pointed questions. A note of sorrow snuck into her voice after War Machine told her that Madame Masque had identified—and neutralized—Bethany's informant.

"Damn," she said. "That's one more thing we owe that gold-plated tramp." There was a brief silence at the other end of the line, then Bethany spoke up. "Still, that's not why I contacted you. We received another transmission from Masque . . . or rather," she corrected herself, "a computer simulation of Masque. This one gave us the location of the drop-off site for the chip. It's an abandoned castle somewhere in England. Iron Man is supposed to deliver the chip at one o'clock, our time, or else. He's supposed to come alone, naturally."

Let's see, Jim thought. One PM, California time, would be nine PM in the U.K., which was roughly nine hours from now. Switching off his microphone for a second, he groaned loudly. All this zone-hopping was making his head hurt. Nine hours, he thought. Just about the length of time needed to fly from Florida to England, assuming no tricky suborbital maneuvers. Blank Screen, as Tony referred to their unseen adversary, had seemingly calculated this operation down to the last minute.

"Of course," Bethany was pointing out, "we now have the chip *and* Tony, so we don't need to make the meet at all."

"Negative," Iron Man said brusquely. "That's not an option. I don't want a stalemate. I want to take the battle straight to the enemy."

"But, Tony," Bethany protested "you don't know what sort of welcoming committee they have waiting."

"With any luck," Iron Man said, "they think Tony Stark is still their captive. That gives me an edge. Transmit the coordinates, Bethany."

Bethany knew better than to argue with her boss and ex-lover when he was in this kind of mood.

Minutes later, the coordinates began scrolling onto a LED display inside Jim's helmet. He assumed Tony was receiving the same information.

"England," War Machine said aloud, activating his microphone. "I'm sure racking up the frequent flier miles on this caper."

Iron Man turned his head towards War Machine, not far enough to affect his flight path but just enough to look Jim in the eye across the several feet of open sky separating them. "You don't have to come along for this part, Jim," he said. "You've done more than your share."

"You kidding?" War Machine replied. "I haven't come this far to drop out now."

"At the risk of being indelicate," Iron Man said, "your armor looks like it's seen better days."

It was true, he had to admit. Between A.I.M. and the Maggia, his War Machine suit had taken quite a beating. Even with Pym's emergency repairs, his chest beam still looked like a smashed headlight and his repulsors were offline. According to his latest diagnostic read-outs, the sealant Pym had applied allowed the suit to maintain its basic structural integrity, but he was all too aware that the exterior of his armor was covered with nicks, gouges, and abrasions, any one of which might lead to a more serious armor breach under combat circumstances. Still, he remembered all the grief he had gone through purely because of the selfish machinations of Blank Screen, not to mention the heartwrenching sight of Tony coughing up liquid slime in an oversized vacuum tube, and he knew that he'd never forgive himself if he didn't get a chance to do unto Blank Screen as Blank Screen had done unto Tony and himself. "Forget it," he told Iron Man emphatically, "I want to see this case through to the end. Let's head over to Merrie Olde England and find out who is *really* behind this."

Tony nodded solemnly. "I think I already know," he said. "Listen...."

SATURDAY. 8:02 PM. BRITISH STANDARD TIME.

To save their strength and energy for the coming battle, they only flew as far as New York, then took one of Stark's private jets from there to London, arriving at Heathrow less than an hour before their enemy's deadline. The sun, which had barely risen in New York when they took off the runway, had long since set in the British Isles. It was cold and wet and foggy—typical English weather. Stepping out onto the runway, warm and snug inside his armor, Iron Man remembered the foggy mist that had swirled around the Golden Gate Bridge during that tense hostage crisis. Had that really been only a day or so ago? He felt like he'd spent days in that blasted white room, sleeping and eating and slaving away in front of what turned out to be a computer-generated simulacrum of a computer. How could it only be Saturday? Blank Screen's virtual reality program had really messed with his sense of time. He felt like Ebenezer Scrooge, waking on Christmas morning to discover, awestruck, that spirits had "done it all in one night."

Unlike the jubilant Scrooge, however, he felt like hell. The flight had been a tiring one. After shaving and showering in the jet's private bathroom, he had tried to sleep on the way over, only to fail miserably. He had squirmed and tossed about in his seat, unable to relax; it was as though his body, kept forcibly immobile for countless hours in the cramped confines of the life support module, was determined to make up for lost time. Although he was physically and psychologically exhausted, his body quivered with excess energy. At times, he wished he could separate his head from his rebellious, impatient limbs.

It was more than that, though. *Admit it, Stark,* he told himself. *You can't get used to having a body again.* After his timeless sojourn in cyberspace, existing in a platonic realm of pure logic and mind, the everyday aches and pains and sensations of fleshly existence were strange, alien, and distracting. His hands, as he had once anticipated, were sore and bruised from punching Victor's armored faceplate when he was aboard *Athena.* His muscles felt weak and sore from disuse. His skin itched. His mouth tasted like industrial waste. Unregulated hormonal reactions, ranging from homicidal rage at Blank Screen to sudden flashes of physical desire for Anastasia, stirred up his thoughts, compromising his concentration. He found himself longing wistfully for the rigorous geometrical lines, and cool objectivity, of the world of data and command codes. In its own inhuman way, there was something terribly seductive about escaping your own body, especially after all the physical ailments, from heart disease to alcoholism, that had afflicted him over the years. *To say we end,* he thought, quoting *Hamlet* once more, *the heartache and the thousand natural shocks that flesh is heir to. . . .*

Within his armor, Tony shuddered. He was human again, and glad of it. Wasn't he? He strode across the rain-drenched tarmac. His legs still felt rubbery, his body weak, but his armored exoskeleton supported him, let him walk tall and straight in the world no matter how wretched he felt. Created from the workings of his brain, his armor, it occurred to him, was perhaps the perfect compromise between his mind and his body: his imagination and creative ability given form to enhance, rather than supplant, his physical abilities. The best of both worlds, perhaps. The incorporeal serenity of cyberspace still beckoned to him, but, shielded by his invincible armor, he faced the physical world confident that he could endure all those celebrated natural shocks to which his flesh was heir. For now, at least, that would have to be enough.

A heavy iron finger, black as anthracite, tapped him gently on the shoulder. Iron Man looked up from his reverie to see War Machine standing beside him. Rain ran down the surface of War Machine's armor, pooling in the cracks and crevices. ''We'd better get going,'' Jim said.

Iron Man inspected War Machine's armor. The outer enamel layer was chipped and scratched in more places than Tony could count. The palms of his gauntlets looked as they'd been assaulted with a power drill; according to Jim, a Maggia dreadnaught had done the damage, which probably made a drill seem like a feather duster in comparison. The tri-beam projector in his chestplate had been thoroughly trashed. The best Tony had been able to do by way of repairs was to patch up the hole with a fresh layer of armor plating. None of the beams worked, but at least War

Machine's chest didn't look so bloody vulnerable anymore.

Fortunately, Jim had done a much better job of resting up during their transatlantic flight. He had devoured a large in-flight meal and then slept for at least six hours. In a way, it was ironic, Iron Man thought. *My armor is in tip-top shape, but my body's a wreck. Jim's armor is trashed, but he's physically fit. Together, we make one perfect iron man.* But would that be enough to defeat Blank Screen, especially if he was who Iron Man suspected he was? There was no time like the present to find out.

When in London, he thought, do as the Londoners do. "Come, War Machine," he said loudly. "The game's afoot."

War Machine caught the reference. "Elementary, my dear Iron Man," he replied. He blasted into the stormy sky, executing a perfect vertical takeoff. Iron Man launched himself after him.

A few minutes' flight brought them over London proper. They rocketed over the large, bustling city, the streets laid out in a confusing, crazy-quilt pattern that made no logical sense at all. Someone had once told Tony that if you wanted to know what a street map of London was like, just throw a handful of wiggling worms onto a piece of paper and watch how they moved. It was one of the truest things he'd ever heard. Hundreds of feet below them, red double-decker buses, packed with tourists, drove through the bright lights and flashing neon of Piccadilly Circus.

British cabs, looking like small black beetles from above, darted around buses and pedestrians. The pedestrians themselves could not be seen, only an army of upraised umbrellas crowding the sidewalks. Despite the downpour, the streets were packed. *Of course*, Iron Man thought. *If the British stayed indoors during bad weather, they'd never get outside at all.*

They veered away from Buckingham Palace, for fear of alarming the Palace security forces, but passed directly over the Houses of Parliament. Atop a glittering tower, Big Ben looked out over the Thames. Iron Man glanced at the giant clockface as he flew by it. According to Big Ben, it was now eight-sixteen in London, or sixteen minutes after twelve back in California. Blank Screen's deadline was less than forty-five minutes away. Iron Man thought about the precious energy chip, now tucked away in a golden utility storage module attached to his hip. Jim had given the chip to Tony shortly after they left New York. Blank Screen was expecting Iron Man, after all.

Heading east, they left Parliament miles behind, soon passing high above the Tower of London itself. The gray stone fortress, once the most terrible prison in England, cast a pall over Tony's heart. He knew what it was like to be trapped in captivity, with no reprieve in sight. Many innocent men and women had been tortured and executed with the walls of the Tower. He had no doubt that Blank Screen was responsible for countless similar tragedies. *But not anymore,* he thought fervently. *Tonight it ends.*

They turned north eventually. According to his suit's location finder, the rendezvous point was an old castle in the English countryside, midway between London and Cambridge. Soon, the lights of the city receded into the distance behind them, and Iron Man found himself soaring above rolling green hills, dotted with occasional herds of sheep. Beneath the light of his searchlight, the green was even more vibrant than in the swamps of Louisiana, but there the resemblance ended. Where the bayous were wild and mysterious, the grassy fields beneath him were conspicuously cozy and domesticated. Amazing, he thought, the difference several centuries of civilization can make. The climate was radically different, too: cold and clammy, where New Orleans was hot and muggy. All the two regions had in common was their wetness. Both England and Louisiana had more water than they knew what to do with, which probably accounted for all the green that characterized both locales.

Dark, billowing clouds surrounded the two heroes. A cold wind blew rain against their faceplates. With the storm raging around them, it was a challenge to keep each other in sight. War Machine banked closer to Iron Man. His voice echoed within Tony's helmet. "So what's the plan?" Jim asked him.

"I want you to stay out of sight," Iron Man said, "at least at first. Blank Screen's expecting Iron Man to arrive alone. You're my ace in the hole."

"Should be easy enough," War Machine observed, "especially with all this cloud cover. You don't think the other team's going to call the game on account of rain, do you?"

"I doubt it," Iron Man said. "Blank Screen's put too much time and trouble into this scheme. Besides, he wants the chip." *What he's going to get, however,* he thought, *is something else again, namely a great big dose of revenge.* His heart sang at the prospect of feeding Blank Screen a mouthful of iron knuckles, and Tony found himself amused by the savage joy he felt at the mere concept of striking back at his foe. Come to think of it, he thought, maybe there were advantages to all those unruly glandular responses after all. . . . A stray thought of Ana, stretched out on a deck chair in her silver metallic bikini, passed through his brain on its way to the rest of him, warming his blood and reminding him of the undeniable pleasures of biological existence. The sooner he defeated Blank Screen, the sooner he could get back to Anastasia. He just hoped she felt the same way, despite her frightening experience aboard *Athena.*

At ten minutes to nine, Waverly Castle loomed on the horizon. Although only half as large as the Tower of London, it was constructed along the same basic principles. High stone walls, dark and forbidding, stretched between a quartet of mighty towers that guarded each of the castle's four corners. The jagged crenellation running along the battlements of the castle made the tops of the walls resemble the fanged lower jaw of some immense mythical beast. A wide, deep ditch, which Iron Man suspected had once held a moat, circled the castle, so that the only way in or out was across an old stone bridge, through the castle's front gate, and beneath a rusty, spiked portcullis. At least that was the only *visible* entrance; Iron Man recalled that most of these ancient fortresses contained hidden bolt-holes and tunnels through which the inhabitants of the castle could flee in the event their fortifications fell before an invading army. None of the castle's defenses, of course, could possibly keep out an invader who could fly. His boot jets rendered the ancient rockpile singularly obsolete.

Storm clouds, black and swollen with rain, gathered above the castle. Lightning bolts zigzagged across the sky, illuminating the looming towers in strobe-like flashes that gave the scene an appropriate Gothic atmosphere.

War Machine pointed towards a large courtyard just past the gate of the castle. "I'm reading four, maybe five targets down there," he told Iron Man. "Still want me to make myself scarce?"

"For now," Iron Man said. "Keep a close eye on what goes on. If it looks like I need help, make like the cavalry."

"Got it," War Machine responded. "Good luck. To be honest, I'm hoping Blank Screen isn't who you think he is. For your sake." Altering his trajectory, War Machine swung left into a heavy, black cloudbank.

"Me too," Iron Man said quietly. He checked his internal chronometer. It was one minute to nine, almost twenty-four hours exactly since the bogus "Madame Masque" delivered her original ultimatum to Stark Enterprises. *Time to meet Blank Screen,* he thought. *Let's not keep the man waiting.*

Descending from the clouds, Iron Man zoomed over the parapets of the castle, then came to rest in the central courtyard. The courtyard floor was paved with cobblestones, many of which were now cracked or missing. The ground felt bumpy and uneven beneath his boots. Weeds grew in the cracks between the cobblestones. Falling rain formed deep puddles in depressions formed by the absence of various missing stones. High granite walls surrounded him on all four sides. Within the walls, squat, one-story structures of brick and timber had collapsed into heaps of debris. Iron Man assumed these junkpiles had once been the castle's living quarters: homes and workshops that had long since succumbed to the ravages of time. Only the walls and the four sky-high towers remained, dutifully enclosing a scene of utter desolation.

The courtyard was dark when he landed. Clouds concealed the moon from sight. Only intermittent flashes of white-hot lightning lit the interior of Waverly Castle. His motion detectors alerted him to five figures approaching him from behind the crumbled ruins, but Iron Man could not see anything. He was about to activate his infrared lenses when flames suddenly sputtered to life in every direction. Torches blazed upon the battlements, supported by metal sconces that gleamed like brass. Flickering orange flames cast eerie shadows upon the courtyard. The torches resisted the pouring rain, remaining lit despite the wet conditions. Perhaps Waverly Castle was not as derelict as it looked.

He heard clanking sounds drawing nearer. Looking away from the fiery torches, Iron Man saw four people clad in heavy suits of metal plating and chain mail striding towards him, looking for all the world like medieval knights. The torchlight reflected off their armor, throwing streaks of red and orange along the molded contours of their metal suits. Iron-shod boots rang against the irregular, cobblestone floor. Their gauntlets held a variety of maces, broadswords, and battle-axes. The visors on their helmets were closed, hiding their faces, but Iron Man suspected, from their number and individual heights, that these were the same four commandoes that had survived the assault on *Athena*. The unfortunate Victor, dead from a self-inflicted electrical accident, was probably somewhere at the bottom of the Gulf of Mexico now, weighed down by his heavy, reinforced scuba gear.

"Like armor, do you?" Iron Man taunted them. "I'm rather fond it of myself, as you can see."

The counterfeit knights did not respond. Cranking up his audio receiver, Iron Man listened for the sound of squeaking metal joints. Instead, he heard the subdued mechanical hum of miniature servomotors. Obviously, his opponents's armor was not as archaic as it looked. *Careful,* he warned himself, *don't under-estimate them or their weaponry.* That mace, for instant, could very well be a particle beam weapon in disguise. He readied his own repulsor rays, targeting the largest knight with the beam projector in his chestplate. Large metal rivets appeared to hold the knight's armor together; Tony assumed they were largely decorative.

The knights did not attack him immediately. Forming a line in front of him, they quickly parted to allow a fifth individual to walk between flanking pairs of knights. The newcomer was a tall figure wearing a voluminous green robe. The hood of the cloak obscured his face. His arms were crossed above his chest, his hands tucked into the sleeves of his robe.

"You have the chip?" he demanded. His voice held a distinct Teutonic accent. Iron Man recognized it instantly. Suddenly, his most dire suspicions were confirmed. The robed man was definitely Blank Screen, but that was not his true name.

"Not so fast, Strucker!" Iron Man said boldly.

The robed man fell silent for a moment, then a chilling sound emerged from the shadowy recesses of the olive-colored hood. The sound began softly, then grew to a maniacal pitch. It was the harsh, cruel laughter of Baron Wolfgang Von Strucker, Supreme Commander of Hydra.

Heedless of the rain, Strucker threw his head back, shedding his hood. He was a bald man, with a narrow nose and cold blue eyes. A dueling scar ran down the left side of his face from his forehead to his cheekbone. The scar appeared to bisect his left eye, which was covered by a monocle. Strucker's complexion was white and pasty and marred by several dark purple blotches just beneath his skin. Iron Man recalled that Baron Strucker had been infected with his own Death-Spore Virus during a pitched battle with Nick Fury and his agents of S.H.I.E.L.D. Unfortunately for the world, Strucker had not succumbed to that deadly bacterial weapon; instead, he had become a carrier for the Death-Spore Virus, a malevolent, modern-day Typhoid Mary capable of transmitting the disease through the merest touch of his infected flesh—except that, unlike the historical Typhoid Mary, Strucker spread his contagion deliberately. Reacting instantly, Iron Man sealed all the vents in his armor.

Even before contracting the virus, Iron Man reflected, Baron Strucker had always been a carrier of sorts, spreading the pestilence of crime and terrorism throughout the world. Hydra, his greatest and most terrible creation, had inflicted incalculable havoc upon humanity, often endangering the very existence of life itself for the sake of Hydra's own twisted ambitions. By contrast, he thought, Madame Masque and the Maggia were mere petty thieves and murders.

An icy smile played across Strucker's scarred visage. On him, it looked like a sneer. "An excellent deduction, *Herr* Iron Man," he declared. "I am impressed. May I ask, *mein freund,* how you detected the hidden hand of Hydra?''

"The clues were all there from the beginning," Iron Man explained. *Get him talking,* he thought silently, activating a recording chip in his helmet to preserve any confession that Strucker might make. Granted, Strucker was already wanted all over the globe for crimes beyond number, but one more piece of damning evidence couldn't hurt—if and when he dragged Strucker to justice.

"First, there was the Hydra agent on the Golden Gate Bridge," he continued, "luring me to San Francisco so that your underwater assault team could abduct Tony Stark. That didn't convince me, though, until an investigation stumbled onto some of your old financial records, referring to an account identified only as the Second Labor Party." Iron Man paused, choosing his words carefully. He didn't want to reveal too much about Tony Stark's ability to traverse cyberspace, or inform Strucker that they had uncovered his base on Dumaine Street. "According to Greek and Roman mythology, the Second of the Twelve Labors of Hercules was defeating the Hydra."

"Fascinating," the Baron commented. "I shall have to have my accountant killed for his sloppiness. Still, that is neither here nor there. The chip, if you please." Strucker withdrew his right hand from the left sleeve of his robe and reached out his hand expectantly. Iron Man saw the ugly violet splotches mottling Strucker's bare palm. Despite his airtight armor, he recoiled involuntarily. Strucker's left hand remained hidden in the capacious folds of his olive robe.

"Later," he said gruffly. "It's your turn to explain. What's this all about, Strucker?"

Baron Strucker withdrew his hand, smirking at the Golden Avenger's obvious revulsion. "There is no earthly reason I should tell you, *Amerikaner*," he said, "except for vanity and my own Prussian pride." He laughed out loud. "Very well! You cannot truly appreciate my genius unless you fully understand the overlapping complexities of my latest offensive. For indeed, my objective was three-pronged. Why be content with one victory, I ask you, when the same stratagem will secure you multiple prizes?" An insane gleam came into Strucker's arctic blue eyes. Dancing red flames were reflected in his monocle.

"First," he said, raising one discolored finger, "I wanted to obtain the energy chip from my former allies at Advanced Idea Mechanics. Fools! They should have never divorced themselves from the unholy glory that is Hydra. What is mere scientific ingenuity without the strategic brilliance—and the iron will—necessary to truly create fear?" Consumed with disgust, Strucker spat upon the crumbling paving stones. His saliva, Tony noted, was a greenish black. "Of course, had you failed to wrest the chip from A.I.M. I would have had to content myself with the death of Iron Man, a worthy goal in its own right.

You see what I mean, *mein freund*. Plans within plans. . . .

"Second, I am attempting to extort from Anthony Stark the secrets of your own magnificent armor. Failing that, I will at least succeed in keeping Stark, a perpetual busybody and persistent thorn in my side, from interfering with my other objectives.

"Third, and most importantly, I intend to launch a secret war against both A.I.M. and the Maggia. Already, thanks to my inspired misdirection, you have inflicted considerable damage upon both organizations. Now, with the power of the chip at my command, Hydra will obliterate all our rivals and assume utter control of the entire international underworld! My first step will be to order the assassination of both the pretender, Madame Masque, *and* the Supreme Scientist of Advanced Idea Mechanics. After that, Hydra will reign supreme—and all the governments of the world will tremble before our might!"

Listening to Strucker's ravings, Iron Man was horrified by the nightmarish potential of the robed man's ultimate vision. A super-powered gang war among Hydra, A.I.M., and the Maggia, fought with the latest developments in technological destruction, could cause untold carnage and kill thousands of innocent civilians. Once before, at the instigation of the new Madame Masque, all three criminal organizations had turned on each other—and it had taken all of Iron Man's strength and resourcefulness to nip that bloody conflict in the bud before the body count rose too high. *Never again,* he vowed.

"You can't be serious," Iron Man protested. "Even if you win, a war like that would cost everyone involved more than they could possibly afford. You would inherit only devastation, and a mountain of casualties."

"And survival!" Strucker crowed. "Survival of the fittest! Nature red in tooth and claw! That is the only dream I hold dear, Avenger. That is my ideal." He stalked towards Iron Man, his eyes aflame with madness. Inky spittle sprayed from his mouth. "You think Hydra is about money, greed, power? If so, you are mistaken, *mein* metallic pawn. Perhaps in the past, under lesser commanders, Hydra pursued such baubles for their own rewards, but no more! I have passed through the valley of death, experienced personally the endless oblivion at the heart of the universe, and returned from the void carrying the crimson banner of pure animal survival. Only through fire and blood can the strong prove themselves and the weak be culled from the species. That is the one true vision I brought back from the abyss: a glorious world of total anarchy.

"Power, treasure ... those are but tools," he sneered. "Under my visionary leadership, the hordes of Hydra shall create bloodshed and terror *for their own sake!*"

Strucker's mad oration reached a crazed crescendo, and Iron Man shuddered within his armor at the sheer, unmitigated insanity of Baron Wolfgang Von Strucker's malignant crusade. "I already knew you were a sociopath and a fanatic, Strucker," he said angrily, "but now I realize that you are also a complete and total lunatic." *You're not the only one who has died and come back, Baron,* Tony thought privately. *Thank God that, when Abe and Erica thawed me out from the cryo-sleep, I didn't wake up as a drooling psycho.*

"A lunatic?" Strucker echoed him. "I accept that epithet proudly from the likes of such as you. True genius appears as insanity to those of limited vision." His left hand slid out of its sleeve; it was a blood-red, metallic claw whose razor-sharp pincers struck sparks off each other whenever they clashed together. Strucker's real hand, Tony recalled from Nick Fury's files, had been severed at the wrist during a battle with S.H.I.E.L.D. Now the Baron wore a variety of deadly prosthetic hands, each equipped with all manner of destructive weaponry. He called them his Satan Claws.

"Now then," Baron Strucker said, brandishing his Claw. All trace of sardonic amusement and false *bonhomie* dropped instantly from his voice. His human hand unfastened the collar of his robe. The robe separated down the front, the loose ends flapping like a cape in the wind and giving Iron Man a glimpse of a brown paramilitary uniform underneath the robe. "The chip," Strucker demanded.

"Never," Iron Man said. He had heard enough.

There was no way he was letting this maniac get his hands on another potential weapon. "You're coming with me. One way or another."

"Then Stark will die," Strucker threatened. Either he didn't know that his prisoner had escaped or he was bluffing shamelessly. Iron Man didn't really care.

"It wouldn't be the first time," he said.

SATURDAY. 9:24 PM. BRITISH STANDARD TIME.

Circling five hundred feet above Waverly Castle, War Machine observed the bitter confrontation transpiring within the imposing stone walls of the ancient fortress. Lightning crackled around him. Peals of thunder boomed in his ears. War Machine's telescopic, infrared lenses easily penetrated the roiling storm clouds drifting between him and the castle. He watched intently as Iron Man faced off against what looked like four suits of animated armor, as well as a sinister figure in a flowing green robe. When the figure removed his hood, War Machine concentrated his 'scope on the man's head, zooming in on his face. Jim's eyes widened at the sight of a hairless domed skull—and a scarred face oozing malice with each new expression that crossed his predatory visage.

So, War Machine thought sourly, his lips forming a tight line beneath his mask, *Tony was right after all.* Blank Screen was Baron Strucker. Madame Masque had been telling the truth, he realized. Jim figured he should feel sorry about trashing A.I.M.'s undersea laboratory and Madame Masque's opulent New York penthouse, but, somehow, he couldn't work up too much guilt about either exercise. *Sometimes,* he consoled himself, *bad things just happen to bad people.*

What with the thunder and all, War Machine could not make out what was being said below, nor could he eavesdrop via Iron Man's audio receptors.

He and Iron Man had chosen to maintain radio silence except in absolute emergencies, for fear of having their communications detected by the opposition. Still, he expected they weren't having a pleasant chat about the weather. "C'mon, Tony," he muttered. "Get on with it." This wait-and-see routine was chafing on his nerves. He wanted action.

Then, just when Jim thought he was going to explode, Baron Strucker waved a vicious-looking scarlet claw in ShellHead's face. The armored knights flanking Strucker lurched forward, raising their weapons. War Machine saw a heavy metal mace, covered with spikes, swing towards Iron Man.

That's my cue, he thought. His afterburners fired, and War Machine dived through the clouds, plummeting straight towards the castle.

The time for talk was over, Iron Man concluded as the *faux* knights of Hydra came at him. The closest knight took the lead. The contours of his armor suit implied a lean man of compact dimensions; Tony guessed he was the same man who had defeated him on the deck of *Athena*. The knight raised a huge metal mace, bristling with sharpened spikes, over his head. Iron Man quickly evaluated the potential threat. A genuine medieval mace wouldn't even scratch his state-of-the-art, diamond-hardened suit, but who knew what surprises the mace might have in store. Those spikes could be tipped with adamantium, he thought, the hardest known substance. Better safe than sorry.

His right arm snapped up, blocking the mace's descent. The impact rocked his body. Hydra's armor obviously enhanced its user's strength. *But not as much as mine does,* he thought, smiting the bogus knight with a left-hand punch to the abdomen. His iron knuckles left deep indentations in the knight's metal breastplate. The *cuirass* it was called, Tony remembered; not surprisingly, he had made an extensive study of antique armor.

His blow staggered the knight, but did not drop him. Iron Man was impressed; the archaic-looking metal suit was tougher than it looked. The knight held a broadsword in his other hand. He jabbed the point of the sword at Iron Man's mask. Iron Man thought he saw a sparkle of shimmering energy flash at the tip of the blade. *That looks bad,* he thought. His repulsor beam shot from his chestplate, striking the knight solidly in the midsection. *Now that's what I call a kick in the cuirass,* Iron Man thought. *Pun definitely intended.* The lean knight stumbled backwards, his boots splashing through the puddles, his arms pinwheeling wildly in a desperate attempt to keep his balance. The violet force-beam remained focused on his breastplate, keeping the pressure on until the knight backed into a semicollapsed stone wall at top speed. He hit the wall with a resounding crash that could probably be heard all the way to London.

Before Iron Man could savor his victory, however, a heavy weight hit him between his shoulderblades. He fell forward, throwing out his hands. He would have hit the rough, stone pavement face-first except that his chestbeam, still in operation, fell upon the rocky floor first. The repulsor effect pushed him back onto his feet, just in time to receive another savage blow in the side of the head. This time he caught a glimpse of a battle-ax, glowing with iridescent sparks of azure energy, out of the corner of his vision. His temple throbbed even beneath several layers of padding. He heard his teeth rattle.

Caught offguard, he struggled to orient himself. The remaining three knights had fanned out around him, enclosing him in a deadly triangle. Try as he did, he could not keep them all in sight. Through sheer luck, his peripheral vision spotted another knight charging at him, wielding another super-charged broadsword. From the shape of her cuirass, he guessed this knight was a woman. *King Arthur might not approve,* he thought, *but this is no time for chivalry.* Spinning on his heels, he grabbed her blade with both hands; he felt its unleashed energy surging in his grip. He unleashed a portion of his own solar power reserves into the blade, reversing the ion flow. A white-hot glow suffused the entire length of the sword as a powerful jolt of electricity rushed up the shaft of the sword into her chainmail gauntlet. A shrill scream erupted from behind the woman's visor. She stiffened, then dropped her sword like a hot potato. Smoke rose from her glove and she waved it frantically in front of her. Harsh curses assailed Iron Man's ears.

Blast, he thought when he saw she was still standing. *She's better insulated than I thought.*

Frustration filled his throat with bile. *I don't have time for this, blast it! Where's Strucker?* That madman could be getting away. He tried to locate the Baron amidst the conflict and confusion, but the knights kept getting in the way. He glanced towards the wall he'd knocked the first knight into; to his dismay, no armored form rested among the debris. The lean knight must have gotten back onto his feet and rejoined the fray. What was it going to take to defeat these bastards? There were too many of them, and, to be brutally honest, he was still exhausted from his long captivity.

The battle reduced itself to fragmentary images, and instant, reflexive actions. A battle-ax flew towards his face. Iron Man ducked under the ax, then lashed back with a repulsor burst from his right gauntlet. He heard a grunt of pain, followed by the sound of crashing metal. A sword whacked against his hip; it didn't slice through his armor, but his leg stung as though whipped with a heavy switch. *I can't take this much longer,* he thought desperately.

Suddenly, the loud report of automatic gunfire filled the courtyard. Chips of stone flew from the pavement, joining the spray of water from a dozen small puddles. Iron Man heard shouts of anger and surprise escape his armored foes. He looked up eagerly.

War Machine dropped from the clouds, guns

blazing. His minigun was in place above his left shoulder, and he strafed the castle grounds as he buzzed by overhead. Fire exploded before him. Thunder roared in his wake. Ironclad in stark black-and-white steel, looking like the very avatar of mechanized fury, War Machine zipped over the courtyard, flying below the uppermost levels of the castle's guardian towers. Bullets bounced off Iron Man's armor-plated adversaries, but not a shot hit the Golden Avenger himself, who stood amidst the rain of ammunition as though protected by an invisible bubble. Even though he'd designed War Machine's targeting computers himself, Tony Stark was still amazed by the lethal precision of War Machine's weapons.

Jim's voice came through the headset in his helmet. "Looked like you could use a hand," he said.

"And then some," Tony said gratefully. "Good timing."

The bullets didn't appear to penetrate the knights' armor, but the sudden onslaught of high-intensity gunfire certainly threw them off-balance. For the first time since the fight began, Iron Man had a chance to take a breather without having to worry about yet another weapon being flung at him. His eyes, safely lodged behind industrial-strength lenses, searched the scene before him, looking for Strucker. The Baron had disappeared from his view as soon as the first knight tried to bludgeon Iron Man with his mace. Where was he now? Surely, Iron Man thought, Baron

Strucker would not leave without his precious energy chip, would he?

But Strucker was nowhere in sight. Iron Man feared that the insidious Hydra leader had indeed fled the castle, leaving his steel-encased minions to finish up his dirty work. Then a blinding flash of lightning drew his attention to the battlements overlooking the courtyard. An ominous brown figure stood upon the high grey wall, partially silhouetted against the storm-tossed clouds. A steel claw flexed its incarnadine pincers. A monocle glinted in the night.

"Come, *Amerikaner*," Baron Strucker called out to him. "Let us finish this *verdammt* business now!"

You want it, you got it, Iron Man thought furiously. "War Machine," he instructed his ally via radio. "You take care of these Round Table wannabes. I'm going after Strucker."

"Got it," Jim confirmed. "Think you can handle Strucker on your own?" Tony heard the concern in his friend's voice. He couldn't fool Jim; Jim knew that he still hadn't fully recovered from his confinement in Hydra's virtual reality trap.

"Don't worry about it," he said firmly. "Strucker's mine." A sudden afterthought occurred to him. "And, War Machine, seal your armor against biological weapons if you haven't already. I'll explain later." That was another good reason for taking on Strucker himself, Iron Man thought. War Machine's much-abused armor was vulnerable to Baron Strucker's dreaded Death-Spore Virus. According to Fury, the virus was incurable, and instantaneously fatal, and just one miniscule crack in War Machine's armor could spell his doom. *Let Jim take out the knights*, he affirmed. *I'll beat the Baron—or die trying.*

Firing his jets, his lifted off from the courtyard, relinquishing the battleground to War Machine. A greater struggle now awaited him. And a more personal one.

Blank Screen, he thought. *Here I come.*

War Machine cruised over the rain-soaked courtyard, peppering the knights with automatic weapon's fire. The 3.9-mm shells were supposed to be armor-piercing, and had certainly proved that claim during his contest with A.I.M.'s submarines the day before, but they only seemed to stun the knights. *What are those suits made of?* he wondered. Advanced Idea Mechanics needed to talk to its suppliers; Hydra was obviously getting the better product.

He considered deploying his missile launcher, but felt oddly reluctant to do so. *Why is that?* he asked himself, then realized the answer. It was Tony. As irrational as it sounded even to himself, Iron Man's presence inhibited him from using deadly force— which was what firing his missiles at single individuals probably entailed. War Machine and Iron Man both hated killing, but, as far as Jim was concerned, Tony was positively obsessed about the subject, particularly where his own technology was concerned. The subject had strained their friendship more than

once, and even though they had now been square with
other for quite a while, he didn't feel like rubbing Tony's nose in the brutal realities of combat, not after all
he'd gone through lately. His gaze fell upon the armored thugs several feet below him. All four knights
were up and about, waving their archaic, museum-
quality weapons at the man-shaped dive-bomber cruis-
ing above them. *You suckers lucked out,* War Machine
thought. *Tonight we're playing softball.*

Instead of launching his missiles, he rolled onto
his side and fired another volley to cover Iron Man's
retreat. Out of the corners of his eye slits, he saw Iron
Man rise towards the battlements to keep his appoint-
ment with the infamous Baron Strucker. *Good luck,
pal,* he thought, before returning his attention to his
own foes.

At the moment, he seemed to have achieved a
stalemate with the knights on the ground. They
couldn't fly, but his ammo did little more than faze
them. If he wanted to keep them away from Iron Man
and the Baron, a closer engagement looked inevitable,
but was he ready to take on all four knights at once?
He'd seen what a rough time they'd given Iron Man
when they all ganged up on him simultaneously. Convinced he was safely out of their reach, he hovered
momentarily, considering his options.

Then one of the knights—the lanky man with the
mace—hurled his weapon like a spear. *What the hell?*
War Machine thought, startled. The spiked ball flew
towards him at an amazing speed. Reacting instantly,

War Machine batted the mace away with his fist. *Spikes,* he thought angrily. *Why does it always have to be spikes?* However, its pointed protrusions failed to penetrate his weakened gauntlet, though it probably didn't do the already-damaged repulsor projectors any good.

Before he had a chance to recover, two of the other knights—one man and one woman—aimed their swordspoints at War Machine. Prismatic beams of pure energy leaped from the swords, crossing the distance between the knights and War Machine, and catching the hero in a vicious crossfire. Rays of searing heat baked Jim within his suit, while straining the magnetic fields that held his armor together. *Lasers,* he guessed. He had to get out of the line of fire . . . and fast. Already, alarms were going off inside his helmet, warning of imminent system collapse.

War Machine executed an immediate power dive, pitching and yawing to escape the rainbow-hued lasers that dogged his path. His laser blade sprang from his left gauntlet, a shaft of radiant red slicing through the rain. *Okay,* he thought, warming to the challenge. *You want to play with swords? Let's play with swords.*

He was in the knights' midst instantly, slashing out with his blade of light, like a guided missile rocketing horizontally over the floor of the courtyard. His laser blade stabbed one knight in the leg. She dropped onto the wet cobblestones, clutching her knee, but War Machine had zipped past her before she had even cried out. Another knight crossed his path: the skinny one who had thrown the mace. War Machine let out a ferocious snarl; amplified at three times his usual volume, it sounded like the roar of a tyrannosaur in an old Ray Harryhausen monster movie. The back of Jim's hand still smarted where the mace's spikes had gouged him. *Here's where you get yours, pal,* he thought vengefully. Extinguishing his laser, he cannonballed into the thin knight at close to Mach One, grabbing on to him by the shoulders and flinging him backwards over his shoulders. The knight went flying over the heads of two of his compatriots only to smash into the third as though hurled by a catapult. But War Machine wasn't done with the mace-man just yet. Doubling back, he rough-lifted the skinny knight off of his fallen ally, then tossed him straight up with all his considerable strength. The man rose to a height of nearly fifty feet, but he didn't come down. War Machine accelerated after him, catching up with the knight at the peak of his rapid ascent. The man's visor had come loose during his previous crash. In the split-second before gravity could yank the knight violently to the earth once more, War Machine stared into the man's exposed face. A ruddy face with a broken nose looked back at him, the knight's expression almost comically bewildered.

''I don't like spikes,'' War Machine said, drawing back his fist. A single blow sent the knight sailing over the battlements, arcing above the English countryside like Halley's comet. *Just like hitting the open-*

ing serve in a tennis match, War Machine observed, *but a hell of a lot more satisfying.*

He didn't wait to see the flying knight hit the ground who knew how many miles away before executing a perfect loop-the-loop in the wind and the rain and diving down again, fists first, towards the floor of the courtyard. He quickly took stock of the enemy's situation. One knight was down with a wounded leg. War Machine felt a twinge of sympathy; knee injuries could be nasty and almost impossible to fully recover from. Another knight still rested flat on his back where the thin knight had landed on top of him. That left only one knight still holding the field: an impressive-looking woman holding a sword in one hand and an ax in the other. Judging from the size and proportions of her armor, War Machine guessed the Hydra agent was a bodybuilder in her spare time.

She pointed her sword at War Machine. Expecting another laser blast, he banked to the right. But her move with the sword turned out to be feint; the minute he veered in one direction, she cast her ax directly into his path. The ax rose through the air as straight as an arrow, the axhead glowing as if electrified. He accelerated to avoid it, but the ax hit him squarely on his left boot. He felt a smashing impact in his ankle, followed by an intense electrical shock. The turbines in his boot shorted, throwing him into a tailspin. He tried to compensate using the jets in his other boot, but it was too late. The paving stones rushed up to greet him, smacking him in the face so hard the innermost layer of his mask slammed into his nose. Stunned, he blacked out momentarily.

War Machine's crash landing shook the entire castle. It threw up rocks and dirt, and dug a large crater into the floor of the courtyard, over two feet deep. Rain streamed rapidly into the crater, creating a shallow pool where War Machine lay dazed. The chilly water, seeping through countless minute cracks in his armor, revived Jim. Dizzy, his head spinning, War Machine staggered to his feet, just in time to see the female knight running towards him, swinging her broadsword at his neck. Her metal cuirass was splattered with dirt and mud; she must have been standing nearby when he hit the ground, War Machine guessed. The edge of her blade threw off angry white sparks as it sliced through the night towards his throat. Decapitation seemed a heartbeat away; in his mind, Jim saw an instant image of his head, still wearing his iron helmet, impaled atop a rusty steel pike, while ravens pecked fruitlessly at his metal eye slits.

His response was instantaneous. A single cybernetic command restored his laser blade. A length of ruby light materialized over his wrist even as he swung his arm to block the oncoming sword.

Laser blade met broadsword. Laser light collided with electrified steel. There was flash of color and an explosive discharge of energy so powerful it sent both combatants reeling backwards. Despite his tinted lenses, Jim saw blue spots before his eyes, as though he had stared directly at a flashbulb. His eyes watered. His left hand tingled and felt slightly numb.

His opponent looked similarly jarred. She stood only a yard or two away, shaking her head. She raised her visor for a second, and dabbed at her eyes with the back on an armored glove. War Machine caught a glimpse of a pale white face; two dark, kohl-lined eyes; green lipstick, and a shock of hair dyed a fluorescent shade of chartreuse. She looked like a punk rocker on steroids. The color scheme—green lips, green hair—struck War Machine as vaguely familiar. He couldn't place the memory at first, but then it hit him: the woman's look was clearly inspired by the notorious super-villainess known as the Viper, the original Madame Hydra. The Viper, a murderous *femme fatale* affecting green attire and lipstick, had commanded Hydra for a brief but significant period following Baron Strucker's apparent death; next to Strucker himself, Madame Hydra had been one of the terrorist group's most feared and legendary masterminds. The real Viper had parted company with Hydra years ago, but clearly her example still lingered in the memory of some of today's Hydra agents, as demonstrated by the female knight's disturbing *homage*. War Machine wondered if Baron Strucker approved.

She glanced up and saw him looking at her. Her dark eyes glared at him. Emerald lips curled back in a sneer. She pulled her mud-spattered visor back into place, then tugged on the fingers of her chain mail gauntlet. *Now what's she up to?* War Machine thought, puzzled. The gauntlet came off her hand, revealing long, lime-green fingernails. With a palpable aura of disdain, she flung the gauntlet at War Machine's face. The metal glove clanged against his mask, then slid harmlessly into the mud.

Oh, he thought. *So that's how you want to play it.* He took advantage of the lull in the battle to clamber out of the water-filled crater. Already the newly-formed pool was ankle-deep, and the cold rain kept coming down. War Machine ignored the fierce weather raging about him. He stood opposite the female knight, who raised her sword expectantly. On level ground, she was only a few inches shorter than he. He held his laser blade outstretched in front of him. *So be it,* he thought, getting into the spirit of the scene. If Lady Hydra wanted a full-fledged duel, he was ready to oblige her.

"En garde," he roared, then thrust his laser blade at the armored woman. She parried it easily with a stroke of her own super-charged sword. Bursts of energy flashed whenever their swords crossed, but this time War Machine was ready for the jolts, as was his foe.

Parry. Thrust. Feint. Riposte. Like old-time duelists, they matched each other's blows stroke by stroke. The storm-drenched cobblestones were slippery beneath War Machine's iron boots, but he stayed grounded, reluctant to experiment with his wounded jets in the middle of a fight. The ground was just as wet for Lady Hydra, he reminded himself, and it sure didn't look like she was wearing sneakers.

After a few more parries, however, War Machine wearied of their little swordfight. *The hell with it,* he thought. His missile launcher snapped into place. *Who do I think I am, Errol Flynn?* He fired a single, anti-tank missile directly into the knight. She went flying into the sky, propelled by both the explosive force of the missile and its attached solid-fuel rocket. She crashed into the top of the castle's northwest tower, shattering one wall. Falling masonry dropped like boulders on the courtyard. He wondered briefly if there was any way in the world the female knight could have possibly survived. *Probably not,* he realized, *unless her armor was very, very good—of course, knowing Hydra, it probably was.*

Slowly, painfully, he clambered to his feet, carefully extricating his left boot from the muddy crater bottom. Water crept through the nicks in his armor, chilling him to the bone. *Doesn't it ever stop raining in this stupid country?* he thought. Los Angeles was sounding better and better. Winded by the duel, he paused to catch his breath.

Then an explosion on the battlements rocked the castle, and he remembered Tony.

Twenty-five minutes earlier:

A narrow walkway, less than the width of two people standing side by side, ran along the top of the castle wall, forming a bridge of sorts between two towers. Heavy stone blocks, each three feet high and spaced about a foot apart, formed a jagged crenellation facing the rolling green hills surrounding Waverly Castle. Across from these battlements, a spiked iron parapet had been installed to prevent careless guards from falling off the wall and onto the courtyard, roughly forty feet below. *A nasty drop,* Iron Man thought. He was tempted to see how high a career terrorist would bounce, especially if he landed on top of his bald, cracked, boiled egg of a head. He flew closer to the battlements. In a way, the narrow, elevated causeway reminded him of the upper levels of the Golden Gate Bridge, where this entire sorry saga had begun. Iron Man clenched his fists as he soared through the thunderstorm. *Time to end this,* he thought.

Baron Wolfgang Von Strucker stood midway across the bridge, watching Iron Man approach. He had discarded his green robe somewhere along the way. Despite the wind and the rain, he wore only a brown uniform similar to one worn by the nutso hostage-taker back in San Francisco, except that Strucker's uniform was bedecked with paramilitary stripes and ribbons, befitting his rank as Supreme Commander of the forces of the Hydra. A segmented belt, made of the same crimson metal as his Satan Claw, circled Strucker's waist. Black leather boots, polished until they shined like dark mirrors, rested firmly upon the walk. Hydra's new insignia, resembling nothing so much as a Rorschach drawing of a squid, its tentacles coiling around its bulbous head, was outlined in black upon Baron Strucker's chest.

Strucker saluted Iron Man with his right hand, while resting his Satan Claw on top of a weathered stone battlement. "I see you disregarded my instructions to arrive alone," he taunted Iron Man, "risking the life of your employer by calling surprise reinforcements from the heavens in order to save yourself. You have no honor, Iron Man. I admire that. What is honor except a foolish illusion when compared to utter ruthlessness that is the true essence of existence?" He stared at Iron Man through his monocle, displaying no sign of fear or trepidation. "But your treachery cannot save you. I, Baron Strucker, *am* Hydra. And, like the nine-headed serpent of legend, I am immortal. Strike me down and I grow more powerful still. I have conquered death itself, and no lowly, servile bodyguard can defeat me." He laughed at Iron Man. "If you were a true warrior, Avenger, you would have slain Stark yourself years ago—and seized his empire for your own!"

Iron Man ignored Strucker's bluster. He landed solidly on the elevated walkway, his boots slamming into the centuries-old stone approximately five yards from where Strucker was standing. "I'm giving you one chance to surrender, Strucker," he said. "Give up now and I'll see you get a fair trial, followed by life imprisonment in the strongest prison Nick Fury and Tony Stark can devise. Resist, and you're looking at a world of hurt."

Part of Iron Man hoped the Baron would surrender. Although he longed to pay Strucker back for all the pain and hardship he'd endured over the last twenty-four hours, Tony was sensible enough to realize that he was in no shape for another extended battle. His arms and legs ached with every sudden movement. A headache pounded behind his eyes; he felt the veins throbbing in his temples. His injured right hand had grown stiff and sore. He could really use an easy victory this time around, he knew, and several hours of intense R&R.

Even as he issued his warning to Strucker, however, Iron Man knew his wish for a quick and peaceful resolution was a futile one. Fanatics like Baron Strucker never gave up without a fight.

"*Nein*," Strucker declared. "The only thing that will be surrendered this evening is the chip that rightfully belongs to me." He raised his Satan Claw defiantly. A carmine glow suddenly formed around the metal pincers, surrounding the Claw like a halo of radioactive fire. The Claw crackled loudly with unmistakable destructive potential. Talons of blazing red metal pointed at Iron Man.

Forget it, Strucker, Iron Man thought decisively. *I'm no sitting duck.* Still hoping for a fast finish to this fight, he struck first—with a vengeance. Raising his gauntlets as quickly as a Wild West gunfighter, he blasted Strucker with two fistfuls of repulsor beams. The purple rays raced across the bridge at close to the speed of light, their paths coming together directly in front of Strucker so that a single, unified beam struck the Hydra leader right in the middle of the symbolic squid emblazoned on his brown tunic. Iron Man fully expected to see Strucker go flying backwards from the force of his beams, only coming to rest, perhaps, against the granite face of the tower at the far end of the walk.

None of that occurred. Instead a faint red radiance outlined Strucker's body the instant the repulsors should have knocked him flat, the iridescent tracery growing momentarily brighter as it seemingly absorbed the violet light of the repulsors, then winking from sight as if it had never existed at all. Untouched and unharmed, Baron Strucker stood triumphantly between the parapet on his right and battlements on his left. He shook his bald head sadly, as though disappointed by the inconsequentiality of Iron Man's opening move.

A force field, Iron Man realized, dismayed: from the looks of it, a neutron-absorption field conforming to Strucker's exact dimensions, probably bonded to the bioelectric field generated by Strucker's own body. The field appeared to instantly recalibrate itself to match the intensity level of each attack; the red flashing effect caused by release of energy discharged on the quantum level during the absorption process. . . . Iron Man contemplated the metal belt encircling the Baron's waist. He suspected it was the source of Strucker's protective shield. *Well,* he thought. *This makes things trickier.*

"Is that the best you can do, *Amerikaner* dolt?"
Strucker gloated. "Perhaps Stark's vaunted technology is not so formidable after all." His metal pincers clacked together. The hellish glow encasing his Satan Claw flared dramatically. "Let me give you a taste of real power," he said.

A searing bolt of red energy hit Iron Man head-on. He cried out at the sudden heat, even as his armor's automatic cooling systems went to work, protecting the suit from a sudden meltdown. Energy conversion cells transformed the thermal attack into reserve electrical power, channeling the energy of Strucker's heat-ray away from the point of impact, dispersing it throughout the entire suit. Radiation suppression tiles, layered into every inch of his armor, protected Tony from any unseen contamination. The blast from the Satan Claw hurt like blazes, but Iron Man refused to retreat even a single step.

"I can take anything you can dish out, Strucker," he barked. "You wanted to steal the specs for this armor? Let me show you what it can really do."

Forgetting his repulsors for the moment, Iron Man tried a different tack. The golden tri-beam projector mounted in his chestplate lit up, producing a bright white beam. He sent his armor a terse, cybernetic command: *Activate directional magnetism. Forty-five percent dispersion. Maximum power.* He directed the beam not at Strucker, but towards the rusty metal parapet running along the lefthand side of the walk: the railing was made up of a row of four-foot spikes linked by shafts of iron. Controlled magnetism nagged onto several spikes at once, yanking them from their posts. Cold iron screeched as the parapet twisted in the beam's magnetic grip. Behind thick, opaque lenses, Tony's eyes darted back towards Baron Strucker. *I don't need to touch you to hold you,* he thought.

Before Strucker could react, Iron Man reversed the polarity of his magnetic beam, sending the up-rooted parapet hurling towards his foe. The metal rails wrapped around the Baron, pinning his arms to his sides. Iron Man ran forward, eager to tie the parapet into a knot around Strucker, trapping the insane criminal genius in an impromptu straitjacket woven from solid iron. Force field or no force field, Iron Man resolved, Baron Strucker wasn't going anywhere but jail.

But he'd underestimated Strucker's Satan Claw. The crimson prosthetic tore upwards through the parapet, shredding it into slivers of cauterized metal a heartbeat before Iron Man reached him. He swung the Claw in an fiery arc towards the oncoming hero. A trail of red-hot energy streamed behind the Claw as it cut through the air. Iron Man felt the heat through his armor, a fraction of an instant before the Claw slapped him across the face with the force of an earthquake. He went reeling backwards, recoiling from the powerful blow. No protective railing stood between him and an abrupt, forty-foot drop; instead the parapet now lay in a shambles at Strucker's feet. The heel of an iron boot hung suspended over the precipice. Iron

Man sensed empty space at his back. Throwing his shoulders forward, he halted his backwards flight, then planted his boots carefully upon the walk.

That was close, he thought. If he flew off the wall, he wanted to do so under his own power. He paused and gasped for breath. Every muscle in his body ached. His throat was raw. His lungs burned with every breath. *Got to wrap this up quickly,* he thought urgently. *I'm falling to pieces in here.*

A few yards away, the Baron sneered at Iron Man. The livid white scar zigzagged down his face like the jagged lightning dividing the stormy night sky above the castle's towers. His monocle wasn't even cracked. "Fool! Buffoon!" he shouted harshly. A black leather boot kicked the torn and twisted remains of the parapet off the castle wall. Seconds later, Iron Man heard them clatter loudly upon the courtyard below.

"Did you truly think to trap me thus?" Strucker asked. Bending his elbow, he raised his artificial hand above his head. Coruscating, crimson fire enfolded the Claw, throwing off sparks. "Hah!" Strucker laughed. "I have perfected my Satan Claw a hundred times over the years, each new Claw more powerful than the one preceding it. Nothing can stand against it now. Nothing!"

"Big words," Iron Man challenged him. "But that's all your kind is good for, isn't it? Frankly, I'm not convinced." Clenching his fists, Iron Man braced himself for the next round of the battle. *I can hold it together a little while more,* he thought. *I have to.* Technology and determination kept him standing, despite a growing sense of weakness and fatigue. He wondered how Jim was coping against the knights.

Baron Strucker stalked towards Tony, his Claw held high. The heels of his boots clicked against the uneven stones beneath. To one side, the walk dropped away towards the courtyard. Strucker did not look down.

"Have you read Nietzsche, Iron Man?" Strucker asked haughtily. "*'Man is a rope stretched between the animal and the Superman—a rope over an abyss.'* Look at the abyss that awaits you, this narrow stone bridge stretched like a rope above your doom, and tell me which of us is truly superior."

"I think you've looked into the abyss too long," Iron Man responded. "I'll give you a rope alright, enough to hang you by your rotten neck."

Iron Man directed his magnetic beam upon the Satan Claw itself, hoping to tear Strucker's steel hand from his wrist, but the glowing red metal of the Claw resisted the magnet's pull. *Very well,* Tony thought. He still had plenty of other options. Switching off his chest beam, he raised his repulsors once again and let loose with a continuous, high-intensity repulsor blast. *Maybe I can overwhelm his force field*, he theorized, *by giving it more juice than it can possibly absorb.*

A tidal wave of purple light washed over Strucker. In response, the glowing red outline reappeared around him. His mad blue eyes grew wide.

His teeth ground together and green-black saliva oozed over his lips, dribbling down his chin like liquid gangrene. Iron Man kept the pressure on, hitting Strucker with as much force as his repulsors could muster. The glow around Strucker flared brighter and brighter, until his entire body seemed silhouetted against a shimmering, scarlet backdrop. But Strucker did not falter; his force field showed no sign of collapsing. Slowly, arduously, he advanced against the constant press of the repulsor rays, bending into the cascade of purple energy like a man fighting his way through a steady wind. Step by step by step, he drew closer to Iron Man, swinging his Satan Claw back and forth in front of him like a machete. Blazing energy trailed in the wake of the Claw like the tail of a comet.

"You-can-not-stop-me!" he grunted, each word escaping his lips only with obvious effort. "Hydra-is-supreme!"

A trace of anxiety, and even fear, chipped at Iron Man's resolve. His repulsors still had plenty of power to draw upon, but Tony Stark did not. The man inside the armor was fading fast. His head felt like it was going to explode, splattering his brains all over the inside of his helmet. He was getting tired and even dizzy. If only he could rest for just a second, take it easy. . . .

Tony bit down on his lip, shocking himself back to alertness. *I've come too far to give up now*, he reminded himself. He kept his repulsors focused on

Strucker, pouring all his power into his gauntlets and out through his repulsor rays.

And still Baron Strucker kept coming. The Satan Claw cut a blazing swathe through Iron Man's repulsors. In a minute, the Claw would tear into Iron Man, too. Iron Man prepared to match his own iron fists against the Baron's potent Claw.

Then nature herself entered the conflict. A thunderbolt crashed from the stormy heavens, striking the castle wall between Iron Man and Baron Strucker. Hundreds of volts of natural electricity came into contact with the unleashed energy of Iron Man's wall of repulsor rays. A resounding boom shook all of Waverly Castle as an awesome explosion went off only feet away from the two warring adversaries. The two men, one protected by his armor, the other by his force field, were thrown apart. Iron Man almost dropped off the wall, but he caught himself in time. He saw Baron Strucker steady himself against one the heavy battlements. The Satan Claw cut deep crevices in the ancient stone as Strucker struggled to keep from falling. Seeing Strucker off-balance, Iron Man knew this was his chance to regain the offensive in this fight, but his weary limbs could not move quickly enough. He watched, despairing, as Strucker rapidly recovered. His eyes still blinking from the sudden glare of the lightning strike, the leader of Hydra released his grip. Behind his monocle, Strucker's eye gleamed with crazed amusement.

"You see, *mein freund,* the elements themselves

have succumbed to the glorious madness of war. This is *Gotterdammerung*, the ultimate battle, the twilight of the gods!'' A cold, heartless chuckle came from somewhere deep within the Baron's corrupt body. ''No offense, man of iron, but it seems the turbulent skies are a far more worthy adversary than you.''

Still stunned from the huge explosion, Iron Man stood hunched over, his gloves resting on his armored thighs. Fixing an angry gaze upon Strucker's smug, contemptible face, he inhaled deeply, fighting to get enough breath to tell Strucker just what he thought of him. ''You choose your enemies,'' he gasped finally, ''as badly as you choose your friends.''

''Friends?'' Strucker arched an eyebrow quizzically. ''I have no friends, you naive idiot. Only pawns and victims.''

''That's your mistake!'' a booming voice declared from overhead. Iron Man looked up and saw War Machine rising above the courtyard. Rockets burst from War Machine's boots, lifting him vertically above the very castle walls. Iron Man assumed that War Machine, having made short work of the knights of Hydra, had come to aid him in his life-or-death struggle against Baron Strucker himself. He felt a sudden surge of relief, followed by a curious sense of foreboding. *But why?* he wondered.

''Ah, the sidekick,'' Strucker observed sarcastically, seemingly unconcerned at being outnumbered, ''come at last to join his master in death.''

''I'm no sidekick, you scar-faced S.O.B.,'' War

Machine growled at top volume. "But I am your worst nightmare: a good man with a mad on." War Machine swooped down towards the castle wall, both his minigun and his missile launcher deployed upon his black iron shoulders. A targeting laser projected a tiny red spot upon Strucker's bald dome. "You hurt my friends, tricked me, and dragged me halfway around the world," War Machine accused Strucker. "Now you're going to pay for all that in a big way."

Watching War Machine take a bead on Strucker, Iron Man felt an icy finger run down his spine. Something about this was very wrong, but he couldn't place why. It wasn't just pride; he didn't care if Jim finished off Strucker instead of him, not anymore. But something bad was about to happen. He could feel it in his bones. *Listen to your body,* he told himself.

His thoughts raced, trying to catch up with his fears. He watched Strucker with wary eyes. He expected the Baron to defend himself with his Satan Claw; to his surprise, he saw Strucker raise his other hand instead, the one of flesh and blood. The diseased purple blotches on Strucker's right hand seemed to shift beneath his skin as though alive. Swelling rapidly, they rose to the surface of his epidermis, forming ugly black pustules that looked like they were about to burst at any second. *Oh my God,* Iron Man thought in an instant of horrifying clarity. *That's it!* Strucker didn't need to touch someone to spread the Death-Spore Virus; he could unleash the deadly microbes into the air at will.

Twisting his head so quickly he could hear his neck assembly squeak, Iron Man looked quickly towards War Machine, now plummeting towards Baron Strucker only a few yards away. Tony's heart sank. He didn't need to make an ultrasound scan to see that the airtight integrity of Jim's armor had been compromised at a number of locations. The sealant that had been applied at Avengers Mansion had cracked in his conflict with Strucker's goons. There was no way War Machine, for all his armor plating and firepower, could defend himself against the invisible menace of the Death-Spore Virus. The best artillery in the world was no match for the ultimate in germ warfare.

Iron Man went into action, his previously exhausted body fueled by alarm and concern for Jim. Every second counted now. There was no time to warn War Machine, but Iron Man knew he had to do something; otherwise, his best friend in the world would die a horrible, senseless death, his healthy body instantly consumed by the fatal effects of the Death-Spore Virus. Thinking faster than he had ever done before, Iron Man realized there was only one thing he could do: he turned his repulsor rays upon War Machine.

The repulsors did more than halt War Machine's imminent strafing run. As Iron Man had hoped, the surprise attack knocked his friend for a loop. Spinning madly through the air, War Machine went sailing over the castle's distant gate, flying further out of reach of

Baron Strucker's natural pestilence. At the same time, Iron Man tried to contact Jim on their short-range communication channel. "Jim," he pleaded into the microphone. "Stay away. It's that killer virus I mentioned before. Your armor's not sealed enough to defend against it. Don't come back or you'll die. Repeat: don't come back. . . ."

But when Iron Man repelled War Machine from the castle, he left Baron Strucker free to attack. Seizing the moment, Strucker shot Iron Man in the back with another pyrotechnic blast from the Satan Claw. The sudden burst of pain startled Iron Man. His spine arched backwards, his jaw dropped open behind his mask, and a howl of agony clawed its way up his throat. He spun around to confront Strucker and another bolt struck him in the ribs. It was the last straw; his weakened, ravaged body couldn't take any more. He dropped forward onto his knees and threw out his hands to keep from falling further. Crimson gauntlets gripped the crumbling stone walkway. He fought to keep his head about his shoulders.

Footsteps clicked in front of him. He tried to lift his head higher, but could see only the polished black sheen of Strucker's boots. The madman's voice seemed to come from miles away. "A noble sacrifice," Strucker said, "but the abyss is no respecter of nobility. In the end, only survival counts. You have lost, Iron Man, but I do not wish to destroy you. Not yet. There are still secrets I must extract from your armor, weapons I must add to my arsenal. Give me the chip—now—and perhaps I will let you live a few days longer.''

Iron Man could barely hear Strucker's offer. He felt seconds away from blacking out completely. The world seemed to be growing darker and darker. His vision was fading. Strucker's boots became a fuzzy, black blur. . . . *Wait!* Something Strucker had said caught his attention. Tony shook his head, trying to clear his thoughts. His helmet, the magnetic links connecting it to the armor growing weaker, rattled around his head.

The chip, he realized. That was it. He mustn't let Strucker get the chip. Hydra could do dreadful, terrible things with the chip. According to Bethany and Jim, the chip was supposed to be a source of incredible power.

Power.

A wild idea popped into his brain. A sudden sense of excitement—and hope—sparked inside him. Adrenaline rushed through his body, inspired by one more chance at life. His mind cleared as he grappled with the potential, and probable pitfalls, of his scheme: *What if he used the chip to power his own armor?*

It was a risky ploy, he knew. The chip had not been tested. At this point, only A.I.M. understood the unknown theory behind the chip and its possible applications. The chip could electrocute him instantly, reduce his armor to molten slag, or do absolutely nothing at all. Still, Iron Man thought, the only other alternative was to turn the chip over to Hydra, and he'd rather die than give Strucker a single used battery, let alone the key to ultimate power.

"The chip," Baron Strucker demanded again. Iron Man could hear the energy crackling around Strucker's Satan Claw. "Be warned, *Amerikaner,* I am not by nature a patient man." He let the rest of his threat go unspoken.

Iron Man imagined a new, improved version of the Satan Claw, this one ignited with the allegedly awesome power of the energy chip. *Never,* he thought. But he said: "Wait. Please. I'll get it for you."

His wounded right hand had grown stiff and crabbed, so he had to make do with his left. It was clumsy, but he managed. First, he lifted a six-inch iron panel over his left hip, exposing the receptor site for his universal power connect system. Then, moving too quickly for Baron Strucker to recognize his actions right away, or so Iron Man prayed, he slipped the chip out of the storage module affixed to his other hip. It looked and felt like just another computer chip to him; could it really be as powerful as everyone said? He did not have time to consider the matter. Taking a deep breath, he shoved the chip into the section of his power receptor that was compatible with the chip's alignment.

"Stop!" Baron Strucker shouted frantically, awaking at last to Iron Man's intent. "What are you doing? Give that to me this minute!"

It was too late. For better or for worse, the chip snapped easily into place. Iron Man waited anxiously to see what happened next. At first, for the space of maybe one heartbeat, he felt nothing at all. Then, before he could even reseal the iron panel over the receptor, his armor seemed to surge to life all around him.

Every system in the suit leaped into maximum readiness simultaneously. Power coursed through the circuitry, producing a loud, angry hum that came from all over Iron Man, from the pumps supplying his boot jets to the cybernetic antenna array in his helmet. Lights, graphics, and data raced before his face; it was like a laser show performed at ten times the normal speed. Tony focused with difficulty on the armor's internal diagnostics displays, and he couldn't believe his eyes. The power levels for every system were way above the norm, and rising.

"Nein!" Baron Strucker cried out in fury. *"Nein! Nein!"* Veins protruded angrily on his forehead. His nostrils flared. He snapped his jaws like a wild animal. In a killing rage, he lifted the Satan Claw above Iron Man's helmet, then slammed it with all his crazed, fanatical strength. Flaming scintillations flew off the Claw as it crashed down onto Iron Man's head—and rebounded back off it, leaving the gold-and-crimson helmet completely unscratched. *"Unglaublich!"* he exclaimed in anger and amazement.

Inside the armor, Tony Stark was just as

astounded. The power of the energy chip had height-
ened, accelerated, and amplified every function of the
armor, including the magnetic field extending over the
surface of the armor. No wonder the Claw was unable
to even touch his armor; at these inconceivable power
levels, even a nuke might have trouble disrupting the
field. The chip had no direct effect on his flesh-and-
blood body, of course, but Tony could sense the
sheer, indescribable power rampaging through his armor. It was like being inside a stampeding elephant
or, even closer, standing on top of a volcano just as
all the raging magma of the earth's core came rushing
to the surface. It was both terrifying and exhilarat-
ing—but mostly terrifying.

Iron Man started to stand, then found himself
leaping into the sky before he had even completed
the thought. *I'll have to be very careful,* he thought.
*Every motion I make will be exaggerated one hun-
dred-fold.* He was afraid to activate his boot jets for
fear of launching himself into orbit and well past
Mars. Instead, he let gravity pull him back down to
the battlements. His boots dug deeply into the
weathered stone when he landed, less than half the
length of the wall from Baron Strucker.

The humming grew louder, transforming into a
pounding roar that rivaled the sound of a fleet of
jets flying side by side. It was the roar of continents
shifting, of an exploding sun. Safety warnings
flashed brilliantly inside his helmet before burning
out completely. Warning sirens pierced his ears then

devolved into thunderous wails of static. Iron Man wasn't built to handle this much power. The armor was tearing itself apart. He needed to discharge the excess energy somehow . . . and fast.

A figure came running down the wall at him. Baron Strucker's eyes were wild, his face contorted with fear and fury. The monocle popped from its place over his scarred left eye; it fell unnoticed to the ground where Strucker heedlessly crushed it beneath his boots. His mouth gaped open, but Iron Man couldn't hear a word he said; the neverending *thrum* of the power surging through his armor drowned out everything else, even the thunderstorm. Strucker swung the Satan Claw at Iron Man's face; it bounced harmlessly off his golden faceplate, driving Strucker to even greater heights of frustration and rage.

Iron Man stared at the hate-filled face of the man futilely attacking him, over and over again without results. Baron Wolfgang Von Strucker. Blank Screen. The same man who had callously planned the raid on *Athena,* who had trapped him for what felt like days in a computer-generated lie, who had tortured him with false images of Anastasia's agony, and then ultimately tried to infect his best friend with a virulent, incurable disease. Anger filled Tony Stark, burning almost as hot as the ever more uncontrollable energy coursing all around him. The anger and the energy became one and the same in his mind. Both demanded release.

He released it at Strucker. Supercharged repulsor

rays burst from his gauntlets. They poured from his chest beam to form one giant repulsor blast aimed only at Baron Strucker. The unleashed light went beyond purple, beyond ultraviolet, to unseeable colors far beyond human perception of the spectrum. Strucker's personal force field flickered briefly, but it was as nothing compared to the seismic power of the energy escaping from Iron Man. That power tore Strucker's force field like a paper suit in a hurricane. There was no way anyone could stand against that barrage of pure energy. Strucker's eyes grew red and bloodshot. His lips mouthed inaudible curses and threats, while bubbling black goo streamed over his chin. Like his force field, Baron Strucker appeared to flicker and fade away in the awful torrent of energy. His entire body, uniform and all, dissolved into its constituent atoms, then disappeared entirely.

Disintegrated or beamed away? Iron Man wondered. Had he reduced Baron Strucker to oblivion once and for all, or had Supreme Commander of Hydra simply teleported to safety at the last minute? *I'm sure I'll find out soon enough,* he thought.

Meanwhile, the seemingly endless power of the energy chip continued to gush through his repulsor beams. Iron Man could not stop the flood now if he tried. The dam had been broken and the power set free. Invisible, unstoppable, the energy flowed out of him, enough to power several major cities for years to come, but the energy did not escape fast enough to save his armor. New circuits burned out every sec-

ond. Tony had to close his eyes to protect them from
the sparks and control chips going off inside his helmet. *How bitterly ironic,* he thought, *if I finally defeat
Baron Strucker only to be killed in the meltdown of
my own armor.* And even more tragic if that meltdown ends up destroying the rest of the world.

Eyes squeezed shut, lost in the darkness, he felt
the castle wall tremble beneath his boots, the tremors
increasing until the entire castle was shaking violently
and coming apart in great chunks of flying stone and
masonry. He heard a centuries-old tower collapse at
last, turning into an avalanche of falling bricks and
mortar. Then the stones he was standing on gave way,
and Iron Man fell into open space, the energy within
him lashing out in all directions, reducing everything
around him to rubble, noise, chaos, and confusion. . . .

The storm had passed and the sun was rising when
War Machine returned to Waverly Castle. It had taken
him much of the night, but he'd found a Stark Enter-
prise research center on the outskirts of London,
where a team of engineers, roused from slumber by
a couple of well-placed smoke bombs, had coated his
entire armor with a fast-drying artificial sealant that
they promised was tougher than what Pym used. If
there were any nasty germs floating around the castle,
as Tony seemed to believe, then this airtight coating
ought to keep them out.

But where was the castle? He looked for the tall
gray towers to rise before him on the horizon, but

nothing appeared as he neared the correct location. At first he was afraid that he had taken a wrong turn or maybe even passed the castle without noticing it somehow. He checked the coordinates Bethany had given them the night before and compared them against his location finder. According to the readouts, he was in just about the right place. *So where—?*

Then he saw the crater and, behind his scowling iron mask, his eyes bugged out. Waverly Castle was gone. In its place was a charred black crater easily a mile in diameter. What looked like debris filled the bottom of the crater, several meters down. At the perimeter of the crater, a solitary tower had partially survived the destruction. The tower lay on its side, stretched out over the grass fields. One side of the tower had been completely pulverized; it looked like a giant hammer had pounded it into tiny, bit-sized pieces.

"Oh, Tony," he murmured, awestruck. He could not imagine what apocalyptic events had occurred here after he had fled the scene at Tony's desperate urging. Whatever had happened, it seemed very unlikely that Tony Stark had survived. War Machine could only hope that Strucker and his vicious Knights of the Wrong Circle had perished in the same disaster. He prayed that Hydra had not in fact killed Tony, then blown up the castle to cover their tracks.

If that's what they've done, War Machine thought, *I swear to you that they won't get away with it. I'll track them to the ends of the earth—and be-yond if necessary.*

He activated his ultrasound imaging system and directed it towards the rubble at the bottom of the crater. Perhaps his sensors could uncover some small clue as to what had destroyed Waverly Castle. It seemed unlikely, though; everything in the vicinity appeared to have been reduced to ash and powder.

When the first readings appeared on the optical display inside his helmet, he was sure he must be seeing things. Then he checked the display again and he felt his heart skip a beat. According to the ultra-sonic probe, there was a body at the bottom of the crater—and it was alive!

War Machine zoomed down into the crater. He dug into the powdered stone with his gauntlets, fling-ing great heaps of rock and dirt and splintered timber aside as he worked frantically to uncover the person beneath the mound of debris. The coarse gray powder reminded him of the volcanic ash thrown up during the eruption of Mount St. Helens. He didn't allow himself to hope or even think. He simply dug and dug until, at last, he thought he heard the sound of some-one breathing. Only then did he permit himself to think about the survivor's identity. *Just my luck,* he thought, *it's probably good old Baron Strucker him-self.*

Then beneath the dull gray ash, the sunlight over-head glinted off an exposed inch or two of smooth, golden armor. Heart pounding, he hastily wiped away more of the ash with his hands, like an archaeologist impatiently uncovering the find of a lifetime. More of the golden metal was revealed, along with stretches of crimson plating as well. As the powder came away, he freed first an arm, then a shoulder, and finally most of a shining golden mask. The faint, but definite, sound of breathing came through the long horizontal groove positioned beneath two smaller eye slots. War Machine couldn't contain his joy any longer.

"Yes!" he cried out, saluting the air with his fist. *Iron Man was alive!*

"Jim?" A weak voice came from inside the mask. He sounded more dead than alive.

"That's right," he said. "Hang on, let me get you out of there." Taking Iron Man's head in both hands, War Machine carefully unfastened the helmet, the same way he had so often removed his own. Beneath the gold-colored iron mask, Tony Stark's face was pale but alert. He took a deep breath, then looked around.

"My God," he said quietly, surveying the devastation. "Jim, it was the energy chip. It did this. It did this all."

The chip? War Machine thought. That tiny little crystal thingie he'd heisted from A.I.M.? He remembered the sheer size of the crater, the way the scene had looked from above. He recalled the massive stone fortress that had stood unconquered for centuries— until now. He let out a long whistle. Suddenly, he felt even better about keeping that chip out of the grubby hands of A.I.M. and the Maggia. Then another thought disturbed his peace of mind. "Tony," he asked, "what happened to the chip?" *If Hydra has it now,* he reflected grimly, *our troubles have only begun.*

Tony must have heard the apprehension in his voice. "Don't worry," he said. With his free hand, he burrowed into the dirt and ash. War Machine heard a latch unsnap, then watched as Tony removed a minute object from the side of his armor. He lifted it up so they both could inspect it. It was the chip alright, but baked and blackened almost beyond recognition. Tony squeezed the chip between his fingers; it crumbled to dust before their eyes. "Completely burned out," he explained. He paused and looked around thoughtfully. "Probably just as well."

War Machine couldn't help but agree with him. For such a tiny object, it had certainly caused plenty of trouble and destruction. He picked up a handful of the powder and let it run through his armored fingers. Just a few hours ago, that dust had been Waverly Castle. His gaze swept the crater. "I still can't believe you lived through this," he said. "Not that I'm complaining, of course."

Tony smiled. He rapped a set of iron knuckles against his golden chestplate. "When I build a suit of armor, I build it to last."

"So I've noticed," Jim said dryly from within his own battered set of Stark armor. "So what you want to do now, guy?"

Tony thought about it for minute. "I think," he said finally, "I need a vacation."

Athena rocked gently upon the waves. Wispy, white puffs of cloud drifted lazily across a sunny sky so blue Tony Stark could hardly believe it was real. This far from shore, no gulls were likely to fly overhead, although a school of dolphins played merrily in the sparkling, green water off the starboard bow, their high-pitched laughter punctuating the gentle lapping of the sea against the hull of the yacht.

Stretched out on a deck chair, the sun gently warming his naked chest, a cup of iced ginger ale in his hand, Tony experienced another mild case of *déjà vu*. This peaceful afternoon at sea reminded him of the carefree beginnings of his most recent voyage upon *Athena*, with only a few minor changes. A fresh coat of paint covered the upper deck, blotting out the damage done by last weekend's brawl with Hydra, while the attaché case containing his Iron Man armor rested securely beneath this very deck chair, within easy reach. *Better safe than sorry,* he thought.

Not that he was anticipating trouble this trip; it was just that some memories were not so easily shed. He turned his head towards the woman reclining in the deck chair alongside his. "I have to say," he told her. "You're a pretty courageous woman to agree to this again, and so soon."

"And why is that?" asked Anastasia Swift. She yawned casually, stretching her arms out above her head and arching her back. She had exchanged last week's silver bikini for a one-piece, black mesh bathing suit that dipped very low in the back, displaying, among other things, the elegant curve of her spine. Tony admired Ana's tan. If anything, it had grown even darker and more lustrous since the last time he saw her. "Are you so important," she teased him, "that you expect to be kidnapped every weekend?"

"Not at all," Tony said, laughing. Someday, perhaps, he would tell her the full story of his strange captivity in the house on Dumaine Street, and of the disturbing role she had—and had not—played in his experience there. But not now. Today the sun was high in the sky, and he was alone at last with Ana. The *real* Ana. "I've been practicing, by the way," he told her.

"Practicing what?" she asked. Her eyebrows hung like question marks above her sapphire eyes. A warm sea breeze ruffled her short blonde hair. Soft golden bangs floated over her unblemished forehead.

"Listening to my body," he said. He glanced briefly at his right hand. A gauze bandage was wrapped around his sprained knuckles. Aside from an occasional twinge, they felt fine.

"That is very good," Ana said. She pursed her lips thoughtfully. "Although, one should not always talk to one's self." She rose from her chair and took the drink from his hand, laying it gently on the floor beside his briefcase. "It's not healthy."

Healthy, Tony thought, *is exactly how you look,*

and how you make me feel. He watched her intently, filled with anticipation. "You know," he said, "there's something I've been meaning to ask you."

"Which is?" she asked. Her blue eyes looked away, her gaze sweeping over the sea around *Athena* as if to reassure herself that only the dolphins could see them.

"Your name. Anastasia *Swift.* That doesn't sound particularly Ukrainian."

"Of course not." Her fingers reached back behind her neck to toy with the delicate black ribbon holding up her bathing suit. "Was my agent's idea. He thought 'Swift' was more commercial."

Tony sat up straight in his deck chair, unable to keep his eyes off her. "So," he asked, his mouth dry, "what is your real name?"

"I will tell you . . . later," she purred throatily. The black ribbon came loose and her suit fell away, fluttering gently to the deck of the yacht. Slowly, gracefully, she stepped away from the clingy black fabric piled around her smooth, bare feet. "A woman must not reveal *everything* at once."

Tony Stark smiled again. It was good to be alive. And free.

GREG COX is the coauthor (with John Gregory Betancourt) of the *Star Trek: Deep Space Nine* novel *Devil in the Sky* and the coeditor (with T.K.F. Weisskopf) of the anthology of science fiction vampire stories called *Tomorrow Sucks*. *Iron Man: The Armor Trap* is his first solo novel. Recent short stories by Cox have appeared in such anthologies as *The Ultimate Spider-Man*; *The Further Adventures of Batman*, Volumes 2 and 3; *100 Vicious Little Vampire Stories*; and *Alien Pregnant by Elvis*. He has also written *The Transylvanian Library: A Consumer's Guide to Vampire Fiction*. Cox lives in New York City where he works as an associate editor for Tor Books.

GABRIEL GECKO was the original artist on Marvel's *War Machine* title, and is currently working on several projects for Malibu Comics. He has an extensive commercial and fine arts background, having attended New York University and the School of Visual Arts in New York City. He now lives out West with his wife and his dog.